CARAMEL CRUSH

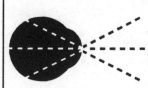

A CUPCAKE BAKERY MYSTERY

CARAMEL CRUSH

JENN MCKINLAY

WHEELER PUBLISHING
A part of Gale, a Cengage Company

Farmington Hills, Mich • San Francisco • New York • Waterville, Maine
Meriden, Conn • Mason, Ohio • Chicago

LIBRARY OF CONGRESS CATALOGING-IN-PUBLICATION DATA

Names: McKinlay, Jenn, author.
Title: Caramel crush / by Jenn McKinlay.
Description: Large print edition. | Waterville, Maine : Wheeler Publishing, 2017. |
  Series: A cupcake bakery mystery | Series: Wheeler Publishing large print cozy
  mystery
Identifiers: LCCN 2017016855| ISBN 9781432840549 (softcover) | ISBN 1432840541
  (softcover)
Subjects: LCSH: Cooper, Melanie (Fictitious character)—Fiction. | DeLaura, Angie
  (Fictitious character)—Fiction. | Bakers—Fiction. | Bakeries—Fiction. |
  Murder—Investigation—Fiction. | Large type books. | GSAFD: Mystery fiction.
Classification: LCC PS3612.A948 C37 2017 | DDC 813/.6—dc23
LC record available at https://lccn.loc.gov/2017016855

Published in 2017 by arrangement with The Berkley Publishing Group,
an imprint of Penguin Publishing Group, a division of Penguin Random
House LLC

Printed in Mexico
1 2 3 4 5 6 7 21 20 19 18 17

Given that I am freakishly tall and a bit of an airhead, I've always had a surprisingly strong sense of self (thanks, Mom!), right up until I birthed the hooligans — my sons. Suddenly, I felt like the stupidest person alive and doubted every single thing I did. I bumbled through the toddler years (it's pretty hard to screw up naps and snack) but then the hooligans started school. Ack! All these other parents seemed to know what they were doing and I was lost — completely lost! But then I found my people at Chesnutt Park on Tuesday afternoons. We were this eclectic group of moms with nothing much in common except our love for our kids, and we gathered every week for several years to share snacks, let the kids run wild (and, boy howdy, did they!), and share our worries, fears, information, failures, and successes with no judgment, just gentle understanding of how freaking hard this parenting gig is. Suddenly, I wasn't so lost anymore. So, this book is dedicated to my dear friends "the Moms." By order of appearance in the park: Sabrina Redden, Betsy Boyer, Laura White, Zarin Fadlu-Deen, and Erin Dahl. You ladies are and always will be the keepers of some of my happiest memories. Thank you for your friendship and your grace, you are all so very beautiful to me.

ACKNOWLEDGMENTS

As the cupcake series goes on, it becomes harder and harder to come up with titles that are punny and blend that perfect mix of cupcakes and death, which is very difficult to achieve, sort of like the perfect cake-to-frosting ratio. This go-round was a doozy. Title upon title was offered, tweaked, twisted and yet nothing worked. Nothing. I was in despair and then I appealed to the Hub to think of something. He blinked at me and offered *Caramel Crush.* Just like that. He didn't even break a sweat! So here's my sincerest thanks to the Hub for the wonderful title and for always having my back. I could never do what I do without you! Also, I want to thank Judi LaRocco Franko for her help with the details of Catholic weddings and for being such a wonderful cheerleader for the series. You're the best, sweetie! And as always, here's a big thank-you to my squad: Kate Seaver, Kath-

7

erine Pelz, and Christina Hogrebe, for making my books sparkle and shine and for keeping me on task. Big thanks to everyone at Berkley for the fantastic covers, terrific design, and for all the sales and marketing pizzazz that get my books in the hands of readers. You are awesome!

ONE

"Why are you hiding in the walk-in cooler?" Melanie Cooper asked her friend and business partner Tate Harper.

"I'm not hiding," he said.

It was hard to understand him as his teeth were chattering, making a sharp clacking noise that drowned out his words. His lips had a tinge of blue around them and his fingers were shaking so badly, he could barely type on the laptop he had set up on one of the wire shelves.

"Liar, liar, pants on fire," Mel said. She looked at him and raised one eyebrow. "Bet that would feel pretty good about right now."

"Wh— wh— where is she?" Tate asked. He blew into his cupped hands and rubbed them together.

"She just left to go look at flowers . . . again," Mel lied. "Now get out of here before you freeze to death."

She pushed open the door to Fairy Tale Cupcakes's walk-in cooler and shoved Tate out into the bakery kitchen. Mel scooped up his laptop and followed him. The thing was like snuggling a block of ice. Brr.

"Sweetie, there you are," Angie DeLaura cried when she caught sight of her groom. "Where have you been? I've been looking all over for you. Sara at the flower shop is waiting for us."

Tate slowly turned and looked at Mel over his shoulder. His eyebrows, which looked to have the beginnings of frost on them, lowered in what she recognized as his seriously unhappy face. Too bad.

Tate and Angie had flipped a coin to see who Mel would stand up for, since they were both her best friends since middle school, and Angie had won, calling "heads" right before the quarter hit the ground face side up. Mel's loyalty now had to be with the bride until the vows were spoken and normalcy returned.

" 'To love is to suffer,' " Mel said to Tate. He glowered and she shrugged.

"*Love and Death.*" Angie identified the movie Mel quoted. It was a game the three of them had been playing since they were tweens bonding over their mutual love of the Three Stooges and Three Musketeers

10

bars, because as everyone knows all good things come in threes.

"Well done," Mel said.

"But wait." Angie frowned. She tossed her thick brown braid over her shoulder. "I don't see the relevance. Tate, you're not suffering, are you? You're enjoying planning our wedding, right?"

Mel gave Tate a pointed stare. If he answered this incorrectly, it would be very bad for all of them.

"Of course, honey, I can't think of anything I'd rather do with the sixteen hours a day I spend conscious and breathing than have in-depth discussions on the merits of freesia in the bouquet," he said. Mel noted he had his fingers crossed behind his back.

Angie grinned at him and Mel blinked. Wow, the bride thing must be like wearing a suit of sarcasm-deflecting Teflon, because if anyone else had been on the receiving end of Tate's razor-sharp response they would be bleeding out by now.

Mel gave Tate a reproachful look. He bowed his head and she noticed his shivering had subsided somewhat. He ran a hand through his wavy brown hair as if to brush off his bad attitude and when he looked back up his eyes were crinkling in the corners when he smiled.

11

"I'd do anything for you, babe, even days and days of looking at flowers, flowers, and more flowers," he said. This time he sounded sincere.

"You're the best groom ever," Angie sighed.

"That's because you're the best bride," he returned.

Then he grinned and pulled Angie in close for a smooch. She squealed and then the whole thing turned mushy-gushy, saccharine sweet and Mel felt her upchuck reflex kick in.

Tate and Angie's wedding was a little over three months away, and if the past few weeks were any indicator, it was going to be a long three months with Angie, who had shocked them all by morphing into a bride-zilla who was wholly consumed by her upcoming nuptials and all that went with becoming Mrs. Tate Harper. Truly, it horrified.

Mel was trying to be the supportive best friend, but she really didn't know if she could handle much more of this. Possibly, it was because it was summer in central Arizona, and the heat was making her a little bit crazy. But more than likely, it was because Mel had put off her own wedding to Joe DeLaura, Angie's older brother, so that Angie could have her special day and the waiting was making Mel a bit antsy-pantsy.

Mel and Joe had attempted to elope in Las Vegas a couple of months ago, but because it was Mel and she was sure she was cursed in matrimony, the Elvis-impersonator-slash-justice-of-the-peace that her bakery assistant Marty Zelaznik had hired to marry them had turned out to be a fraud, making Mel and Joe's vows worth less than the free limo ride included in the wedding package.

"I love you more," Angie said.

"No, I love you more," Tate replied.

Gag. Mel left the kitchen and headed into the front of the bakery. It was fairly quiet. Marty was restocking the front display case, and Mel blew her blond bangs off of her forehead and began to help him.

"Back so soon? I thought you went to bake something," he said.

"I started to get a cavity."

Marty's bushy eyebrows rose up on his shiny dome, and then Tate and Angie came through the swinging door, holding hands and staring into each other's eyes.

"You're beautiful, puddin' pop," Tate said.

"No, you are, snugglupagus," Angie answered with a giggle.

13

"No, you are, cutie patootie," he insisted.

"Oh, barf on a biscuit," Marty said to Mel. "Those two are revolting."

"Welcome to my world," Mel said. "Honestly, I don't know how much more I can take. Yesterday, they managed three *poopsies* and two *shmoopies* in a five-minute conversation and I swear I needed an airsick bag."

"Tell me when they're gone," Marty said.

He shuddered and then turned back to the display case. He looked like he was going to shove his whole body from the shoulders up into the glass case to avoid looking at Tate and Angie as they rubbed their noses together and murmured more lovey-dovey sweet nothings.

Mel was not to be abandoned. She wedged herself in beside Marty and helped him offload the chocolate cupcakes with peanut-butter frosting that she had baked fresh that morning. Sometimes in life there was nothing better than chocolate cake with a fresh dollop of peanut-butter frosting on top. This was one of those moments.

"Hey, find your own display case," Marty grumbled at her. He nudged her out of the case.

"But this *is* my display case," she protested.

"I was here first," he argued. "Besides, you're the maid of honor; you have to put up with that."

Mel gave him a look that she hoped clarified how she would not have a problem pelting him with cupcakes until he surrendered control of the glass barricade between them and the sickening bride and groom.

"There are limits to what a maid of honor can manage," she said. "And I draw the line at listening to the two of them call each other —"

"Martin!"

"Huh?" Marty went to stand and smacked his head on the top of the display case. "Ouch!"

Glaring at him over the top of the glass shelving was Marty's current girlfriend, who was also Mel's baking rival, Olivia Puckett, owner of Confections bakery. She was in her usual blue chef's coat with her gray corkscrew curls bouncing on top of her head in a messy topknot.

Marty rubbed his head as he faced the woman across the counter. He looked wary; she looked irritated, although in all fairness Olivia always looked irritated so she might be as happy as a clam, for all Mel knew.

Mel frowned. Were clams happy? Would anyone be happy stuck in a shell with mostly just a belly, some sinew, and one muscly foot for a body? She shook her head. *Focus!*

"Hi, Olivia," she said. "What brings you by?"

"Not the food," Olivia snapped.

Mel pressed her lips together to keep from saying the first thing that came to mind, which was not nice. Her mother had raised her better than that; still, it was an effort.

"Now, Liv," Marty said. "You know we're not supposed to visit each other's place of work. I stay out of your bakery and you stay out of mine."

"Yeah, that'd be fine," Olivia snapped. "Except someone filled up our DVR with reruns of *Magnum, P.I.*"

Marty blinked at her. "So?"

"So?" Olivia's arms flapped up in the air like she was trying to achieve liftoff. "I can't record my cooking shows because it's all full of Mustache Guy."

"Mustache Guy?" Marty echoed the words as if she had blasphemed.

Mel ducked back down behind the display case to hide her smile. She noted that Tate and Angie had ceased the PDA and were actively listening to the conversation.

"Yes, Mustache Guy," Olivia said. "You know, what's-his-face."

"What's-his-face?" Marty repeated faintly.

16

He clutched his chest as if he couldn't believe what he was hearing and it was causing him a severe bout of angina. "His name is Tom Selleck and he is a god among men."

"Pish," Olivia said. "He's overrated."

Now Marty staggered back and Mel jumped up to grab him in case he stroked out on the spot. There were few things that Marty held sacred, but Tom Selleck was one of them.

"He is not —" Marty began, but Olivia interrupted.

"Yes, he is," she said. "So I deleted all of the episodes on the DVR and reprogrammed it to cover just the Food Network."

"What?" Marty cried. He clapped his hands on top of his bald dome as if trying to keep the top of his skull from blowing off.

"You heard me," she said. She looked quite pleased with herself and Mel had a feeling this was not going to end well.

"But . . . You . . . That . . . We . . . I . . ." Marty was so upset, he was babbling.

Mel wondered if she should slap him on the back to help him get the words out. There was no need.

"That's it!" Marty shouted. "When I get home tonight, I am moving out!"

Olivia crossed her arms over her chest. She glowered at him. "No, you're not."

"Oh, yes, I am," he declared.

"Puleeze," Olivia sniped. "Where would you go? Who is going to take in a man who thinks the floor is a laundry basket, snores like a donkey, and never cleans the bathroom?"

"Says the woman who can't leave a dirty dish in the sink, thinks washing windows is a daily chore, and who writes her name on every single edible item in the fridge," Marty retaliated.

Mel met Angie's gaze over the counter. Marty had moved in with Olivia, at her request, just a few months ago. It appeared the honeymoon phase of their live-in period was dusted and done.

"You're impossible," Olivia snapped.

"No, you are," Marty said.

Mel looked at him. As far as comebacks went, that one was pretty lame. He shrugged and turned his back on her.

"Give me until the end of tomorrow, and me and my stuff will just be a fuzzy memory," he said to Olivia.

"Yeah, fuzzy because it's growing mold on it like everything else you leave on the counter," she said.

18

"That's it!" Marty said. "We're done here."

"We're not done until I say we're done," Olivia argued.

"Too late," Marty said. "Done."

With that, he strode through the kitchen door, leaving it swinging in his wake.

"Hey!" Olivia shouted. "I'm not done with you yet."

She charged behind the counter and followed Marty into the kitchen, where a clang of pots and pans sounded with a bang and a crash. Mel looked at Angie and Tate in alarm.

"What do we do?" she cried.

"Uh . . . nothing?" Tate said.

Crash!

"But my kitchen," Mel said.

She twisted her apron in her hands. More ominous noise came from the kitchen but it did not sound like any more pots and pans were being tossed about.

"Will survive," Tate said. "But you'll never be able to unsee whatever you walk into behind that door."

"I'm with honey badger on this one," Angie said.

"Honey badger?" Tate asked her.

"It's cute," she said.

"If you say so," he said. "I think I'm

19

partial to honey bear."

"How about honeybee?" Angie offered.

Mel blew out a breath. She wasn't sure what was worse, the couple in front of her canoodling or the couple behind her brawling. Either way, she wondered if it was too early in the day, at ten o'clock in the morning, to require an espresso-infused cupcake or two.

The door to the bakery banged open again, but this time a tall, thin woman in a snappy aqua skirt and suit jacket paired with beige sandals and a matching purse strode into the room looking like she was on a mission. She scanned the room and then her deep brown gaze landed on Mel like a laser beam on lock.

A man, also in a suit, came in behind her and Mel had a moment of panic. Was this another couple? Were they looking to book a wedding? Were they going to be fussing or fighting or goopy in love? She genuinely didn't think she could take much more coupleness, no matter how well it paid.

"Melanie Cooper," the woman said. Obviously, she knew Mel from somewhere. "You're just the woman I need. Lucky for me, you owe me one, don't you?"

Two

It took Mel a second to remember the voice. It was sharp, direct, and took no prisoners. She knew that voice. She glanced back at the woman's face. A thick blond bob framed a heart-shaped face with an upturned nose and full lips. Could it be? Diane Earnest? Her old roommate? The woman strode forward and it was the walk that clinched it. Despite the heels, she moved with a familiar bow-legged stomp, not unlike a dinosaur, that always made Mel think there would be cracks in the flooring upon her departure.

"Diane," she said. "Is it really you?"

"In the flesh!" Diane answered with a toss of her bob. She enfolded Mel in a perfumed hug, the scent of which lingered long after Diane let her go. "How are you, roomie?"

Mel stared at the woman who had been her college roommate during her first two years at UCLA. Diane Earnest had looked amazing then and she looked equally so now. Blond, tan, well muscled, and in her perfectly fitted suit, she looked the very essence of the successful marketing executive that she was.

It slapped Mel upside the head. This was what she had studied in college. This was what she'd thought her life would be. Power clothes, power cars, power meals, making and breaking products and companies as they came to market. Diane looked as if the life suited her. She positively crackled with energy as she took in Mel's humble bakery. It was all Mel could do to keep from throwing her arms wide and protecting her pretty little retro shop from Diane's hard, assessing gaze.

"I heard you're franchising," Diane said. "I can see that working for you."

"You can?" Mel squeaked. Her voice came out more hopeful than she would have liked. Darn it! She cleared her throat and consciously lowered her voice. "Yeah, it's overdue."

One of Diane's eyebrows rose and a small smile played on her lips as if Mel hadn't fooled her at all.

The tall man in the suit who had followed Diane into the bakery stepped forward. He wore the jacket and slacks well but there was an aura of nerd about him, obvious in the wrinkled necktie, unkempt thinning brown hair, and dark-rimmed glasses, that the pale gray suit couldn't quite hide.

"Elliott," Diane said. "I want you to meet one of my friends from my college years. Melanie Cooper, Elliott Peters."

Mel held out her hand to shake his. His palm was a bit sweaty but given that it was June in Arizona and the temperature outside was already in the nineties, she couldn't really fault him for that.

"Nice to meet you, Elliott," Mel said. "Diane, I think you met my friends, Tate Harper and Angie DeLaura, back in the day? They are my business partners in the bakery."

Tate and Angie stepped forward and exchanged greetings with Diane and Elliott. Diane smiled warmly at them.

"Of course I remember," Diane said. She gave Tate a flirty look. It was clear to Mel that she was speaking to Tate and not Angie.

"So, did you two ever . . . ?" Diane let the question dangle as she glanced between Tate and Mel.

"No!" Mel and Tate both answered at once. It was hard to say who looked more panicked at the thought. It had taken Mel years to convince Angie that Tate was like a

23

brother to her. She couldn't have Diane undo all of that in one short visit.

"Too bad," Diane said. "I really thought you two would make an adorable couple."

Mel glanced at Angie out of the corner of her eye. Judging by the flat stare in Angie's usually warm brown eyes, she was moments away from schooling Diane in some manners, whether Diane wanted her to or not.

"Actually, Tate and Angie are getting married," Mel said. "In just a few months."

"Really?" Diane looked at Angie as if reconsidering her. She looked her up and down, clearly unimpressed by Angie's jeans and T-shirt. "How'd you manage to bag him?"

Angie was short and curvy, with a head of thick dark curls and a very pretty face. Her pretty girl-next-door looks frequently caused people, usually other women, to underestimate her potential. It was a mistake they seldom made twice.

"I didn't bag him, he bagged me," Angie said. "If you'll excuse us, we're off to pick out our wedding flowers."

She hooked her hand through Tate's arm and yanked him out the door. Obviously, Sara the florist could not be kept waiting a moment longer.

"She's feisty," Diane said. "I like that."

"That's one word for it," Mel agreed.

She paused to listen for any noise coming from the kitchen. There was no more clattering or banging so she could only hope that Marty and Olivia were now having a calm reasonable discussion or maybe they were making up. She wrinkled her nose. She did not want to picture that in her head. Too late. Ugh!

"Can I get you anything?" Mel asked. "The special today is chocolate cupcakes with peanut-butter frosting. It's a real crowd pleaser."

"No, not for me, thanks," Diane said. "I do have a favor to ask you, however."

Maybe it was the way she said it, or perhaps it was Mel's latent survival instincts kicking in — then again, it could just be that Mel had seen Diane in action and she knew, as the hair rose on the back of her neck, that whatever Diane was going to ask her was not going to make her happy. Not even a little.

Mel forced her lips to defy their inclination to turn down and instead she forced them to curve up. She knew the smile didn't reach her eyes; heck, the corners of her lips didn't even reach her nose. Still, it was a valiant attempt to mask the fear that was now coursing through her system.

25

"Why don't we sit," Mel said. She glanced at Elliott. "Can I get you anything?"

"Do you have any gluten- and lactose-free cupcakes?" he asked.

Mel glanced at the display case. Separated from the other cakes were her specialty cakes for those with specific dietary needs. She knew they were low on the vanilla, but there were several freshly made chocolate cupcakes. Oscar Ruiz, her assistant chef who went by the name Oz, had created the recipe himself when he discovered his little brother suffered food allergies.

"How do you feel about chocolate?" she asked.

"I like chocolate," Elliott said.

"I'll be right back then," Mel said.

Diane led the way to a booth in the far corner. She slid into one side and Elliott slid in after her. They had their heads pressed together as they shared a whispered conversation. Mel hadn't gotten a romantic vibe off of them, but as she plated Elliott's cupcake, she noticed that he watched Diane with a look on his face that reminded her of a puppy looking for a belly rub.

Oh, boy, she felt for the guy. From what she remembered about the years she cohabited with Diane, the woman had a habit of chewing men up and spitting them out. Dating wasn't a random event for Diane. She treated it like she treated everything else in her life. It was a competition.

If Diane was going to give a man the time of day, he was at the top of his class; he was handsome with a side of hot; he had to dress well, drive a nice car, and be able to take her out in the style to which she planned to become accustomed. He had to be the best boyfriend, trumping any other woman's man with his wit, wisdom, and wealth.

There were no late nights spent watching bad TV and eating pizza right out of the box in Diane's world. They had been living in Los Angeles and if she was going to spend time with a man, he was going to take her out where she could see and be seen.

Mel remembered feeling in awe of her roommate. She had never met anyone so self-directed. It had been enlightening as much as it had been horrifying. On the one hand, Diane knew what she wanted and she didn't take no for an answer. On the other hand, her life hadn't seemed to be very much fun to Mel. There was no room for spontaneity or silliness, which were qualities she treasured in Tate and Angie.

She put the cupcake plate on a tray and grabbed a clean fork from the service station. It was mid-morning and other than a few orders that had been picked up, the bakery was quiet. Mel knew that she only had about fifteen minutes until the morning lull was over and the pre-lunch crowd started the steady stream of business that would continue on until they closed at eight o'clock tonight.

She put the cupcake down in front of Elliott and then slid into the booth on the opposite side of Diane. Elliott took the fork she had handed him and jabbed at the cupcake as if he was afraid it might bite back.

"Are you sure it's gluten-free?" he asked.

"Positive," Mel said.

"And no dairy or eggs?"

"None of that, either," Mel said. "We use baking soda and apple cider vinegar to make it rise. Also, unsweetened cocoa, not the Dutch processed, is acidic and will act as a leavening agent with the baking soda, so you get a nice fluffy cake."

"Vinegar?" Elliott frowned and his glasses slid down his nose. "What about the frosting? That looks like a buttercream and butter is dairy."

Mel swallowed her sigh. She was itching to find out what Diane wanted but Elliott was clearly untrustworthy of her gluten-dairy-egg-free chocolate cupcake so she

28

needed to put his mind at ease first.

"We use non-dairy spread and coconut milk," she said. "Can you eat those?"

Elliott nodded. He peeled the wrapper off of the cupcake and then slid the fork into the frosting, getting a well-balanced bite of cake and frosting on his fork. He held the fork up to eye level and examined the bite. Mel wondered what he was looking for. She glanced at Diane, who was watching Elliott with an annoyed expression on her face.

"Oh, enough already," Diane said.

She took the fork out of Elliott's hand and ate the bite herself. As she chewed her irritated expression changed into one of pleasure. Mel smiled. A good cupcake will do that for you.

"This is amazing," Diane said. "You can't even tell that there's none of the bad stuff in it."

"Really?" Elliott asked. "Are you sure?"

"Positive." Diane handed him his fork. "Enjoy."

Elliott tucked into the cupcake like a kid finding a candy stash in his sibling's room.

Diane turned to Mel. She reached across the table and took Mel's hands in hers.

"So," she said.

"So," Mel echoed her.

She studied Diane's face. She was smiling, her unnaturally white teeth practically glowing under the shop's fluorescent lighting.

"Tell me if I'm crazy, but I get the feeling this is more than just a social call."

"You always were so smart," Diane said. "Top of our class on every project."

This had actually been a sticking point between them for several semesters, until Diane had scored a coveted internship in New York and had left school for a semester. Mel had taken the opportunity to move off campus and they hadn't roomed together again.

Mel pulled her hands back and folded them in her lap. She knew she wouldn't be able to nudge the purpose of her visit out of Diane until she was good and ready. She had been like this in college, too. There was nothing Diane liked as well as a dramatic entrance or a dramatic pause.

"Now, you know I run my own very profitable marketing company," Diane said. Mel nodded. "Well, I fell in love with one of my clients, Mike Bordow. His family owns Party On!, the party supply company."

"Oh, how ni—" Mel began, but Diane cut her off.

"No, not nice," Diane said. "Turns out, he was a rather poor ROI, in fact."

"ROI?" Mel asked.

"Return on investment," Diane said.

"Ah." Mel nodded.

She'd forgotten how much Diane loved her acronyms, also how she viewed relationships as more of a business concept than an emotional connection.

"He was perfect," Diane said. "Gorgeous, rich, successful, well connected; he had it all."

"Had?" Mel asked. The way Diane was talking she wondered if the poor guy had died.

Diane pursed her lips. "Yes, well, I recently discovered, he wasn't quite as wealthy as he led me to believe."

"Oh," Mel said. She knew her old roommate well enough to know that money, or the lack thereof, would be a deal breaker.

"Which is why I am here," Diane said. "You know how I hate to be played for a fool."

Mel nodded. She did indeed.

"Well, it occurred to me that I need a unique way to get my message across about our engagement —" Diane said.

"Engagement?" Mel cried. "You're getting married?"

"Were," Diane said. "We were getting married. *Were* being the operative word

31

here. So, I want you to bake me some cupcakes."

"For the wedding that isn't going to happen?" Mel asked.

"No, to break up with the big jerk," Diane said. "What I need you to do, Mel, is bake me the freshest, tastiest, most wonderful cupcakes ever."

"Because you're dumping your fiancé?" Mel asked. She didn't want to appear dense but usually people didn't hire her to put this much effort into cutting loose their significant other.

"That's right," Diane said. "After all, nothing says *We're through* quite like a yummy cupcake that says, *It's not me, it's you.*"

THREE

"I can honestly say this is a first," Mel said. "I've baked some specialty cupcakes, sure, but breakup cupcakes to end an engagement, that's new."

Diane smiled while Elliott finished his cupcake. He even scraped the plate with his fork, which Mel took as high praise.

"I'd like you to deliver them tomorrow morning," Diane said. "He's usually at home or at his country club until ten as he likes to work out first thing in the morning, and the club has an amazing gym. I'm going to miss it."

"You don't need to work out," Elliott said. "You look amazing."

Diane smiled at him and Mel wondered if she had any idea that the man was besotted with her. Mel was betting she didn't. Elliott didn't fit the profile of what Diane envisioned for a life partner and therefore he was just an employee, or perhaps a lackey, in her world. It was too bad. Despite his many dietary issues, Elliott seemed like a nice guy and it had been Mel's experience that there was a serious lack of nice guys on the planet.

"All right," Mel said. "I can have Oz, my assistant, drop off the cupcakes on his way to class."

"No, it has to be you," Diane said.

"What?" Mel asked. "Why?"

"Because I want you to call me and give me a blow-by-blow description of his re-action," Diane said. "Film it with your phone if you can manage it."

"Oh, no, I really don't —" Mel protested, but Diane interrupted.

"I would consider this repayment for the debt you owe me," Diane said. "In full."

Mel felt the pinching, piercing, painful twist of the screws against her thumbnails. Now it was all coming into focus. The reason Diane wanted her to do her dirty work for her was because Mel owed Diane a favor, a big one, from their college days. She had never thought Diane would be so mercenary as to cash in on the worst night of Mel's life, but clearly she had misjudged her old friend.

Mel reached into her apron and took a pen out of the large pocket. She snatched a paper napkin out of the silver dispenser on the table and began to sketch a few ideas for cupcake toppers. She figured she could make them in an edible fondant.

She led off with Diane's *It's not me, it's you* and then followed up with a heart broken in two, the word *love* with a circle around it with a line across it, and a pretty cursive topper that read *Love stinks*. She turned the napkin toward Diane so that she could see it.

"A dozen?" she asked.

"Perfect," Diane said. "He loves caramel, so if you could make a batch of those, that would be perfect. I'd like to picture him choking on every bite."

Mel studied her for a moment. "He's not allergic, is he?"

"What do you mean?" Diane asked.

"I'm not delivering caramel cupcakes to a guy who is allergic, am I?" she asked. "Just because you're angry doesn't mean you can put him at risk."

"Mel, what kind of person do you think I am?" Diane put her hand on her chest in a protestation of innocence.

Mel noted that even Elliott gave Diane a dubious look, so he might be besotted but he wasn't completely oblivious to Diane's temperamental nature.

"Your word," Mel said.

"Sheesh, fine," Diane huffed. "You have my word that he isn't allergic to caramel."

"Or milk," Mel said.

Diane rolled her eyes. "Or milk."

"Or gluten, eggs, any dairy, wheat, sugar . . ." Mel started listing all of the ingredients she could think of at the moment.

"He's not," Elliott said. Mel turned to look at him. He fussed with the placement of his plate and fork as if needing them in perfect alignment and said, "He used to make fun of me for my food allergies. He seemed to think it wasn't manly to be lactose intolerant. He gave me a smoothie once with a raw egg and some yogurt in it. I was sick for a week."

Diane patted Elliott's arm. "I should have dumped him then and there. Big jerk."

Mel glanced between them. Elliott's face turned a hot shade of red, but Diane seemed unaware that it was her touch on his arm that caused him embarrassment as opposed to his shame at the hands of her ex. Mel felt bad for the guy. He had it bad.

"All right, so I'll deliver the cupcakes to your ex tomorrow," Mel said. "Do you have a picture or something so I can make sure I deliver them to the right guy?"

"Mel, you met him," Diane said. She sounded exasperated.

"I did?"

"Yes, don't you remember, last year at that magazine gala, Mike was my date?"

"You mean the gala where we made a huge cornucopia of cupcakes with the staff of *Southwest Style* magazine, the gala where I was trapped in a fire and almost died? That gala?" Mel asked.

"Yeah," Diane said, sounding irritated. "I introduced you to Mike and I even told you I thought he was going to pop the question."

"Huh, I must have been preoccupied with fleeing for my life," Mel said.

Diane shook her head at her. "I'm disappointed in you, Mel. That's really self-absorbed of you, you know."

"Yeah, sorry about that," Mel said.

She glanced at Elliott. He blinked at her behind his glasses, reminding her of an owl. Then one corner of his lips turned up as if he knew exactly how she felt. Mel decided she liked him. If he could see the absurdity of Diane and be in love with her anyway, he was good people.

Diane's phone chimed and she glanced at it. "That's my eleven o'clock. I have to go."

"All right," Mel said.

She followed Diane and Elliott to the door.

"Text me a picture of the cupcakes, so I can approve them before you go," Diane said.

She was texting while talking so Mel stared at the top of her head, noting that Diane had the telltale dark roots of a fake blonde showing. For some reason, this gave Mel a boost in the old self-esteem. She had no idea why. It wasn't as if she had anything to do with her own DNA, but still, in a world of fake blondes, it felt nice to be the real deal.

"Oh, and if you really need to remember what Mike looks like, just go on my Instagram account," Diane said. "We did Coachella a few months ago. He's the one with the sad man bun on his head. Honestly, it's the mullet of our age. I made him cut it off as soon as we got home."

"He still has the gross beard, though," Elliott chimed in. "It's kind of thin and scraggly. I don't think all the raw-egg smoothies in the world are going to help him with that."

"Scraggly beard, got it." Mel nodded.

As the door shut behind them, she sagged back down into a seat at one of the tables. She had no idea how she was going to finesse the delivery of breakup cupcakes to the unsuspecting fiancé. Then again, it really didn't matter. She would do it because as Diane had so happily reminded her, she owed her old roommate one, and Mel wanted nothing more than her debt to be paid in full.

"How was your day, dear?" Joe DeLaura asked as he strode into the bakery kitchen via the back door.

Mel glanced up from the steel worktable where she was perfecting her breakup fondant. She had rolled out a large piece of white fondant and cut out round buttons the size of quarters. Now that they were dry, she was using her edible gel markers to draw the pictures she had sketched for Diane. This was the tricky part, which was why she had made extra buttons, because if she pushed too hard while drawing, she'd ruin the fondant.

"Oh, you know, I baked a little, ate a little, sold a lot," Mel said. "How about you?"

Joe put the carry-out bags he'd brought with him on the table and leaned in to kiss Mel. When his mouth lingered on hers, she felt her insides flutter just like they always did when Joe entered her personal orbit. They'd been dating like a normal couple

39

for the past few months and Mel was sure she'd never get used to it.

She lifted her gloved hands like a surgeon who was prepped for an operation and used her elbows to hook Joe in and pull him close. Then she kissed him as if she hadn't seen him in days instead of just that morning.

"I am never going to get tired of this," he said. He hugged her tight before releasing her and glancing around the kitchen. "Where's my boy?"

"Captain Jack is out front, terrorizing Marty while he cleans up," Mel said. She pointed to the carry-out bags. "What's cooking?"

"The best take-out Mexican in the valley," he said. "Two orders of Fiesta Burrito's carne asada French fries."

"I knew there was a reason I loved you," she said.

"And here I thought it was for my good looks."

"Those don't hurt, either."

Joe glanced down at the table. Then he frowned. "Please tell me that is not dessert for you and me."

Mel followed his gaze to the anti-love fondant buttons that would soon be decorating Diane's one dozen cupcakes of caramel-

40

crushing heartbreak.

"No, no!" she cried. "These are a commission from my old college roommate. She's breaking up with her fiancé."

"Via cupcake?" Joe asked. He glanced back at the table. "Harsh."

"Diane isn't known for her subtlety," Mel said.

Joe tipped his head to the side. "Diane?"

"Diane Earnest," Mel said. "We roomed together at UCLA until she went for an internship in New York City."

"Blond? Walks like a T-rex?"

"You know her?"

Joe looked uncomfortable. "We might have dated."

"Might have?" Mel asked. "That's not like sort-of pregnant, is it?"

"Well, it was more like the county hired her company to work on our public image, and I was sent to have dinner with her," he said. He ran a hand through his thick dark hair and then loosened his necktie as if he couldn't get enough air. "She seemed to think it was personal while I thought it was business. I didn't catch on until our third meal where she informed me that she was dining commando."

Mel choked on some spit. "She . . . Oh my god! How does a woman inform you

41

that she is underwear-less in polite conversation?"

"Given that she had me jacked up against the wall, *polite* is not the word that leaps to mind," he said. He shuddered.

"Oh, Joe," she said. "Why didn't you ever tell me about this?"

"I think the psychological damage I incurred caused me to block it out," he said. "Plus, it was five or six years ago and you and I weren't a thing yet."

"Have you seen her since?"

"No," he said. "And I'm not planning to ever again. Are you sure she didn't request poison in any of these?"

"Don't even joke about poison and my cupcakes in the same sentence."

"Noted," he said. "It's just that she strikes me as the sort who might hold a grudge."

"Since she's breaking up with him for his lack of capital, I don't think she's looking for revenge as much as public humiliation, which is why she wants me to personally deliver the cupcakes and report back on his reaction," Mel said.

Joe turned to look at her. A little V formed in between his eyebrows, which was Mel's first clue that he was unhappy about the proposed delivery situation.

"What do we know about this guy?" Joe asked.

"His name is Mike Bordow and his family owns a party supply company called Party On!"

"Doesn't ring a bell."

"I don't imagine it would unless you've seen him in court."

"How do you know he's not going to handle this by going completely bonkers?" Joe asked. "I don't want you in harm's way. I think we've both had more than enough of that."

"No argument there. I don't think Diane would send me into a potentially dangerous situation. I suspect she wants to embarrass him but I can't see her putting me in jeopardy to do it."

"Really?" Joe asked. "Have you stayed in close contact with her? Do you know what she's capable of?"

"I've seen her at events over the years, and we like each other's social media posts." Mel turned back to the table. Her buttons were dry and she started to place them on her cupcakes.

"Social media is lies, all lies," Joe said. "You can't get a real feel for a person who is image-crafting online. Her life probably looks amazing and is actually a complete train wreck."

Mel considered what he said. Diane's social updates were a bit over-the-top, no question, but did she have a dark side that could be teeming with evil plans for vengeance? Mel didn't think so.

"I'm just going to deliver a dozen breakup cupcakes," she said. "What could possibly go wrong?"

FOUR

"Diane, I don't have all day to chase down your ex," Mel said into her cell phone while she juggled the box of cupcakes and her purse.

She was leaving Mike Bordow's country club in the McDowell Mountain foothills under the watchful eye of thc club's hostess. No one had seen Mike and even though it was still early morning it was beginning to heat up. She felt a trickle of sweat slide down her back before being absorbed into her gray tank top, which was probably marred with sweat stains already. Fabulous.

"You've only tried his club," Diane protested.

"And his house," Mel argued.

"Fine, just stop by his office," Diane snapped. "If he's not there then we can discuss an alternative."

"Text me the address, please," Mel said.

"Okay, but call me when you get there,"

Diane ordered.

Then she ended the call without so much as a good-bye. Mel had to admit she was going to be relieved when the cupcakes were delivered, her debt to Diane was paid, and they could go back to being friends at a distance.

She unlocked the door to her red Mini Cooper and climbed in. She strapped the box of cupcakes into the passenger seat and turned on the engine to cool the car while she waited for Diane's text. Her phone chimed and Mel glanced at the address to see that the location was in the industrial section of Scottsdale, near the airport. Great, just great.

She put her phone away and left the country club. If she was lucky and traffic was light, she'd be able to deliver the cupcakes and be back at the bakery within the hour. Then she was done with this whole messy situation.

She wondered how Mike Bordow was going to react to receiving breakup cupcakes. She hoped she didn't have to explain it any more than to say that the cupcakes were from Diane. Oh, god, what if he got mad and yelled at her or, worse, cried?

She didn't think she could handle a strange man blubbering about his breakup.

It was one thing if she knew a person, but this man was a complete stranger. What if he threatened to do himself harm? Was she obligated to stay and make sure he didn't?

Because she was in north Scottsdale, she opted to take the 101 south toward the airport. As she took the exit that would take her to the warehouse, she heaved an irritated sigh. She had so many better things to do back at the bakery than to deliver cupcakes for one very high-maintenance client. Yes, she owed Diane a favor, a big one. At that Mel punched on the radio in the car. Anything to distract herself from thinking about past stupid decisions.

She wondered how the flower shopping had gone with Angie yesterday and knew that when she did return to the bakery, she would have to spend the rest of the day pretending to be listening when Angie hemmed and hawed about the merits of each flower, asked Mel which she preferred, and then spent the rest of the day second-guessing her final choices.

Mel was suddenly relieved to be on the road away from the turbo bride. She could only hope that Tate had offered some strong opinions in the flower-selection process to help her out. It seemed he was the only one who could offer an opinion without making

47

Angie cry.

Then again, this was Tate. He'd probably enjoy using cactus for centerpieces if it moved the ceremony along and scored a laugh. He had pushed for a down and dirty civil ceremony, but his mother had insisted on the full-blown, big traditional wedding for their only child and Angie's parents had been in total agreement for their only daughter. There was no escaping the humongous wedding that was unfolding before them. At last count, Mel had heard the number of guests was somewhere around three hundred and fifty. It made her regret that her elopement with Joe hadn't taken because she really didn't think she could handle that big of a wedding.

Mel cruised past the Scottsdale Airpark, which led her into the industrial district. She checked the address on her phone and knew she was only two left turns away from where she needed to be. Unfortunately, it was two left turns broken up by seven stoplights, which gave her a chance to plan what she was going to say.

"Hi, I'm Mel . . ."

No, there was no point in giving him her name. It wasn't like he was ever going to come to Fairy Tale Cupcakes and order a dozen from them after this. She drove to the next light, which turned red right before she got there.

"Hi, I have a delivery for Mike Bordow," she said. That was better. "These are a gift from . . ."

No, no, no, these were not a gift so much as an icing-covered kick in the man junk. She breezed through the next three lights and stopped, flipping on her signal to take a left.

"This is a delivery from Diane Earnest. If you could sign here," she practiced. There; that sounded nice and professional and blissfully vague. She would have Diane on the phone with her of course, which was weird, but whatever the client wanted the client got, right?

She saw the warehouse for Party On! ahead on her left. The small parking lot in front of the building looked empty so she parked right in front of the main doors, which opened into the business's showroom. The building was huge, so she figured they stored all of their party supply goods here in the huge warehouse beyond.

She wondered if the cupcake business would ever require them to have this much space. She really hoped not. There was no way she could quality control the amount of bakers it would take to fill up a place this large.

She climbed out of her car and felt the heat slap her in the face. It was the start of summer in central Arizona and the weather guys were already calling for record heat. After thirty-three years of living here, Mel knew she should be used to it, but every summer seemed just a little bit harder to get through than the last.

She circled the car and took her cupcakes from the passenger seat. The bright pink box looked so festive compared to the message inside. For a moment, Mel felt really bad about what she was about to do. What if Mike was crazy in love with Diane? This could be excruciatingly awkward. But then, once she did this favor for Diane she would have her old debt paid in full. It was a no-brainer and Mel strode forward, hitting the lock fob on her keychain as she went.

She put away her keys and took her phone out of her purse as she approached the door. With the cupcakes balanced in one arm, she dialed Diane's number and then let the phone rest on the top of the cupcake box as she pulled the front door open.

Cool air washed over her, and Mel felt the sweaty spots on her tank top turn cold. Not necessarily a bad thing. The showroom had high ceilings and loud music playing. Displays of glassware, linens, plastic flowers, and a pergola filled the large room.

Mel approached the unmanned front desk, hoping to find someone who could tell her where to find Mike. She really didn't want to give him his cupcakes in front of everyone. Even if that would make Diane's day, it was not part of the agreement and it would make Mel feel petty and mean.

"Hello?" she cried. There was no answer. She stood awkwardly in front of the desk, hoping someone would appear. The moments ticked by and she heard Diane's voice bark out of her phone.

"What's going on?" Diane demanded. "Where is he? Did you give them to him yet?"

"There's no need to yell," Mel said. "I'm right here."

"What's happening?"

"Nothing," Mel said. "There doesn't seem to be anyone at the front desk. Is that normal?"

"How should I know?" Diane asked. "It's not my business. I don't know their SOP."

Mel blew out a breath. Again with the acronyms; this one for *standard operating procedure.* How appropriate. "Well, what do you want me to do?"

"Deliver the cupcakes."

"Fine. Where is Mike's office?"

"Do you see the door behind the front desk?"

"The one that reads *Personnel Only*?" Mel asked. "Yeah, I see it."

"Go through that," Diane said. "It leads to the offices and the warehouse in back. It could be that they're having a meeting in a conference room or something."

"This is making me really uncomfortable," Mel said. That was an understatement and a half.

"Buck up. I think we both know how "uncomfortable' I made myself in order to save your behind. Yes?"

"Yes. All right. I'm going into the back."

Mel closed her eyes, trying to channel her patience. Had Diane always been this manipulative or was she just seeing it more clearly now that she was on the receiving end of it?

She walked around the vacant desk and into the back. Juggling her purse, her phone, and the cupcakes made it tricky, as the last thing she wanted was to drop the cupcakes and ruin Diane's revenge, thus keeping her debt alive and well. No, no, that sucker needed to be paid in full.

The door to the back was a swinging door.

She pushed it open, fully expecting an alarm to sound because she wasn't an employee. Quite the opposite, it was eerily quiet as she walked down the carpeted hallway. Office doors were open but no one was about. She noticed that the offices got bigger the farther she got away from the front, so she slowed down to read the name plaques beside each office, hoping she would find Mike's.

"Diane, something isn't right," Mel said. "There is literally no one here. It's creepy."

"Have you reached Mike's office yet?"

Mel glanced at the nameplate on the second-to-last door. "I'm standing in front of it now."

"Oh, goody," Diane squealed. Mel was pretty sure she heard her clap, too. "Go ahead in and make sure I can hear him when he reacts to the cupcakes."

Mel heaved a sigh. She shifted the cupcakes and rapped her knuckles on Mike's door. There was no answer. She tried the knob. It was unlocked. Desperate to get out of there, she pushed it open, hoping to find Mike, deliver the goods, and scram. The door swung open and she glanced inside.

"It's empty," she said.

"What?" Diane asked. "Where is everyone?"

"Not here," Mel said.

"Go into the warehouse," Diane ordered. "I bet they're having a meeting. You can surprise him in front of everybody. It'll be even better that way."

"Better for who?" Mel asked.

"Whom."

"Whatever."

"Just go."

Mel turned and left the office. She hoped with all of her might that the door to the warehouse was locked. It made sense that they must all be in there but the idea of humiliating Mike, a stranger, in front of all of his employees made her stomach cramp. Mel wasn't a fan of confrontations unless she was confronting a really big piece of chocolate cake with a fork.

Unfortunately, the door opened with a solid push. Mel stepped into the concrete cavern, expecting to find a crowd of people. Instead, it was as empty as the offices had been.

"Hello?" she called out. Her voice echoed against the large metal shelving units.

At a glance, she saw everything a party planner could ever hope for in their professional life. There were dunk tanks, photo booths, margarita machines, piñatas in every shape imaginable, glassware, tablecloths in every hue of the rainbow, pergolas, plastic flowers, pedestals, tables — truly, the warehouse seemed to go on and on and it was stuffed from floor to rafter with party supplies. Mel was immediately relieved that Angie had not come with her, because it would have caused her to second-guess every single thing she had chosen for her wedding thus far.

"Hello?" she called out again.

There was no answer, not even from the giant blow-up clown in the corner, although honestly he looked a little deflated. Mel could relate.

"Diane, seriously, there is no one here," Mel said. "I could throw a cupcake across the warehouse and not hit a living being. It's a ghost town in here."

At the word *ghost,* a shiver wiggled up Mel's spine and she shuddered. She shook her head. She was being ridiculous.

"There has to be someone there," Diane argued. "The front door was unlocked. Would they really risk having all of their merchandise ripped off by not locking the doors?"

"I can't really imagine who is going to run off with a bunch of deflated bounce houses," Mel said.

"Maybe they're in the back of the warehouse," Diane said. "Just do a walk-through so we know for sure that no one is there. You know, if you don't find him now, you're going to have to wait for him or come back later."

Mel grimaced and clenched her fingers around her phone, pretending it was Diane's neck. Then she cleared her throat.

"Or I could just leave the cupcakes in Mike's office for him to find whenever he gets in," she said.

"No, that is completely unacceptable," Diane said. "I have to hear his reaction to the realization that I am dumping his ass."

"Okay, come clean," Mel said. "I get that you're miffed because you found out he is marrying you for your money, but this gesture seems, I don't know, angrier than that."

"Maybe that's because I thought I'd finally found the one," Diane said. "I really thought he and I had something special and then I find out that it's just my bank account. I . . . I . . ."

Her voice trailed off and Mel heard genuine hurt in her voice. Given that franchising the bakery sucked up every bit of free cash she, Angie, and Tate had at this point, she couldn't really imagine what it was like to have a flush bank account. When she thought about Joe, however, and imagined being loaded with money, she knew it would devastate her to find out Joe was only after her bottom line, as it were. Suddenly, being broke seemed not so bad.

"Okay, okay, I'll walk the warehouse," she said. "I'll find him and you'll get your epic breakup."

"Thank you, Mel," Diane said. "You're the best!"

"Yeah, yeah, says the woman who is getting her way," Mel grumbled, but it was without real complaint.

She strolled down one wide aisle, looking for someone, anyone, who could tell her where Mike was. Tanks of helium were stored by enormous bins of balloons in every conceivable color. For a second she thought about doing the inhale-helium-and-talk-in-a-squeaky-voice thing, but good sense prevailed and she turned around and went down the next aisle.

She was halfway down when she noticed a portable ball pit. It had clear sides of thick Plexiglas and was full to bursting with bright colored balls the size of baseballs. Even more tempting than the helium, Mel had to fight the urge to jump in feetfirst.

"Did you know they have a portable ball pit?" she asked Diane.

"Yes, we set it up for a party once," Diane said. "It was totally fun until some drunkard threw up in it. So gross."

Mel frowned at the ball pit. Vomit would be a buzzkill. Then she felt her breath catch and the blood drained from her head in one big swoosh, making her dizzy. She blinked as she staggered, but there was no denying what her eyes were seeing. Pressed against the clear side of the pit was a man's hand, clutching a bright yellow ball.

FIVE

"Uh, Diane." Mel's voice sounded high-pitched and panicky even to her own ears. "There's a hand."

"What?" Diane asked. "A hand? What are you talking about?"

"In the ball pit," Mel said. Her voice was definitely wobbly now; in fact, her whole body was wobbly as she began to shiver and shake. "Help."

That last part hadn't been for Diane but for anyone who might be somewhere in the warehouse, hearing her have a complete and total meltdown.

"Help? Mel, what is going on?" Diane's voice was a cross between irritated and alarmed, for which Mel really couldn't blame her.

Mel took a steadying breath. Maybe she was panicking prematurely. It could be that one of the guys who worked here was inordinately fond of the ball pit. Perhaps he had just climbed in to play, and while in there he had fallen asleep and was taking a nap. There was no reason to assume the worst.

"Mel, what the hell is going on?" Diane snapped. "You aren't making any sense."

"There's someone in the ball pit," Mel said.

"Is it Mike?" Diane asked. "That would be just like him. He's so immature. If it is, make him get out and look at the cupcakes and switch over to video on your phone so I can see his face."

"Hang on," Mel said. "I need to put the cupcakes down."

She glanced around the area and saw some shelf space nearby. She put the box of cupcakes and her purse on the edge and then returned to the ball pit.

She stood by the hand that was still clutching the yellow ball and knocked on the glass. She braced herself for the person inside to jump when they heard her knock. There was no movement. Mel felt her stomach twist. This was not good. So not good.

Maybe the person was listening to music and didn't hear her. Joe did that all the time. He put in his earbuds, and she didn't see them and then discovered she'd spilled out her whole day to him while he listened to music and heard none of it. They'd had a few discussions about it, which now led to her always starting the conversation with, "Do I have your full attention?" and making sure he answered before she launched into her daily tirade about whatever, although lately it was usually Angie and "the wedding."

"What's happening?" Diane demanded.

Mel ignored her and rapped on the glass again, harder this time. The fingers didn't move, not so much as a twitch. Mel glanced over the side of the ball pit, which sat as high as her nose, causing her to stand on tiptoe to look inside.

She could just make out a tuft of brown hair visible between the balls. The rest of the person was buried — oh, bad choice of words — deep in the pit.

Mel reached over the side, but she couldn't reach the person. She knocked on the glass again. Nothing. She kicked the side of the pit. The balls jiggled a bit in response but the person didn't move.

There was no other choice. She was going to have to go in.

A ladder, like the sort used to climb into an aboveground swimming pool, was perched on the far side of the ball pit. Mel walked around, hoping the person would move before she had to climb in there. They did not.

"Diane, I don't want to alarm you, but the person in the ball pit is not moving," she said.

"What do you mean?" Diane asked.

Stress made Mel's temper short. "What do you mean *what do you mean?* Did I stutter? There's a freaking body in the ball pit!"

"A body?" Diane's normally bossy tone was downgraded to one full of concern.

"Yes, a body," Mel said. Now she sounded like she was on the verge of tears, which was not inaccurate. She could feel the sobs welling up just beneath the surface.

"What are they doing in there?" Diane asked. "Who is it?"

"I don't know," Mel said. "Look, I think I have to climb in there and see if they're okay."

"Yeah, that's a good idea."

"Says the woman who does not actually have to go in there."

"Don't take it out on me," Diane said. "It's not my fault you found a body."

"Really? Because I'm thinking if I wasn't here on this vindictive errand of yours, I wouldn't be here right now, climbing into a ball pit with a body."

"Maybe they're napping," Diane said.

"Huh." Which was the nicest grunt Mel could come up with as she hauled herself up the ladder with one hand.

The ladder was wobbly and rickety and she felt like it would snap under her weight at any second. If ever there was a ladder that was built for children, this was it.

Mel stood on the second-to-top step and leaned over the edge. She reached out a hand to see if she could grab any part of the person in the pit, but her reach was too short and she couldn't see through the balls. She was going to have to dig.

"Diane, I'm putting you on speaker," she said. Then she tapped the screen to do just that and tucked the phone into the front of her tank top.

Once the phone was secure, Mel used both hands to scoop away some of the balls so she could see the body. A black polo shirt was revealed. Much like the hand she'd seen through the side had been big and square like a man's, so was the torso that was revealed. She went up another step on the ladder and leaned farther into the pit so she could follow one of the arms until she found the wrist.

The skin was cold to the touch and she shivered. She put her fingers on the pulse

63

point just above the snazzy silver band of the man's wristwatch. She couldn't feel anything. She started to panic but then remembered she'd never been very good at finding her own pulse, never mind anyone else's.

She climbed up onto the edge of the ball pit. She had to find the guy's face; that was the only way she'd be able to tell what was happening. Mel lowered her feet into the pit, hoping she wasn't stepping on some part of him she couldn't see.

"What's happening?" Diane asked. She sounded worried.

"I'm trying to dig him out," Mel said. "Hang on."

Mel shoved aside armfuls of the happy-colored balls. They poured back, filling the void, making the whole process a bit maddening. The tears Mel had pushed aside now felt like they were roaring back, ready to spill over her eyelids at any provocation. Also, her nose was starting to run.

"Damn it," she cried.

She began to shove armfuls of balls over the side of the pit. The only way she could dig out the body was to get rid of them. She grunted with effort as she sent dozens of balls spilling across the warehouse floor. Finally, she was able to see more of the

64

body, which was angled so that the head was facing up but was lower than the rest of the body.

Mel scooped up armfuls and tossed them again and again until her fingers brushed something sticky and wet. She turned her hands up and noticed that they were covered in blood. A yelp came out of her throat and then a sob. She glanced down and saw that the face had finally been revealed, what was left of it anyway, and it belonged to Mike Bordow. The Party On! owner had clearly jumped into his ball pit for the last time.

Before she could stop it, Mel's breakfast staged a rebellion and just like any kid hopped up on too much junk food and too much time spent playing in the ball pit, she barfed all over the brightly colored balls and Mike Bordow's black polo shirt.

"Mel? Mel? Are you there?" Diane cried. "What's happening?"

Retching, Mel staggered through the balls to the side of the pit. Her hands were shaking as she hauled herself up and out of the ball pit and collapsed onto the cold concrete floor in a heap. Mike Bordow was dead. Deader than dead. And she had found him. Why? Why her? Why? Why? Why?

The snot and tears came out like an avalanche. She was shaking and her teeth

65

were chattering and all she could taste was the bile in her mouth. All around her, at odds with her state of crisis, brightly colored happy plastic balls littered the floor.

"Mel!" Diane was screeching now. "Answer me!"

Mel pulled her phone out of her shirtfront. She used the hem to wipe the tears and snot from her face.

"Hang up, Diane," she said. "Hang up and call 9-1-1. I found Mike and he's dead."

Silence came from the phone.

"Diane, did you hear me?"

"I heard you." Her voice was faint. "Are you . . . su— sure?"

"Yes." Mel pressed the palm of her hand to her forehead. "I need to call my uncle and you need to call the Scottsdale Police Department. Do it. Do it now."

"Uh . . . okay," Diane said. Her voice was shaky and Mel realized that she had just told her friend that the fiancé she had so looked forward to breaking up with was dead.

"I'm sorry, Diane," Mel said.

"Me, too," she said. She ended the call.

Mel scrolled through her contacts until she found her uncle Stan's name and number. He was her late father's younger brother and had been a member of the Scottsdale

66

Police Department for as long as she could remember. He'd been working as a homicide detective for over a decade and Mel had never been more grateful for his line of work than she was right at this moment.

"Cooper," he barked into his phone after the second ring.

"Uncle Stan, it's Mel," she said. Relief swept through her at the sound of his familiar gruff tone.

"So the caller ID said. What do you need, kid?" he asked.

He sounded unhappy and Mel knew that he still blamed her for the departure of his last partner, Manny Martinez, who had relocated to Las Vegas just a few weeks ago. It wasn't Mel's fault that he had fallen head over heels with Holly Hartzmark, the former showgirl turned baker, who had opened their first Fairy Tale Cupcakes franchise on the Strip, but there was no talking Uncle Stan out of his annoyance with her. Still, she needed him.

"Uncle Stan, there's a b— bo—" Mel began, but the words did not come easily.

"Don't say it," Uncle Stan ordered.

"What?"

"Do not say what I think you are about to say," he said.

"But I have to, there's a bo—"

"No!"

"Uncle Stan," Mel cried. "I need you."

He heaved a sigh that sounded as if it came all the way from his well-scuffed loafers.

"It's a body, isn't it?" he asked.

"Yeeeeees," Mel answered on a wail that quickly turned into a second bout of blubbering.

"How is this possible?" Stan cried. "I'm a homicide detective and I don't turn up this many dead bodies. Where are you?"

"I'm in the warehouse of Party On!, the party supply company near the Scottsdale Airpark," Mel said. "No one is here, just me and the —"

"You!" a voice cried from across the warehouse. Mel glanced up to see three people, one woman and two men, all wearing the same black polo shirts Mike was wearing, storming toward her. "Who are you and what the hell are you doing here?"

"Uncle Stan, you might want to hurry," she said.

"Roger that," he said. "Stay on the line so I know you're not in danger. Dispatch will send over the nearest squad car in the area."

"Thanks," Mel said.

"Hey, lady!" the woman yelled at her. "I asked you a question."

"Stop!" Mel said. "I have the Scottsdale PD on the phone. The situation has been called in and I need you to stay out of the area."

"Scottsdale PD?" the woman asked. "On whose authority? I'm Suzanne Bordow. I own this company. If anyone is calling the police for any reason, it's me calling on you for breaking and entering."

"Stan, what do I do?" Mel asked.

"Keep them away from the scene. We need it to remain as untouched as possible," he said.

"Listen, there's been an incident, and I need you to leave the warehouse area," Mel said.

"Incident?" Suzanne asked. "I'm sorry, who are you?"

"Melanie Cooper, I'm a cupcake baker," Mel said.

Suzanne shook her head. She had the same dark curls as Mike and Mel felt her gag reflex kick in as she pictured Mike's blood-soaked hair. She glanced down at her hands.

"Oh my god, is that blood?" one of the men standing beside Suzanne asked.

"Yes, I'm afraid it is," Mel said. "That's why you need to . . ."

"Troy!" The other man shouted the first

69

guy's name and jumped toward him as he went all limp and slid to the ground as if someone had let the air out of him.

"Whose blood is that?" Suzanne demanded. Her eyes were wide and she glanced from Mel to the ball pit, where Mike's hand was still visible, smashed up against the Plexiglas. And since Mel had cleared out half of the ball pit, so was his bashed-in head.

"When I found him, I accidentally got some blood . . . Oh, urgh." Mel's urge to upchuck kicked in again, and she had to swallow swiftly to keep from barfing.

"Mike!" Suzanne cried. "That's my brother Mike!" The anguish in her voice made Mel's heart hurt. The man who had failed to catch his coworker before he hit the floor reached out to Suzanne but she shook him off.

There was no other word for the sight of Mike in the ball pit except *grisly,* and Mel felt really badly that his sister had to see him like that. Suzanne glanced back at Mel as if the shock was making her slow to put the pieces together. "That's Mike's blood on your hands."

"Yes, but I was just delivering cupcakes when I found him, I swear," Mel protested. Suzanne did not appear to believe her. In

70

fact, judging by the crazy light in her eyes, things were about to get ugly. Mel spoke into her phone, "Stan, I need backup, repeat, I need backup."

"We're on our way," he said. "Hang tough, kid."

"You killed my brother!" Suzanne cried. Without any warning, she launched herself at Mel and took her down hard onto the cement floor. Even the smattering of happy, bright colored balls didn't block the impact enough to keep Mel from having the wind knocked out of her.

"Help!" she gasped into the phone before it fell from her grasp.

Six

Suzanne grabbed Mel by her short-cropped hair, knotting it between her fingers as she pulled Mel to her feet.

"You killed him!" she screamed. "You killed my brother!"

Two uniformed officers burst into the warehouse at that moment. One of them was talking into her shoulder radio; the other had his hand hovering over the firearm on his hip.

"Hold it; no one move," the officer with the itchy trigger finger said.

Mel raised her hands into the air. Suzanne released her and strode toward the male officer, while the female officer pulled on blue latex gloves and hurried to the ball pit to examine Mike Bordow. After mere moments, she turned back to her partner with a shake of her head.

"She killed my brother! Look, she has his blood on her hands!" Suzanne shrieked.

The officer pulled his gun and pointed it at Mel.

"I can explain," Mel said. "I'm Detective Cooper's niece and this stuff happens to me all the time."

"Good, then you can explain it to the detectives when they get here," the officer with the gun said. He inched his way around Mel and cuffed her hands behind her back.

"Is this really necessary?" she asked.

"For the moment," he said. "Everyone clear the area. Now."

"But my brother," Suzanne protested.

"I'm sorry, ma'am, but we need to seal the area for the investigators," he said.

"I'm telling you what happencd," Suzanne snapped. "She killed him."

"I didn't," Mel said. "I swear."

Troy was roused from the floor and hauled out of the warehouse by his coworker while Suzanne and Mel were escorted after them back into the hallway of offices. Suzanne and her employees waited in one room, while Mel was led to another. The officer positioned himself in the hallway, making sure no one left their room.

Mel couldn't wait for Uncle Stan to arrive and read these uniforms the riot act for cuffing his niece. As she sat in a hard chair in what appeared to be a conference room, she longed for her phone so she could call someone, anyone, okay, mostly her boyfriend, Joe, to comfort her during this horrible ordeal.

She glanced at the clock on the wall. Stan had said they were on their way. His office wasn't that far away from the airpark. Surely he would arrive in a matter of minutes and get her sprung from this travesty of justice.

When the minute hand had moved past the thirty-minute mark, Mel was pretty sure that Stan was still pissed at her for Manny leaving the department and this was the way he was going to make her pay. Lovely.

She rose from her seat, went over to the wooden door, and gave it a solid kick. There was no way she was going to sit here for another minute, while her shoulders stiffened up from the awkward position and her hands were still caked in a dead man's blood.

No one responded, so she began kicking the door in a steady rhythm that she hoped was like an obnoxious dripping faucet, or a relentless woodpecker, or a kid dribbling his basketball up and down the street, until it started to beat on the brain of anyone within hearing distance.

The door was opened right as she was about to kick it again and her foot shot forward and connected with the navy trouser leg of a short, curvy woman. The woman wore her dark hair in a fat bun on top of her head, her dress shirt was white and completely wrinkle-free, she wore a badge on her belt, and the sour look she gave Mel made her think the woman enjoyed her line of work entirely too much.

"Oh, sorry," Mel said. "You should warn a person before you open the door."

"You shouldn't kick doors like a three-year-old having a tantrum," the woman returned.

"I wasn't kicking it because I was mad," Mel said. The excuse sounded lame even to her own ears. Damn it. "Is Detective Cooper around?"

"He's busy at the scene," the woman said. "What do you need?"

"To get out of these cuffs, to wash the blood off my hands, to go home, take your pick," Mel said. Okay, now she sounded like a three-year-old, but in her own defense, it had been a rough morning and she was not at her best.

"Have a seat," the woman said. "You'll go when we say you can go."

Mel lifted her eyebrows. No one from the Scottsdale PD had ever spoken to her so harshly except Manny when they had first met. She glanced at the name on the woman's badge. T. Martinez.

No freaking way.

"You know Manny Martinez?" she asked.

The woman gave her a look that said perhaps Mel wasn't as stupid as she'd thought. "He's my cousin. I'm Tara Martinez."

"Of course you are," Mel said. Now the woman's hostility was all coming into focus.

"And you are Melanie Cooper, former love interest of Manny. You remember him, tall, good-looking detective who just moved to Las Vegas, transferred to the Vegas PD, in fact," Tara said. "Who does that? Who moves away from all of his family to go shack up with some cupcake baker and her kid?"

"That is not my fault," Mel said.

Tara narrowed her eyes at her. "Of course it is. You could have made him stay, but did you? No. You had your eyes set on a bigger prize, an assistant county attorney. How is good ol' Joe DeLaura anyway?"

"Fine," Mel said.

"Terrific," Tara said. Her sarcasm was as sharp as the edge of the cuffs digging into Mel's wrists. "And I'm sure Joe will be thrilled to hear all about this."

With that, Tara slammed the door in Mel's

face. She wouldn't have thought the day could get any worse. She'd been wrong. So very wrong.

"Really, Uncle Stan?" she asked when he appeared in the conference room fifteen minutes later. "Forty-five minutes I've been sitting here. I get that you're annoyed with me, but seriously?"

"Mel, I need you to let the crime scene technicians look you over," he said.

"Why?" she asked.

"To prove that you didn't have anything to do with Mike Bordow's murder," he said. He reached into his shirt pocket and fished out a roll of chalky antacid tablets. He popped one in his mouth and ground it between his molars as if it were the antidote to a venomous snakebite.

"What's going on?" she asked.

"The vic's sister is raising a hell of a stink about finding you here," he said. "Your bloody hands were not helpful."

"Do I need a lawyer?" Mel asked.

Uncle Stan pressed his lips together. He clearly was torn between helping her out and divulging facts about the case.

"It'll be easier if you let them snap some pics and take some swabs," he said. He lowered his voice. "You can track your moves this morning?"

"Oh, yeah, I was at Bordow's house and talked to the guard at his gate, then I was at his country club and talked to the hostess, and I was on the phone with my client Diane before I got here and found him. Why?"

"The medical examiner puts his death at before seven o'clock this morning, putting you nowhere in the area at the time of death," he said.

"I was at the bakery with Tate and Marty. I didn't even leave there until after eight o'clock." Mel felt her body sag in relief. Then she glared at him. "You could have led with that, you know."

He gave her his first smile of the day. "Now we're even."

Mel gave him a hurt look. "I didn't think you were that vindictive."

Uncle Stan sighed. He turned her around and released her from the cuffs. Then he chafed her wrists between his big callused hands, reminding her so much of her dad it made her heart hurt.

"I'm not," he said. "It had to be handled this way so that I couldn't be accused of cutting you a break because you're my favorite niece."

Mel smiled. "I'm your only niece."

"Doesn't make it any less true," he said.

He opened his arms wide and Mel stepped in for one of his patent-worthy bear hugs.

He was built big and wide just like her father. He even wore the same aftershave. When Uncle Stan hugged her, it was just like having her dad with her, and she squeezed him extra tight, grateful for the comfort that only Uncle Stan could give.

"So, it was by the book to keep things on the up-and-up?" she asked. She leaned back and studied his dear jowly face.

"Mostly," he said.

"What do you mean *mostly*?"

"My new partner really doesn't like you," he said.

"That came out loud and clear," Mel said.

"I'm sure you'll win her over."

"Did you know your right eyebrow always rises a little bit higher than your left when you lie?"

"It does not," he protested.

Mel gave him a look and then turned and headed out the door to go retrieve her purse and her phone. She caught Uncle Stan feeling his right eyebrow in the reflection of the window glass in the door, and she smiled.

While they walked down the hall, Mel described exactly what had happened to the best of her ability. She acknowledged that the vomit in the ball pit was hers and Stan

79

patted her back, letting her know it was understandable.

He handed her the cell phone she'd dropped and Mel gave him a grateful smile. She glanced at the display and noticed she had a call from Diane, two texts from Tate, and a call from Joe.

"Does he already know?" she asked Stan. She knew she didn't have to clarify that she meant Joe.

"I called him on the drive over," Stan said. "If he's coming from downtown Phoenix, he should be here any minute."

"Thanks, Uncle Stan," she said.

"No problem," he said.

He led her over to the crime scene technicians. One of them looked at her hands. Because they'd been behind her back, Mel hadn't been able to remember how much blood she'd gotten on her hands. It was a relief when she looked to see that it was just her fingertips where she'd moved aside some of the balls that had his blood on them.

The medical examiner looked her over from head to foot. Then he reached into a plastic case and handed her several alcohol-soaked wipes.

"No spatter, no signs of an altercation. On the security cameras you're seen arriving hours after he was killed," he said. "As far as I'm concerned, you're free to go."

"Thanks, Hank," Stan said.

"Yes, thank you," Mel said. "And sorry about the vomit."

Hank Whitaker was tall and thin with gray hair that stood up in a mad-professor sort of way on the top of his head. He wore dark-rimmed glasses and his tie was askew, as if it just couldn't manage to stay centered.

"I've dealt with worse," he said.

Mel began to vigorously scrub at her hands, using the entire handful of wipes Hank had given her. When she was finished, she tossed them into a hazmat container, which the crime scene techs would throw their gloves and such into.

She saw Detective Martinez standing by the shelves where Mel had left her things. She walked around the yellow crime scene tape that had already been put up and went to the shelf to collect her purse.

As she put her phone in her handbag, she stared at the bright pink bakery box. She wasn't certain what the ramifications of showing it to Uncle Stan would be. Would he think Diane was somehow involved in this? Was she? Mel shook her head. Diane was an intense personality but she refused to believe she was capable of murder.

"Hey, baker, what do you have there?" Detective Martinez asked.

Mel frowned. She didn't want to think of this woman as Detective Martinez, as that title was reserved for her friend Manny.

"My purse, Detective Tara," Mel said. She made a show of opening her bag and checking the contents.

Tara pursed her lips. She was a handsome woman rather than pretty, but with her hair down and a smidgen of makeup she could pass for attractive. Of course, she would also have to off-load the tractor-trailer full of attitude she seemed determined to haul around with her. Not that Mel was judging or anything.

"Yeah, right, and what's that next to it?" Tara asked. She was talking to Mel in a high-pitched singsong voice, the sort that was meant to be condescending and irritating at the same time, which it was.

"Why, look!" Mel returned in the same singsong voice. "It's a box full of cupcakes."

She paused to dramatically slap her hand on her forehead. Tara curled her upper lip, looking like she wanted to take a bite out of Mel's hide. Mel ignored her.

"Oh, silly me, while tossing my cookies upon finding a body in the ball pit, I completely forgot that the only reason I'm even here is because I was hired to bake some cupcakes. Gee, it's a good thing you're here, Detective Tara. Whatever would we do without you?"

Tara crossed her arms over her chest. Now a low growl was coming from deep in her throat.

"Listen, baker, just because you're dating a county prosecutor and you're my partner's niece, don't think I'm going to go easy on you," Tara snapped. "I find it highly suspicious that you were the only person here and you were the one to find the body. That big-blue-eyed, blond thing you've got going might work on everyone else but it isn't going to work on me."

"Really?" Mel asked. "And here I was thinking you must have a crush on me given the way you've been so eager to tie me up and get me alone and all."

Tara took a step forward, looking like she wanted to use her Taser on Mel. Mel refused to back up. Instead, she set her chin, daring the smaller woman to try it.

"Mel, sweetheart." Joe appeared at her side and spun her around to give her a quick hug. "How are you? Sounds like it was a rough morning. Please excuse us, Detective Martinez."

Tara stared at Joe as if her tongue had just

gotten stuck to the roof of her mouth. It was a look of surprise, but not an unwelcome one.

"Hi, Joe. I didn't know you were coming to the scene," Tara said. Her voice was breathy and not in a hostile way but more in an I'm-picturing-you-naked-while-we-talk way.

"Not in an official capacity," Joe said. "I'm just here for her."

He glanced back at Mel and the concern in his eyes was almost her undoing. Almost. She was too busy watching Tara, who gave a jerky nod, spun on her heel, and stomped over toward Uncle Stan and the other crime scene investigators.

Mel knew that look. She had worn that exact expression from the first moment she had planted her peepers on Joe DeLaura when she was twelve and he was sixteen. Tara Martinez had a crush on Joe. Now her blatant hostility was coming into focus. This wasn't about Manny at all. It was about Joe. Oh, for the love of buttercream. Mel did not need this. Not now.

"How are you, cupcake?" Joe asked. He was studying her face as if looking for any signs that she was about to have a complete meltdown.

"I'm fine, or I will be as soon as I can get

out of here," she said. "I barfed in the ball pit."

"Oh . . . ew," he said. He hugged her close.

Mel hugged him back, happy that her hands were clean so she could get a good grip on him. She needed to feel his solid warmth right now.

"Uncle Stan had Hank Whitaker, the ME, look me over," she said.

Joe stepped back and looked her over from head to toe. "I'm assuming it's to rule you out as a suspect?"

"Yeah, the victim's head was bashed in," Mel said. "Whoever did it would most definitely have some sort of blood spatter on them."

He looked at her shirt. "You're clean."

"That's what Hank said," Mel said. "So, what do you think? Should I have let them?"

He nodded. "I trust Stan's judgment on this."

"Me, too," she said. "Joe, I'm a little worried about the cupcakes I was supposed to deliver."

He tipped his head to the side. "Not sure I understand."

"They're the breakup cupcakes you saw me working on last night," she said. "If the police see them, they'll know Diane was dumping Mike and they might think . . ."

"She killed him?" he said.

"Yeah," she said.

"Well, let's hope she has a good alibi for his time of death then," he said. "Because speaking as a lawyer, I am quite positive that the cupcakes are going to be considered evidence."

SEVEN

Joe drove Mel back to the bakery when they were done with the crime scene. She didn't ask him to, but he didn't really give her any option, which was a good call because even after she was cleaned up, she was shaky and edgy and guilt-ridden. There had been no way to avoid giving the cupcakes to Uncle Stan, and she'd seen Detective Tara's eyes light up at the possibility that Mel had just handed them their prime suspect.

Joe gave his keys to Uncle Stan, who agreed to drop off his car at the bakery on his way back to the station. Mel didn't think she imagined Detective Tara looking disappointed that Joe didn't ask her.

She wondered how long Joe had known Detective Tara and under what circumstances they had met. Not that she was jealous; no, not at all. Still, Joe had never mentioned her, just like he had never mentioned "dating-not-dating" Diane.

"What?" Joe asked as he opened her car door for her.

"What what?"

"You're giving me side eye," he said.

"No, I'm not."

"Yeah, you are."

He fell into step beside her as they crossed from the small parking lot behind the bakery, through the alley to the back door of the kitchen.

Mel was not going to get into it. She wasn't going to say a word. Things had been so lovely between them for the past few months. She really didn't want to ruin it with petty jealousy when she was still so rattled from finding Mike Bordow's body that she could barely think straight.

"Detective Tara totally has the hots for you," she said. *Doh!*

"Okay, I didn't see that coming," Joe said. He paused by the staircase that led up to Mel's apartment above the bakery.

Mel frowned. "I didn't, either. Sorry."

"Don't be," he said. "I don't think Detective Martinez has the hots for me, as you so delicately put it, but it wouldn't matter if she did as I belong totally and completely to you."

Mel felt her heart turn over in her chest with a cartwheel of joy. Even after their aborted wedding, Joe was still hers. Sometimes she just needed to hear him say it.

"All right then," she said. "That's that and I think I need to go shower and burn my clothes or something."

A small smile lifted one side of his mouth. "Yeah, don't burn anything. It looks suspicious."

Mel returned his smile. They had had this discussion before. Didn't every couple?

"All right." She hugged him tight. Something about the solid build of Joe DeLaura and the feel of his big man hands on her back always made Mel feel more grounded. "Take my car to work. I don't want you to get busted for going AWOL."

"Meh," he said. "You know the county prosecutor has a soft spot for you."

"That's because your boss has a weakness for my Key Lime Cupcakes," Mel said. She kissed him and then let him go.

"She's got good taste," he said.

"Says the man who's never met a cupcake he didn't like," she said.

"I'd give them all up for you," he said.

It was a totally corny thing to say and, yes, Mel's heart went squish at the words. Mostly, because Joe's sweet tooth was legendary but also because the look in his warm brown eyes was 100 percent sincere.

Goodness, she loved this man.

"Go," she said. She turned and walked up the stairs to her apartment. "Before I drag you up here with me."

Joe made to lunge after her and Mel jumped and then laughed. He grinned at her but then grew serious.

"Call me if you need me — for anything," he said.

"I promise."

He watched her until she went into her apartment and shut the door behind her. It was little things like that that meant so much to Mel. She didn't need a man to take care of her; she was perfectly capable of running her business and meeting her responsibilities all by herself, but there was something nice about having a man, who loved her, watch over her just as she did him.

Then she frowned. He hadn't really explained how he knew Detective Tara, though, had he?

After a hot shower and some therapeutic playtime with Captain Jack, Mel felt almost normal. It was amazing what an affectionate head butt from a kitten could do to lift a gal's spirits. Captain Jack, named for Captain Jack Sparrow, natch, had been rescued out of the bakery Dumpster just a little over a year ago.

He was so named because one of his black patches of fur covered one eye, giving him a decidedly piratical look. Mel loved him all the way to her squishy middle and given that he had been with her through some of the darkest days of her life, she wondered sometimes who had rescued who.

With a last kiss and a squeeze, Mel grabbed her phone, locked up her apartment, and headed downstairs to tell the bakery crew what had transpired that morning. They had to be wondering where she had gone since she should have returned two hours ago.

She unlocked the kitchen door and strode inside. Angie was seated at one of the steel worktables with her cousin Judi LaRocco Franko. The two of them had their heads pressed together, looking at an enormous binder.

"Look at how they decorated the pews with pewter tulle here," Judi said. She tapped the page and Angie nodded enthusiastically. "We could absolutely do something like that."

Judi was a short and blond version of Angie. She had a laugh that was contagious and eyes that twinkled, and, like Angie, she

91

was fierce about protecting those she loved, especially her husband, Chris, and their two beautiful daughters, Ciera and Arianna.

"Oh, I like that," Angie said. "Fancy but not over-the-top. But what about the wedding favors? I have no idea what to do for three hundred and fifty people."

Judi furiously flipped through the book until she got to the page she wanted, which she then turned to show Angie.

"I can take care of that for you. We'll go traditional Italian — your mother will be so happy — and I'll make the *bomboniere* for you."

"Oh, Judi, I love you," Angie cried, and she hugged her cousin in a hold that strangled.

"No problem, sweetie," Judi said. She smiled at Mel over Angie's shoulder, then she looked alarmed. She patted Angie's back. Hard. "Can't breathe."

"Sorry, sorry!" Angie let her go. "I'm just so grateful. You're really saving my life."

Mel frowned. Really? Who had been dragged to fifteen bridal shops until they found the dress? Who had smelled eight bazillion flowers until Angie settled on one? Who had baked five thousand sample cupcakes for Angie's cupcake tower? Okay, that was a slight exaggeration, but still. Mel had.

Mel had been all in and now, now she was being replaced by Judi?

"Hi, Mel, how are you?" Judi asked.

She smiled at her and it was so genuine and warm, Mel couldn't be mad at her. She could, however, be annoyed at the bridezilla.

"Hi, Judi." She smiled at her and then turned to Angie with a frown and said, "Since you asked, Judi, I've been better, given that just a few hours ago, I was hip-deep in a ball pit at a party supply store with a dead guy."

Both Judi and Angie sat staring at her. Then Judi shut the big binder with a snap.

"Look at the time. I've gotta go," she said. "Angie, I'll call you later."

With that, Judi tucked her binder under her arm and headed for the swinging door that would lead her into the bakery and out the front to freedom from the crazy.

Feeling bad for being so blunt, Mel called after her, "Be sure to take some cupcakes for the girls, on the house."

Judi gave her a wave and a worried smile and fled. Mel couldn't blame her.

Angie pushed the stool Judi had vacated toward Mel and said, "Explain."

Mel never got the chance. There was a shout out front and Marty's voice barked like a guard dog, "Hey, you can't go back there!" right before the door Judi had just left through was slammed open and Diane strode into the kitchen with Elliott on her heels.

"Hey!" Marty was right behind them, looking like he'd drag her back by the hair if he had to. Mel held up her hand to stop him.

"It's okay, Marty," she said.

He glared at Diane. "Next time you wait until I get the boss for you. Got it?"

Diane glared back at him. "Whatever, old man."

Marty opened his mouth to argue, but Angie, obviously sensing big things were unfolding, spun him around and shoved him back out into the bakery.

"Is that the service bell?" she asked. "Sounds like you have a customer."

Once Marty was gone, Angie looked at Mel with wide eyes. Well, at least Mel had gotten Angie's mind off of her wedding for a moment.

"Mel, what happened?" Diane cried. "I made the 9-1-1 call like you asked but then because I wasn't at the scene, the dispatcher ended the call and I haven't heard anything from anyone."

"You might want to sit down while you

hear this," Mel said. She glanced past Diane and saw Elliott standing behind her. She nodded at him to sit, too, but he was too fixated on Diane to pay her any attention.

Diane slid onto a stool and Angie did, too. Elliott remained standing at Diane's back while Mel paced as she talked.

Mel recounted the morning's events from the time of their phone call. She told Diane what Mike had looked like and that the police had arrived and she'd been detained. When she got to the part about being handcuffed, Angie let out a few colorful expletives that Mel appreciated.

Diane, however, waved at her to continue. Mel tried to keep the gore to a minimum and explained that she hadn't had her phone much of the time. As if it was a show-and-tell, she took it out of her pocket and held it up, then she noticed she had missed several calls and texts from Diane.

"Sorry," she said.

Diane sagged dramatically against the table, buried her head in her arms, and began to weep. Elliott patted her back and made soothing sounds. Given that Diane had sent her to dump the guy, Mel found her hysterical weeping a little over-the-top.

Angie moved to stand beside Mel. She put

95

her arm around her shoulders and gave her a solid half hug.

"Tough morning," she said. "Are you okay?"

Mel slumped onto an available stool and rested her head on her shorter friend's shoulder.

"I'll be okay." An image of Mike's crushed *cabeza* flashed through her mind and she shivered. Angie tightened her grip and Mel took comfort in that.

Diane's weeping was getting quieter and Mel stared at the back of her head. Her blond hair was in lovely disarray. Her outfit was a cute floral sundress and strappy pink sandals. All she needed was a parasol and she'd look the perfect part of an ingénue, a poor innocent, incapable of murder.

Mel frowned. Suddenly she felt as if she'd been played.

"Diane," she said. Diane kept her head down. That wasn't going to work. Mel needed to see her eyes. "Diane, look at me."

"What?" Diane asked with a dramatic hair toss. Mel noted her makeup wasn't even smudged.

"Did you kill Mike Bordow?" Mel asked. "Did you kill your fiancé?"

EIGHT

Diane gasped. She put her hand over her heart as if she had just taken a bullet to the chest.

"I am shocked," she cried. "How could you, Mel? How could you think that after all that we've been through together? You know what sort of person I am, especially after what I did for you."

Angie glanced at Mel. It was a speculative look. Mel had never told her about the debt she owed to Diane. She had brushed it off as a silly college thing, but now she could see that Angie suspected more. It made Mel feel guilty squirmy inside and frankly she'd felt all the feels she wanted to feel for one day.

"I'm sorry, it's just that you had me track him down to deliver breakup cupcakes," Mel said. "That doesn't speak well of a relationship and usually in a case of murder —"

"Murder?" Diane gasped. "Why would you say he was murdered?"

"Um . . . because his head was bashed in," Mel said.

Diane clapped her hands over her ears and Elliott gave Mel a reproving look. Mel looked at Angie for backup but Angie shook her head and whispered, "Harsh."

"Okay, fine, given the nature of the way I found him, it appeared he was encouraged toward his end. Better?"

Diane let out a wail and buried her face in Elliott's shirt-front.

"Or not," Angie said.

A knock on the back door of the kitchen made Mel start. No one but employees used that door and they all had keys; even Joe had a key. Mel exchanged looks with Angie and rose from her stool to go open the door. As if sensing something was amiss, Angie went with her.

Mel unlocked the door and opened it. Standing on the back stoop was Uncle Stan and, oh goody, Detective Tara.

"Mel, we're looking for your client Diane Earn —" Uncle Stan began, but Tara didn't wait for him to finish as she opened the door wider and pointed inside.

"Oh, and look at that, she's here," she said. "Shocker."

Detective Tara pushed past Mel and Angie and strode into the kitchen. Uncle Stan gave Mel a sheepish smile and followed his new partner into the room.

"Who is that?" Angie whispered to Mel.

"Long story," Mel said.

"Really? I can't wait to hear it," Angie said.

"Diane Earnest?" Detective Tara barked.

Diane leaned back from Elliott and swiftly swiped at her eyes. Mel noted that this time her makeup had given up its water resiliency and was now streaked down her face. Mel tried not to dwell on why this made her feel relieved. She believed her friend; really, she did.

"Y— yes?" Diane blubbered.

"We've been looking for you, Ms. Earnest," Tara said. "Any particular reason you came running here to see your . . . friend?"

Mel did not like the way she said that word. It was full of innuendo and not in a good sexy way; more like a creepy you-hired-your-friend-to-kill-your-fiancé icky way. She gave Uncle Stan an outraged look and he shrugged.

"Can you tell us where you were this morning?" Tara asked.

"I . . ." Diane glanced at Elliott for reassurance and he nodded. "I was at work."

"And did you hire Melanie Cooper for a

99

job?" Tara asked.

Diane nodded.

"I'm sorry, what was that?" Tara held her hand to her ear as if she was hard of hearing.

Mel turned to Uncle Stan. "Okay, enough. Take charge of her or I'll call Steve Wolfmeier and have him shut you down."

"Ah," Uncle Stan gasped and put a hand over his chest in mock outrage, looking very much like Diane had moments ago, except he was older, grayer, a dude, and clocked in easily at double Diane's weight. Mel glared and he added, "All right, relax."

"Again, Ms. Earnest, what were you about to say?" Tara continued to badger Diane.

Stan moved to stand beside Tara. "Excuse me, how do you do, ma'am? We haven't been introduced. I'm Detective Stan Cooper and this is my partner, Detective Tara Martinez."

Angie looked at Mel and mouthed the name *Martinez* with a questioning face and Mel nodded.

"Hello," Diane said. "I'm Diane Earnest and this is my head of technology, Elliott Peters."

No one shook hands but they all nodded at one another — well, everyone except Tara. She was too busy glaring, a look that now included Stan as well.

"I understand you were engaged to Mike Bordow," Stan said.

Diane nodded.

"I'm very sorry for your loss," Stan said. He looked sincere and that was all it took to reduce Diane to a blubbering mess.

She started to cry and this time Mel had no doubt that the tears were genuine, and she felt herself soften toward her bossy, demanding friend. This surely hadn't been how Diane had planned the day to go.

"Thank you," Diane said. "I was in the process of breaking off the engagement, but I never . . . I would never have wanted any harm to come to him."

"Where were you this morning?" Tara asked.

"At home and then I went into work about nine o'clock," she said.

"Did anyone see you before nine?" Tara asked. Her words had the *rat-a-tat-tat* of gunfire and Mel noticed that they all jumped a little bit when she spoke.

"No, I was alone, but I didn't do anything wrong," Diane said. "I didn't harm Mike."

"Uh-huh," Tara said.

She looked unmoved and Mel found herself really disliking the little terrier. As soon as they left, she was going to call

Manny in Las Vegas and tattle on his snippy little cousin. So there.

"I wouldn't hurt him, I swear," Diane insisted. "Tell them, Mel."

Feeling Tara's dark gaze turn to her, Mel glared right back. "Nope, she would never."

The staring contest continued for a moment and then Uncle Stan cleared his throat.

"Perhaps this conversation would be better held at the station," he said. "Ms. Earnest, if you'd come with us?"

"Am I under arrest?" she asked. Elliott stepped closer to her as if he could shield her from the detectives.

"Do you need to be?" Tara countered.

"We're just going to have a conversation, and we'd really appreciate your cooperation," Stan said. "Nothing to worry about, I promise."

Mel noticed that his right eyebrow was higher than his left and she had to squash the urge to tell Diane to run for it.

"Well, I suppose that would be all right," Diane said.

She looked hesitant and Mel suddenly remembered that whether she liked it or not, she owed Diane for saving her bacon back in college.

"I'll have a friend of mine meet you down

102

at the station," Mel said. "He'll get you through this."

Uncle Stan gave her an incredulous look, but Mel jerked her head in the direction of his partner and she did not feel one iota of guilt for helping Diane out. She had a feeling Tara was the sort of detective who decided who was guilty and then worked the case to make it true, unlike Uncle Stan, who worked the case to find the guilty party.

Since Tara had such a chip on her shoulder about Manny and clearly a thing for Joe, Mel would not be at all surprised to see her take her unhappiness out on Diane, since she was Mel's friend and client. Mel couldn't let that happen.

"Thanks, Mel," Diane said.

"Don't mention it," Mel said. "In fact, don't say anything until Steve gets there."

Tara looked like she wanted to smash Mel's cupcakes. If Mel hadn't had her good sense kick in right in the nick of time she would have dared her. Luckily, she just smiled, a closed-lip passive smile that made it more than clear whose side she was on.

"We'll talk later," Uncle Stan said.

He gave Mel a look that told her she was not going to enjoy the conversation. Mel would have felt bad about disappointing him, but she didn't like his new partner.

She didn't like that Tara blamed her for Manny leaving Scottsdale and she didn't like the way she looked at Joe. If they were going to have a conversation, they could start with her.

"Fine," she said. She tipped her chin up and turned her cheek toward him.

Uncle Stan shook his head and kissed her cheek as if he knew the conversation was not going to go the way he planned and now he was dreading it. Mel was okay with that.

"I'll drive you," Elliott said to Diane, and his tone made it clear it was not open for discussion.

Again, he put himself between Diane and the detectives and Mel liked that about him. He wasn't easily intimidated but she supposed he'd have to be like that if he worked for Diane.

"We'll see you there shortly," Stan said.

He led his partner out the back door. Mel could tell by her stiff-legged gait that she was unhappy with the way things had gone. Too bad.

When the door shut behind them, Diane hugged Mel close. Mel hugged her back, thinking it was just Diane being her usual overly exuberant self.

While they were locked together, however, Diane whispered, "Someone is setting me up. You have to find out who is trying to frame me for Mike's murder. Promise me."

She released Mel as quickly as she'd grabbed her and when Mel would have spoken, Diane shook her head ever so slightly. Not knowing what else to do, Mel gave her the tiniest of nods.

Diane flashed her a relieved smile and with that, she swept out of the bakery with Elliott in her wake.

"What's going on?" Angie asked as she sank onto a stool beside their large steel worktable.

"I'm not exactly sure," Mel said. "But I think I may have just agreed to find out who killed Mike Bordow."

NINE

"No," Angie said. "Absolutely not. I forbid it."

"What?" Mel frowned at her friend. "You can't forbid it."

"Yes, I can. I'm your friend. 'You find out who your real friends are when you're involved in a scandal,' " she said.

"Are you quoting Elizabeth Taylor to me? That's not even from a movie. I think that's a foul."

"Whatever. Now listen, we have bigger things going on than your old college roommate and whether she whacked her fiancé or not," Angie said.

"We do?" Mel asked. Mostly she did it because she knew it was going to make Angie's eyes bug right out of her head. Not nice, she knew, but she'd had a really rough day and she wasn't really in the mood to play nice right now.

"Ah!" Angie gasped, giving her a wide-eyed stare. "Today is the day we go to the dressmaker for my final fitting."

Mel crossed the kitchen to the coffeepot. Bless Marty's heart, it was full of piping hot go-juice. Why did she have to go to the dressmaker's? Wasn't that something Angie could do on her own?

"You are coming with me, aren't you?" Angie asked. "You promised."

"I know I did," Mel said. She kept her back to Angie so she wouldn't have to see the hurt in her friend's eyes. "But that was before the dead body du jour."

Mel could feel the waves of sad confusion pouring off of Angie all the way across the kitchen. She lowered her head and sipped her coffee. She turned around and strode across the kitchen into the former closet she had remodeled into an office.

"Listen, I have to call Steve," she said. "We'll talk later."

"Okay," Angie said. "Sure."

Mel closed the door behind her without ever really looking at her friend. She moved around her desk, ignoring the piles of paperwork that needed to be dealt with, and sat in her cushy rolling office chair. She didn't even open her laptop or pull out her cell phone. She simply leaned against the back of her chair and drank her coffee, wishing this day had rolled out differently.

She didn't want to have images of Mike Bordow's dead body burned onto her retinas for the rest of her life; she didn't want to have to get involved with Diane's messy situation, nor did she want to spend her afternoon at a bridal salon, watching her best friend get pinned and primped for her big day when Mel's own big day should have happened a few months ago.

Ack! That was it. That was the thought she hadn't allowed herself to think since they'd returned from opening their first franchise in Las Vegas a few months ago. She was supposed to be married to Joe and she wasn't, and even while she was having a great time dating him, because they'd never really seemed to manage that before, she really wished she was Mrs. Joe DeLaura and she was a teeny tiny bit jealous that Angie was getting married and she wasn't.

There, she admitted it. Funny, she thought a little self-honesty would make it easier to bear. It didn't. It just made her feel bad about herself. Huh.

There was a sharp knock on the office door but before Mel could invite the person in, it banged open with enough force to bounce off of the interior wall.

"Hey!" Mel yelped.

Two heads, one bald and shiny and one long and shaggy, peered around the door-frame.

"You should be ashamed of yourself," Marty, the bald one, said.

"Yeah," Oz, the shaggy one, added.

Mel sighed. Marty was her main counter help and culinary student Oscar Ruiz was her baker in training. Much as she wanted to shove them out of her tiny office and shut and lock the door, she knew for the morale of the bakery, she needed to hear them out.

"What?" she asked. "Did I not use enough buttercream on the Blonde Bombshells?"

"Do not make light of this, young lady," Marty said. His bushy gray eyebrows were pulled together in a stern V, indicating he meant business.

"Yeah," Oz repeated.

Mel glanced at her young chef. Without his toque on, his black hair hung in a fringe down past his nose, making it impossible to see his eyes or know what he was thinking. He must have just arrived, as he was still in jeans and a Ramones T-shirt and was clutching his skateboard in one hand.

"Okay," Mel said. She held her hands out wide. "What's the matter?"

"You are a terrible friend," Marty said.

Mel snapped her head back. *Ouch!*

109

"Angie needs you," Oz added. "And you're letting her down."

"Um, is this about the dress-fitting thing?" Mel asked. "Because I've been to the dress-maker's like three times."

"So what?" Marty asked.

"So, I think I've done more than my share of bridal duty," Mel said. "There is other stuff going on, you know."

"Yeah, yeah, we heard," Oz said. "Another dead body, big deal."

"Big deal?" Mel croaked.

"Angie is only getting married once," Marty said. "While your track record for finding bodies, well, let's just say this probably won't be your last."

"You need to get your priorities in order," Oz said.

Mel stared down at her coffee. They were right. She was being a selfish jerk.

"Mel, you and Joe will have your day," Oz said. His voice was kind and not judgy, but it was also very firm.

Mel glanced up at the behemoth who was her sous chef. His large stature and enormous hands hid the fact that he was gifted in the culinary arts and was capable of sculpting the most delicate butterflies out of the thinnest fondant. The other truth about Oz was that he had the purest heart of

110

anyone she had ever known. If he was calling her out on her behavior, he was right.

"Is Angie out there?" she asked.

"No, she left for her fitting," Marty said.

Mel stood, grabbing her coffee and her cell phone. The bridal shop was just two streets over. She'd call Steve Wolfmeier for Diane while she hoofed it.

"Fine, I'm on my way," she said. The two idiots beamed at her and Mel found herself reluctantly smiling back. When she reached the doorway, she paused to kiss them each on the cheek, causing both of them to blush ridiculous shades of pink. "Thanks, guys."

"Just go," Marty said. "Before she has another episode of bridal self-doubt and scraps her gown and makes the poor dressmaker cry."

Oh, good grief, Marty was right. What had she been thinking letting Angie go solo to her fitting? She ratcheted her pace up to a jog and bolted out the door, shouting, "Call me if you need me!" as she went.

Mel ran down the sidewalk, passing the tattoo joint on the corner at the speed of a blur.

"Hey, hold up there, Mel!" Mick Donnelly popped his head out the door of the place. He had just opened up shop, so the steady buzzing of needles inking skin wasn't as loud as usual since there were no customers as yet.

"No time to chat, Mick," Mel said. She did slow down a bit so she could explain. "Angie. Dress fitting. Emergency."

"Gotcha," he said. At well over six feet tall, fully inked, and chock-full of funky body jewelry, Mick would have scared the dookey out of Mel if she didn't know that he had a passion for opera and coconut cupcakes.

Mel resumed her pace, but Mick called her back.

"Hey, do me a solid?" he asked.

"Sure."

"Tell Angie the wedding tattoos she wants are on the house," he said. "My little gift to the bride and groom."

Mel's eyes widened. This was news. But instead of grilling Mick like she wanted to, she just nodded and said, "Okay."

With a wave, she hurried toward Scottsdale Road and Marshall Way, hoping to get to the dressmaker's before Angie had another bridezilla moment as Marty had predicted. While waiting for the crossing light to turn into the walking person instead of the stop hand it was now, she took a moment to call Steve. His phone rolled over to voice mail after one ring, so she left a detailed message about what was happening and told him to call her if he had any questions. The walking person appeared and she bolted across the street.

She rushed through Old Town, passing a coin collector's shop, a Native American art gallery, a tiny café, and a Western-wear shop before she banged into Madame Amour's bridal salon. Judging by the expression on the face of Madame Amour, she was just in time.

Madame Amour, whose real name was Kimberly, was kneeling beside the hem of Angie's gown with a pin cushion strapped on her wrist and the look of someone who was seriously debating stabbing herself in the eye with her own pins to end the agony she was being forced to endure.

Angie had her back to Mel and didn't see her come in. Also, she appeared to be consumed with her own reflection and her unhappiness with what she was seeing, which was obvious in the way she flounced her skirt and frowned, looking petulant.

"I don't know what I want but this isn't it," she said.

Now Kim looked like she might stab Angie instead.

"I think we should change it to an empire waist," Angie said. "You know, very *Sense and Sensibility.*"

"A quality that is sorely lacking here right now," Kim said around the pin she had clamped between her lips.

"I'm sorry, what was that?" Angie asked.

"Nothing," Kim said. She rose from her knees and looked at Mel. She took the pin out of her mouth and jabbed it into her wrist holder. "Talk to her before I throw her and her gown out."

Mel watched Kim stomp away.

"Hey, where are you going?" Angie cried.

Kim didn't answer, which was probably for the best.

"Oh, Angie," Mel sighed. "You look amazing. Tate is going to die, simply keel over on the spot dead when he sees you."

Angie glanced up at her reflection and saw her friend. "Mel! You're here!"

"Of course," Mel said. "Where else would I be?"

"Helping your other friend, Diane," Angie said. She sounded the teensiest bit put out.

"Oh, you mean the one accused of a murder she didn't commit," Mel said. Her gaze met and held Angie's in the mirror as she attempted to stare her down.

"Dress fitting, wrongly accused, dress fitting, wrongly accused," Angie said as she held her hands out as if they were a scale.

114

"All right, I can see where you might have had to help her first."

"Thank you," Mel said. "Now, what is going on with your dress, which is perfect by the way? Why are you planning to change it?"

"I saw a picture in a magazine —" Angie began, and Mel interrupted.

"Okay, that's it, no more magazines for you," she said. "We have to make a rule, once you pick flowers, you can't look at any other flowers. Once you choose the music, no more listening to any other music. This whole ceremony is about commitment; you need to start committing."

Angie opened her eyes wide. "Hey, you're right. It's like every decision is a test putting me one step closer to being committed to Tate. Huh, I never thought of it like that."

"Does it help?" Mel asked. She was hoping it did instead of making her friend's anxiety even worse.

"Maybe . . . No."

Angie let loose a sigh that sounded as if it came all the way from her pretty pink toenails. Then she sank onto the ground in a pouf of organza and silk. With her big brown eyes and long brown curls, she had the look of a fairy-tale creature who had

115

been plopped into the middle of a bridal salon.

Her gown was simple with a fitted bodice, halter top, and a pretty poufy skirt that was embroidered with white silk thread all along the hem in an eye-catching pattern of vines and leaves entwined with flowers.

The dress complemented her skin tone and her curvy figure, making it look innocent and sexy all at the same time. This was no small achievement for a dress but Madame Amour had nailed it. Mel didn't wonder why Kimberly felt the need to walk away from Angie and her bridezilla moment. It was a perfect dress.

She approached Angie warily, waiting to see if her friend was going to have another episode or not. It was a lot like approaching a strange dog. She wondered if she should hold out her hand and let Angie sniff it, but thought that the joke might not be appreciated by the woman sitting in a wad of tulle-stiffened crinolines in front of her.

"I just want it to be the best wedding," Angie sighed.

"It will be," Mel said. She sank onto the raised dais beside her friend. "Because it's you and Tate, getting married and pledging your lives to each other. Everything else is extra."

"Extra? How can you say that? Do you have any idea how critical the wedding is? I've read article after article that states if a bride is unhappy with her wedding, she will end up divorced in five years."

Mel suspected that the source for that information was sketchy. Sort of like those wedding vendors who tried to squeeze every dime out of brides and grooms by telling them that this was the most important day of their life and that they were only getting married once when statistically everyone knew that wasn't true. She didn't think now was the moment to point this out to Angie, however.

"Angie, what is the worst thing that can happen?" Mel asked.

Her idea was simple: Go through Angie's list of worries one at a time and talk her out of them. Clearly, her friend was suffering wedding anxiety and the only way to talk her down was to address each phobia as it came up. It seemed like a simple solution. She should have known better.

When Angie fixated on a problem, she was like a heat-seeking missile locked on a target. Nothing would get her off course until, well, kaboom.

"What if the food gives everyone food poisoning and we all end up in the emergency room?" she asked.

"You're having the reception at a five-star resort," Mel said. "A world-renowned chef, Tessa Duchamp, is cooking. It's going to be amazing."

"What if I set fire to the church during the lighting of the unity candle?"

"Tate will throw himself on the flame and save us all."

"What if he dies in the fire?" Angie wailed.

"He won't," Mel said. "I'm your maid of honor, I'll carry a fire extinguisher."

"It will clash with your dress," Angie said. Her agitation was rising and Mel was running out of ideas for how to talk her down.

"My dress is blue," Mel said. "Nothing clashes with blue."

"Go try it on," Angie said. "I won't feel better until I see it."

"We just did the fitting last week," Mel said. "I'm sure Kim hasn't had time to finish it yet."

"Please," Angie begged. "For me, please. I need to see us together to be sure I like the dress."

"Ange," Mel said. "Your wedding is a little over three months away. You can't change the dress. It's perfect."

"I need to see it," Angie insisted.

Mel stared at her friend. Her pretty heart-shaped face was set in stubborn lines and Mel knew she wasn't going to get out of this bridal salon without putting on the dress. She closed her eyes, praying for patience, and thought about Marty and Oz telling her she was being a bad friend. When she got back to the bakery, she fully intended to kick both of them in the derriere.

"Okay, I'll go ask Kim if she's willing," she said. "But you are not allowed to change your mind. I like this dress — heck, I picked the dress. You have me and four other bridesmaids who've already paid for our dresses; you are not changing it."

Angie clapped her hands, giddy that she was going to get her way.

"Thank you," she said.

"Huh," Mel grunted and stood up. Casting her friend a dark look, she left the main fitting room to go find Kim in the back. She wasn't sure if she hoped Kim would go along with the idea or not.

"I am really sorry," she said. She figured it was best to lead with an apology at this juncture. "But I need a favor."

She found Kim stabbing her pins into a small bride doll that, while it looked like it was a pin cushion, also resembled a chubby voodoo doll.

Kim glanced up at Mel over the top edge

119

of her black-framed reading glasses. Her dark hair was twisted up into a stylish knot on top of her head, while random chunks hung down over her face in what could have been artful disarray or the product of a woman who had been about to rip her hair out.

"What favor?" she asked. Her cherry-red lipstick did not turn up in a smile but rather stayed in a flat line of suspicion.

"Angie wants me to try on my bridesmaid dress again," Mel said.

The cherry-red lips now turned down at the corners in an out-and-out frown.

"I'm sorry. I wouldn't ask but she's going round the bend with anxiety," Mel said.

"Is she going to make me redo the bridesmaid dresses?" Kim asked. Her voice was now a low growl.

"No!" Mel said. "In fact, I think if she sees the dress and her gown together, I can reassure her that they are perfect and get her out of your hair."

"Fine, follow me," Kim said. "But do try to calm her down because Angie is rapidly becoming my most high-maintenance client and I really thought that title was going to stay with Diane Earnest for a lot longer."

"Diane Earnest?" Mel asked. "She bought her gown here?"

"Doesn't everyone?" Kim asked.

Mel nodded. Madame Amour was the place where everyone said yes to the dress.

"And all of her bridesmaids' dresses," Kim said. She led Mel to the dressing rooms in back. "Wait here."

She returned in minutes with a garment bag draped over her forearm. She handed it to Mel as she gently shoved her into the curtained fitting room.

"So how do you know Diane?" Kim asked.

Mel hesitated. She wasn't sure why. But she thought Kim might share more if she thought Mel was more a passing acquaintance of Diane's rather than her former roommate.

"She used to date my boyfriend," Mel said.

"Joe?" Kim asked. "Really? I can't see him with someone like her."

Mel felt her feelings for the dressmaker become warm and fuzzy, and if they weren't separated by the thick cloth curtain she would have hugged her.

"Well, I don't think it was ever serious," Mel said.

Kim was quiet and Mel could picture her nodding in understanding. Mel quickly stripped down and pulled the pretty blue dress over her head. It still had some pins

121

in it but was perfect in a fit-and-flare look that flattered every figure and made Mel feel ridiculously feminine.

"That makes sense," Kim said. "You know, I don't particularly like her but you have to feel sorry for a woman like that."

"For Diane? Why?" Mel asked. Diane had caused Mel to feel many things over the years but pity had not been one of them.

"Well, I don't like to gossip but since she canceled her wedding and is trying to stick me with the cost of all of her dresses, I am less inclined to be as professional as usual. Plus, she tried to hook your Joe; that gives you a vested interest."

"Okay, so what's the dish?" Mel asked as she pulled the curtain back and stepped out.

Kim looked her over and adjusted the fabric around her waist with a gentle tug.

"Well." Kim paused for dramatic effect. "Rumor has it — and by *rumor* I mean we heard it from the woman herself — that Diane's fiancé was having a smoking-hot affair with one of her bridesmaids."

TEN

"No way."

"Way."

"That's horrible," Mel said. "Who was it?"

"Nicole Butterfield. She straight-up told one of my seamstresses that she had her eye on Mike and was fully intending to bag him and stop Diane's wedding. She said his party supply business looked to be making a nice profit and after her last two divorces, she needed someone bankable."

Mel gaped at her and Kim looked at her knowingly.

"I know. Pretty ballsy, right?"

"It's not that — well, it is that — but also I know Nicole," Mel said.

"Oh, no," Kim groaned. "Please do not tell me she dated Joe, too."

"No!" Mel said a bit more vehemently than she meant to, but the idea of Joe and Nicole horrified, like walking through a cobweb and doing the skeeved-out jitterbug of horror.

"Yeah, she's awful," Kim said. "Joe would've had to have suffered a severe head trauma to date a woman like that. The other bridesmaids were all nice enough. I sort of got the feeling they were doing the bridesmaid thing more out of a sense of obligation than any real affection for Diane — not a big surprise."

Abruptly, Mel felt a sudden need to run into the other room and hug the fluffernutter out of Angie. Having a bestie, a true girl's girlfriend, the sort who would hold your hair out of the toilet when you puked; punch an overly grabby admirer in the throat when he needed it; who would show up with several pints of gelato when it was required, such as a hideous breakup, bad career decision, or mean reading on the bathroom scale — well, women like that were quite simply priceless.

Nicole Butterfield was not one of those women. Quite the opposite. She had gone to college with Mel and Diane but she had been there more to acquire her MRS degree than to actually study for a career.

She had resided on the same floor as Mel and Diane during their first years together. Like them, she had also majored in marketing, but where Diane had clearly been born

124

to the field and Mel had worked her butt off to try and fit in, Nicole had been much more invested in her sorority and all the socializing and background checking of the pedigrees of frat boys that went with it. As far as Mel knew, Diane had never liked Nicole. How had it come to pass that Nicole was in Diane's wedding? It boggled, truly.

Nicole had been very pretty and well connected. Last Mel heard, she had just gotten divorced from husband number two. What would have possessed Diane to have her in her wedding? And if Nicole was telling the truth and she was making a play for Mike, did Diane find out? Was that why she was really calling off the wedding? How angry would Diane be if Mike cheated on her?

Mel shivered. She didn't like knowing this information. She didn't want to have to ask Diane about it and she didn't want to have to tell Uncle Stan. But then she thought about Mike. He'd been murdered, his skull crushed in. If Diane found out about Mike and Nicole, how far would she go to stop it?

Diane was tough. There was no other word for it. Even when Mel had lived with her, it was clear that Diane had a vision about how life was supposed to be and that was it. There was no wiggle room, no deviating from the plan, no excuses, and failure was never an option.

"Wow," Mel said. "I guess you just never know what people are truly capable of."

"Ain't that the truth?" Kim asked. "Now, come on, let's go show Angie your dress before she has another episode."

By the time Mel and Angie left Madame Amour's, Angie and Kim had made up and Angie was once again in love with her wedding dress.

Mel wished this was her only problem. Unfortunately, in the time they were with Kim, her phone started to blow up and it soon became apparent that whatever had happened at the police station had not gone well for Diane and she was now being held as the person of interest in the investigation into the murder of Mike Bordow.

Mel wanted to go back to the bakery and pretend that her phone had died and she hadn't received the haboob of texts and voice mails by an increasingly panicked Diane. She wanted to bake something gooey and yummy and calorically satisfying. Instead, after she and Angie walked back to the bakery, she checked on Marty and Oz, who were fine, and then looked up the address for Nicole Butterfield.

As Diane kept pointing out, Mel owed her

one, and Mel figured if she could get Nicole to admit to her affair with Mike Bordow, she might be able to throw another suspect in the police's direction, taking the heat off of Diane and making things square between them once and for all. After all, wouldn't Nicole be a suspect if Mike had rejected her and foiled her plan to land a bankable man?

Surely, visiting the mean girl from her college days couldn't be as bad as all that, right? They'd all matured and grown up. Perhaps it would be a lovely social call and Mel had nothing to worry about.

The festering pit in the bottom of her stomach begged to differ, but Mel tuned it out by scarfing a Coconut Cupcake on her way out the door. There really was nothing that a good Coconut Cupcake couldn't cure, even facing down the woman who had made her cry, repeatedly, her first year in the dorms.

Nicole Butterfield lived in a gated community north of 24th Street and Camelback Road. The guard at the gate had to call Nicole's house to give Mel permission to enter and Mel was more than a little surprised that Nicole gave the okay.

She drove her Mini Cooper through the

decorative orange trees that lined both sides of the road. Their trunks had been painted bright white to keep the bark from being sunburned and their canopies of bright leaves were clipped into lush mushrooms of greenery. Mel was sure it was supposed to be soothing with its very precise aesthetics, but she found it stifling. She enjoyed a little wildness in her vegetation and this was a bit too militaristic for her liking.

She followed the directions on her phone's GPS until she reached Nicole's house. It looked exactly like every other house on the street. The exact same types of desert bushes on the gravel front yard, each maintained with the same precision as the trees on the main drive. Was it supposed to feel like a prison? she wondered, because it sure had that vibe.

She parked in the short driveway in front of the garage and walked around the side, following the cobblestone path to the front door. The large wooden door with massive iron hinges looked as if it had been designed to intimidate — or maybe that was just Mel having second thoughts about the whole situation.

The last time she had seen Nicole, the other woman had just dropped out of school to go and marry the son of a Greek shipping tycoon. She had been throwing out all of her clothes, tossing them to anyone in the dorm who wanted the designer duds, because her man had promised to buy her an all new haute couture wardrobe as befitting her new station as his wife.

When Mel had stopped by her room to wish her well, Nicole had shrieked with laughter.

"Oh, Mel, surely you don't think I have anything that would fit you, do you?" Nicole had chortled. The posse of friends she had in her room all howled with laughter as well. It had been devastating.

This had been during one of Mel's plus-size stages, and the shame she had felt at Nicole's scorn had made her pale skin turn fiery red and she'd hid her face behind her much longer hair, pulling it over her face as if she could hide the extra seventy-five pounds she was carrying around with a hank of hair.

"No," Mel said. "I just wanted to wish you well."

The words had about choked her and she had turned and fled from Nicole's room, wishing not for the first time that she could just curl up and blow away like an autumn leaf on the wind.

She had gotten halfway down the hallway,

when Nicole caught up to her. She had grabbed Mel by the arm and spun her around. Tears had been coursing down Mel's cheeks and she kept her head down, refusing to let Nicole have the satisfaction of seeing her cry.

"Hey," Nicole said. "I was just kidding, okay? Don't be so sensitive."

Mel hadn't been able to form words around the lump in her throat, so she shrugged, just wanting Nicole to let her go and leave her alone.

"This is for you," Nicole said. "It's like the only thing I have that might fit you, so don't say I never gave you anything."

With that she grabbed Mel's hand and pressed a silver cuff bracelet into it. Mel wanted to refuse it, to shove it back at her, or, even better, throw it at her and hit her square in the face. Instead, she just stood there, saying nothing. Nicole ran back to her room and Mel never saw her again.

Ironically, the bracelet became a talisman for Mel. She used it to motivate herself into working out like a demon. She was determined to never again be the butt, or have the butt, of anyone's cruel weight jokes ever again.

It had been an unhealthy anger-induced diet that had helped her to lose the pounds but didn't really teach her to love her body or value her health. Changing careers to go to culinary school and studying cooking in Paris, where there was a healthy love of food, did that. Still, it had been the first time Mel had successfully put something, rage, ahead of eating and she supposed in some crazy way, she owed Nicole for that.

She approached the door, trying to pull together her frayed bits of courage. It was like trying to weave a blanket out of panic and she was breathing hard by the time she lifted her fist up to knock.

A second before her knuckles connected, the door was yanked open and there stood Nicole Butterfield, looking just as curvy and seductive as she had ten years ago as an undergrad.

Nicole wore her thick brown hair in a half-up-half-down hairdo that made her neck look longer. Her makeup was thick, as if she spackled it on while trying to achieve that contouring thing that was all the rage. She had long, thick false eyelashes and eye makeup that Mel assumed was supposed to make her look like a cat but really made her look narrow-eyed and squinty.

Her top was a bright turquoise halter that thrust the girls out front and center, her pants were a leopard-spotted yoga pant sort of thing, and she wore turquoise Manolo Blahnik sandals that made her almost as tall as Mel. Her jewelry flashed from her wrists, earlobes, and ankles, winking at Mel as only true diamonds can. Divorce number two had clearly been good to her.

"May I help you?" Nicole asked. She looked past Mel as if she was looking for someone else.

"It's me, Nicole. Melanie Cooper," Mel said. "I don't know if you remember me —"

That was as far as she got before Nicole interrupted her.

"Shut up!" Nicole looked her over, up and down and from side to side, as if she was looking to see what Mel was hiding.

"Okay," Mel said. She didn't want to offend Nicole by speaking, but it was going to make asking her questions about Mike rather challenging.

"Melanie Cooper, I see it now. You have the same eyes and nose, but wow, you are missing some chins. I never would have believed it was you," Nicole said. Then she grabbed Mel's hand and dragged her into the house. "Come in, we have so much to catch up on."

The panic Mel had been feeling before she knocked now seemed as if it might have been warranted, sort of like the heart-stopping moment right before a boat sank, leaving no survivors.

ELEVEN

"So, how are you?" Nicole asked. "Diane mentioned that she was still in touch with you but she didn't give any details. Look at you, you've lost an ass ton of weight. How much? Fifty, seventy-five, one hundred pounds; somewhere in there, right?"

Since she had Mel in an unforgiving hold, reminiscent of a manacle, Mel had no choice but to follow her across the Italian marble foyer and down the stairs into the sunken living room, much like a hostage.

Mel took a moment to scout the room for alternative exits. At a glance, it was clear that whatever else Nicole was into, drapes were definitely a passion of hers. Floor-to-ceiling French doors lined one wall, which presumably led outside, although Mel couldn't be sure because the two sets of drapes on each door, done in eye-watering shades of raspberry pink and black, were all drawn shut. So there went that plan.

The furniture was black with drapery-matching pink throw pillows and the thick area rug that covered the floor was also black. She supposed she should be grateful it wasn't pink, but it didn't need to be because an enormous cursive letter N was painted on the far wall in, yep, more of the bright pink with stylistic black swirls painted all around it. Wow, just wow.

"So, how about a strawberry daiquiri?" Nicole asked. She released Mel's wrist and motioned for her to take a seat on one of the puffy black chairs. "I make one that's to die for."

"No, thanks. Since I have to drive . . ." Mel's words trailed off as she turned to sit and caught a glimpse of the portrait hanging over the fireplace on the opposite wall.

Nicole followed her gaze and grinned. "Amazing, isn't it?"

"Um . . . I . . . It," Mel stuttered.

Mel didn't want to look at the painting. In fact, her life could have gone on quite happily if she had never seen such a thing, and yet it was like the time she and Angie caught the baboons fornicating at the zoo — once witness to such a thing she couldn't seem to look away.

In the portrait, Nicole, wearing nothing but thigh-high leather boots, a red thong, and matching bustier, was posed in the painted portrait as if she were Spider-Woman climbing down a wall, with her hands reaching forward, a come-hither look on her face, and her butt and the boots following her like the back end of one of those slinky-dog pull toys.

"Gino, the artist, really captured my essence in this piece, don't you think?" Nicole asked.

If butt floss is your essence. Mel bit the inside of her right cheek to keep the words from escaping and opted to nod instead.

"You know, not that many women are comfortable with their sexuality," Nicole said. She put her hand on her hip, thrust out her breasts, and tossed her hair back. It was a move that had likely been perfected after hours of practice in front of a mirror. "I like to think I'm a bit more evolved than most women."

Mel forced herself to look away from the portrait, only mildly wrenching her neck in the process, and turned her head so that she could only see Nicole, who took the seat beside hers.

"It's a really good likeness," she said. That was the best she could do. Nicole could take it or leave it.

Nicole hugged herself as if she just

couldn't contain her joy. "Thank you. I think so, too. But enough about me, let's talk about you."

"Actually," Mel began, but Nicole interrupted her.

"You know, I don't understand why you weren't asked to be in the wedding. I mean, duh, of course I know why, but now that I've seen you I really don't see why Diane was concerned."

Mel felt her temples contract as she tried to keep up with Nicole's verbal gymnastics. Had she always been like this? Mel couldn't remember, mostly because she had chosen to block out all of their previous interactions over the years, but still, she didn't remember her being this chatty.

"I'm sorry, are you saying Diane was concerned about me?" Mel asked.

"Yeah," Nicole said. She frowned. "When she asked me to be in her wedding and I asked her if you were going to be in it, she said no, because . . . well, you know why."

A tiny voice inside of Mel told her not to go there, but the voice was so tiny, like a Who down in Whoville, and Mel's curiosity was so strong, she went there.

"No, I don't know," Mel said.

"You know, in case you went on a food bender and got fat before the ceremony,"

Nicole said. As if to illustrate her point she took a deep breath and ballooned out her cheeks to emphasize what she thought Mel would look like after a binge.

It took every ounce of Mel's self-control not to poke Nicole in both cheeks just to see her face pop. To ensure against it, she clasped her hands together in her lap. Perhaps this was why some people from the past needed to stay in the past; they were terminally rude, stupid, and mean.

"Well, it's too bad she didn't pick me," Mel said. "I mean, at least I'm not shtupping her fiancé."

"Ah!" Nicole gasped as if Mel had told her what she really thought about her. Sadly, there was not enough time in the day, er, week for that. "I don't know where you got your info —"

Mel held up her hand, gesturing for Nicole to stop. To her surprise, Nicole did.

"Enough," Mel said. "I know you. You can deny it all you want, but if I found out about it anyone could. So tell me, did Diane know?"

Nicole glanced away, staring at her gaudy drapes as if looking for an answer or stalling to think up a lie. Mel settled back into her seat. The bakery was in good hands. She could wait here all day if she must.

"I don't know who is spreading such vicious rumors —" Nicole began.

"No." Mel shook her head. If Nicole thought she could bluff her way out of this, she was seriously mistaken. Mel was in full-on shut-down mode.

"Jealous people gossip about the people they envy —"

"No."

"Was it Diane's cousin Hannah? She has been just awful to me since the day we met. Had I known I was going to have to put up with judgment from the self-righteous, I never would have agreed to stand up for her."

"No."

"Who is trash talking me, then? Who? I demand to know."

Nicole stomped one high-heeled sandal into the thick black carpet. Her lips were pressed into a hard thin line that looked like they'd only be pried open by a daiquiri straw.

"Did you have an affair with him?" Mel asked. "Yes or no?"

"What does it matter?" Nicole asked. "I talked to Diane a few days ago and she said she was calling off the wedding."

Mel gave her a steady look, the sort that made it clear that she wanted details without her saying a word. Nicole rolled her eyes. Her bogus thick eyelashes and heavily made-up cat eyes looked particularly funny with her eyeballs tipped up as if studying her hairline.

"Did she say why?" Mel asked.

"She said something about her return on investment not being what she had planned on," Nicole said. She lowered her head and looked at Mel. "She was very vague and now that I think about it, she was very short with me on the phone. I thought it was because, well . . ."

"Because you were sleeping with Mike," Mel said.

"You're not going to let it go, are you?" Nicole asked.

"Nope," Mel said.

"God, you were like this in college, too, such a badger," Nicole said. "No wonder your best friend was a box full of Oreos. Who could stand to live up to the mighty Melanie Cooper's scrutiny?"

Mel frowned. "Me? Scrutinize? Ha!"

"You did!" Nicole accused. "You always had that pinched look of disapproval on your face. If I missed a class, you gave me the look. If you caught me sneaking a boy out of my room past curfew, there it was again. You were so judgy."

Mel blinked. "I wasn't judging you. I was shy. You all had so much personality and you were always giggling and gossiping together, and there I was, the chubby girl who no one would talk to or hang out with, except Diane, and that's probably because as my roommate she had to."

"Shy?" Nicole asked. "I thought you just didn't like anyone."

"No, I was terrified of you all," Mel said.

"Huh," Nicole said. "I thought the fat girl was always supposed to be the fun-loving, good-time girl; you know, the pretty girl's sidekick."

"Thank you, Hollywood, for giving plus-sized girls a purpose," Mel said. She knew Nicole was missing her sarcasm but whatever. "You might try losing *fat girl* from your vocabulary, Nicole, and change it to *plus size, curvy,* or even *bodacious.*"

"Yeah, whatever." Nicole shrugged. "Hey, you're not fat now so you must have put down the bucket of chicken and backed away at some point, right?"

"I really think I hate you," Mel said.

Nicole wrinkled her nose. "That was mean."

"Listen, if you didn't bag Mike, that's fine," Mel said. "I just came to find out what was going on with Diane since she hasn't seemed to be herself. I'm sure she'll be relieved to hear that you couldn't manage to sink your hooks into her man. Even though she's called off the wedding, this might make her less bitter about the whole thing."

Yes, Mel was out of patience. Yes, she was playing a calculated risk. She knew Nicole. Vanity was her weakness and Mel was pretty sure that she wouldn't be able to abide the idea that people thought she hadn't been able to steal Diane's groom from her.

It was a terribly manipulative maneuver to make, and Mel didn't care. Not one little bit. She wanted to get out of this hellhole of black and pink and she'd do whatever it took to get the information she needed to make it happen.

Nicole pursed her lips as if trying to keep herself from talking. Yeah, she'd have about as much luck holding back Niagara Falls with a spoon.

"I thought Mike and I were in love. He told me he loved me at any rate," she said. "But there was someone else."

"Diane?" Mel asked. "You remember, the woman he was supposed to marry."

"No," Nicole said. Her look was sly. "And I'm betting Diane found out about the other woman and that's why she called off her

142

wedding. It's one thing to lose your man to a woman who is as young and beautiful as you are — well, let's be honest, more beautiful — but it is another to lose him to . . ."

Mel was on the edge of her seat but Nicole stopped talking.

Mel stared at her and Nicole looked at her with a closed-lip smile that did not reach her eyes.

"Seriously?" Mel asked. "You're holding out on me now?"

"I can't help it," Nicole said. She shook her long dark hair and wriggled in her seat. "It's just so delicious."

"Well, let me give you some incentive," Mel said. "There's one thing I didn't mention about Mike Bordow. He's dead."

The smile slid off Nicole's smug face like a scoop of ice cream falling off a cone. Mel could almost hear the *splat!*

"That's impossible," Nicole said. "I just spo—"

Mel raised her eyebrows but Nicole wisely did not continue speaking.

"I imagine the police are going to hear the same rumor I did," Mel said. "And they're going to be very interested in talking to you about your relationship with Mike, so tell me, who else might have had a motive to kill him?"

"Kill him?" Nicole's eyes went wide. Her lips trembled, and as the color drained away from her face, it left her makeup looking more like a clown's face paint than a grown woman's cosmetics. Mel didn't think she could fake a response like that.

"I found him," Mel said. "I won't give details except it was most definitely not an accident. So, who else did he have queued up as a little side bit?"

Nicole was breathing hard and she put her hand over her heaving bosom. "It was Cheryl, Diane's mother."

TWELVE

Mel sat in her car, staring at the dashboard as if there was an answer for her there that might make the fact that she had just discovered that Diane's mother was having an affair with her future son-in-law okay. Yeah, there was no way that could ever be all right. What sort of a mother slept with her daughter's fiancé? The thought horrified.

She had met Diane's mother, Cheryl, only once when they were moving into their dorm room as freshmen. While Mel's parents and her brother had schlepped all of Mel's belongings up to their room, Diane's mother had sat on the edge of Diane's bed and filed her nails. When it was clear that she wasn't going to help her daughter, Mel's father and brother had stepped up and hauled the rest of Diane's belongings to their room.

Joyce, Mel's mother, had tried to engage

145

Cheryl Earnest in conversation but Cheryl was engrossed in the latest issue of *Glamour* magazine while she filed her nails into talon-sharp points and had only given her cursory answers until Joyce had given up, shrugging at Mel as if to say she had no idea what to say to the other woman.

Cheryl was not what one expected of a college freshman's mother in her spiky high heels and slinky wraparound silk dress in a shade of emerald green that enhanced the green of her eyes. Her wavy blond hair hung halfway down her back and she moved with the predatory grace of a jungle panther. When she spoke, Mel had almost expected the voice of Jessica Rabbit.

In contrast, Joyce, with her bobbed hair, light makeup, ironed cotton blouse, beige capri pants, and sensible running shoes, looked like she was made for giving hugs, slapping on Band-Aids, and doling out chocolate chip cookies. Up to that day in her short eighteen years, Mel had never been as grateful for her mother as she was at that moment.

When all of their belongings were piled waist-high in their room, Cheryl had un-curled herself from Diane's bed and looked around the room as if seeing it for the first time.

"Well, looks like it's time for me to go," she said. She beamed at her daughter. "Freedom beckons! Man, I've been waiting eighteen years for this. Woo-hoo!"

With that, she kissed Diane's cheek and swept from the room without even pausing to thank Mel's family for their help.

"But, Mom, wait . . ." Diane's voice trailed off as her mother never broke her stride, never looked back, and as far as Mel knew, never stepped onto campus again.

Diane clutched the sweater she'd been holding to her chest and then turned away from Mel and her family and began to unpack, busily hanging her clothes in her half of the wardrobe as if it were a timed competition. Mel got the feeling it was so no one would see that she was on the brink of tears.

While her dad and Charlie went to scout the local food situation — it was a Cooper family rule to always check out the local take-out joints in any new neighborhood — Joyce helped Mel unpack. After a few awkward moments, she began to help Diane as well, saying something lame about more hands, less work. Mel had remembered being afraid Diane was going to think they were hopelessly dorky.

Instead, Diane started to warm up under

Joyce's attention and when Charlie and her dad arrived back with a variety of takeout, Diane happily joined them in trying out the local pizza, Thai food, burger joint, and sub shop. Her dad handed over the take-out menus as if he were giving her the key to the city, and Mel and Diane found a spot for them on the bulletin board by their door.

When her family finally left a few hours later, they hugged Diane like she was one of their own and she hugged them in return. A very different parting than she'd had with her own mother. When they were falling asleep that night, Mel was almost unconscious when Diane spoke, breaking the silence.

"Your family is really nice," she said. "Thanks for letting me be one of you tonight."

"Anytime," Mel said.

Seeing her family through Diane's eyes, Mel had been filled with love for her people and in a strange way it made the homesickness that had been dogging her ebb. She had them. They had her. Nothing could change that. Not the miles in between them. Not even death, or so she had thought with the innocence of youth. Losing her father a few years later would change her perspective on that, but still, seeing what Diane had

148

at home had made her love her family all the more.

Mel took her phone out of her purse and turned on her virtual assistant. She knew she should probably tell Uncle Stan what she had learned instead of doing what she was thinking of doing. She knew it and yet she couldn't help but feel that if she got to Cheryl first, she might be able to find out more than Uncle Stan would.

She could just imagine how Detective Tara was going to react to her going to see Cheryl Earnest. Instead of deterring her it spurred her into making what some — Joe — might call a rash decision. As always, Mel consoled herself that it was always easier to get forgiveness than permission.

The simple fact was that with both her bridesmaid and her mother playing hide-the-salami with her fiancé, it made Diane look like the winner in the Most Likely to Whack the Groom competition. Despite knowing what a hard-ass Diane could be in life and business, Mel couldn't believe that she killed Mike.

It just didn't make sense. Why would Diane have hired Mel to bake specialty breakup cupcakes and have Mel personally deliver them so she could give Diane the blow-by-blow of the dumping if she was planning to kill Mike first? Showing her animosity toward the man with the "It's over" cupcakes was not a well-thought-out move, and if there was one thing Mel knew about Diane it was that she always thought everything through. Everything.

From the clothes she wore, to the jobs she took, to where she invested her money, Diane was an overthinker of the first order. Playing chess with Diane was the most excruciating way to spend a rainy afternoon Mel had ever had the misfortune to experience. She'd rather stand in line at the Department of Motor Vehicles than watch Diane agonize over her strategic maneuvers.

Bottom line: If Diane was going to murder Mike Bordow, it would have been planned to the tiniest, pickiest detail and would likely involve poison. Mel just couldn't see Diane smashing a person's head in no matter how miffed she was. That was entirely too messy. Also, she would make it look like an accident and not some rage-fueled bashing of his skull.

Having come to this conclusion, Mel looked up Cheryl Earnest's current address. With luck, she still had no idea that Mike Bordow was dead and Mel could spring the news on her and see how she took it.

Cheryl's address came up on her phone

in an instant and Mel engaged her GPS navigation to talk her through the directions. As luck would have it, she lived in a swank neighborhood not too far from Nicole's. Mel frowned. She wondered how convenient that had been for Mike Bordow.

She knew she should feel bad that he was dead — no one deserved to have their cabbage squashed — but still, what a pig!

Who sleeps with their bride's mother and bridesmaid? Was there anyone else with whom Mr. Loose Zipper was canoodling? Seriously, what if one of them wanted him all to herself and found out about the others? She might have killed him in a fit of rage, which, judging by the sight of him, seemed pretty likely.

A shudder rippled through Mel's body from the top of her head to the tip of her tailbone. The sort of rage and strength that it would take to do what had been done to Mike Bordow was not something she would have associated with a woman scorned. Not that a woman couldn't crack a guy's melon if she was motivated, but it seemed more like something a man would do.

She pondered what other men were in Diane's life and she immediately thought of Elliott Peters. He was a scrawny, IT-nerd type, but that didn't mean he didn't have enough muscle to crush Mike's head and toss him into the ball pit. Mel swallowed hard. The way Elliott looked at Diane, it was clear to her that he was smitten with his boss. How did Diane not know?

Or did she know? Had she discovered that Elliott cared for her in a way the personnel department would frown upon, and had she used that knowledge to get Elliott to do her dirty work for her? And if she had, then had she set Mel up to find the body? Was that what the whole breakup cupcakes plan had been about? Putting Mel in the position where she could say she was on the phone with Diane at the time Mike was found?

Mel shook her head. No, it didn't make sense. Diane wouldn't have had her drive all over Scottsdale to Mike's house and his country club, trying to track him down. She would have sent Mel right to his place of work. And even that made no sense because anyone Mike worked with might have found him before Mel did. And where had everyone been when she arrived? She had never gotten a good explanation for why the company had been wide open with no one on the premises that morning.

With that, Mel started her car and followed the directions to Cheryl Earnest's house. It was a short drive and her neighborhood, while still in the pricier bracket, was not as nice as Nicole's. Mel parked in front of the ranch house, hoping Cheryl was home and that she hadn't yet heard the news.

She strolled up the concrete walkway, wondering how she could start this conversation. She had only met the woman once and while it had been a memorable meeting for her, she doubted that Cheryl would have spared any brain cells to retain the look or name of her daughter's college roommate.

She pressed the button by the front door and waited. The sound of barking, not big-dog barking but rather ankle-biter barking, filled the air. Mel braced herself for a tiny fur ball to come flying at her, and wondered if the dog would smell Captain Jack on her and chomp her just for principle's sake.

"Toots, stop," a voice commanded.

The barking didn't waver, not even a little, so it was easy to see who was actually in charge of this abode. The door was pulled open and Mel barely got a glimpse of the person before she bent over and scooped up a tiny little black-and-brown dust bunny of a pooch.

"Toots, enough," the woman said as she straightened up and looked at Mel. "Can I help you?"

The ten-plus years since Mel had seen Cheryl had not been kind. While it seemed at a glance that she hadn't aged a day, with the same curvy figure, long blond hair, and wide-eyed gaze, there was a sheen to her skin that was unnatural and everything looked extra tight. Mel wondered if Cheryl's face would split right open if she grinned too wide or, heaven forbid, laughed.

"Hi, Ms. Earnest," Mel said. "I don't know if you remember me."

"The name is Mrs. Kelly," Cheryl corrected her. "Earnest was three husbands ago."

"Oh," Mel said. "Sorry."

She studied Cheryl's face. She didn't know if Cheryl was angry at the wrong name or if her pencil-filled eyebrows always looked irritated; maybe it was just today. Did she draw on her eyebrows according to mood? It would be a nice early warning system if she did, but Mel suspected this was not the case.

Toots barked at Mel as if chastising her for the name blunder and Mel held out her fingers to the little puppy. If she couldn't win over Cheryl maybe she could get to her through the dog. Toots bared her teeth and snapped at Mel.

"She doesn't like you," Cheryl said.

"Sorry," Mel said. Although what she was apologizing for she had no idea. It must be that knee-jerk thing most women did: When confronted with a puzzling situation and all else failed, apologize. Ridiculous but true.

"Don't worry about it." Cheryl shrugged. "She hates everyone except me. Right, baby?"

Cheryl lifted the oversized hamster up and began to make kissy noises. Toots licked her face and Cheryl smiled. Much to Mel's relief her face did not split wide open. Still, it looked painful and she was relieved when Cheryl turned back to her and her smile disappeared.

"So, what do you want?"

Mel blinked. "I'm Diane's old college roommate, Melanie Cooper, and I wanted to talk to you about her wedding."

Cheryl tipped her head to the side to study Mel. She frowned, or at least Mel thought it was a frown. It was hard to tell since her face muscles didn't really move that much.

"I don't remember you," she said. "Huh, I don't think I even knew Diane had a room-mate."

Given how little attention Cheryl had paid to the moving-in process, this did not shock Mel. On the upside — and unlike Nicole since Cheryl didn't remember her — she didn't remember her as the fat girl, either. So there was that.

"We roomed together for two years," Mel said. "Right up until Diane took that internship in New York."

"Oh," Cheryl said. She looked confused. "Diane went to New York?"

That was it. Mel was going straight to her mother's house later and telling her how very grateful she was that she got Joyce Cooper in the mama lottery. Honestly, her mother could drive her batty with her worrying and lecturing, but at least she cared, she showed up, and she was invested.

The woman standing in front of Mel right now had shown more interest and affection for the hairy rat in her arms than she did her daughter. Truly she was an insult to mothers everywhere.

"Yes, she had an internship," Mel said.

"Who knew?" Cheryl shrugged. Cheryl turned and led the way into the house. "Well, come on in, roommate. If you're going to ask me what Diane wants for her wedding, I have no idea. She and I had a bit of a falling-out the other day, and she's not speaking to me at the moment."

Mel followed Cheryl into the opulent house. Gilt picture frames, velvet wallpaper,

156

crimson velvet furniture — *bleck,* the interior looked like one of the tackier décors from one of the Real Housewives shows. Honestly, it was amazing how little taste or sense of aesthetic those people had.

Cheryl led the way to a formal sitting room on the left of the front door. The nicest thing Mel could say about it was that with floor-to-ceiling north-facing windows, it had a wonderful source of natural light. This feature was greatly diminished by the animal-print fabrics that swathed every piece of furniture, and as she sat on the squashy leather love seat she tried to keep her gaze confined to the glass coffee table, which was one of the least eye-popping pieces of furniture in the room.

Cheryl sat across from her with Toots on her lap. Toots had stopped barking but every now and again she stared at Mel from under a tuft of eyebrow and growled, showing her little rice teeth. Mel tried not to take it personally.

Instead, she fixed her gaze on Cheryl and said, "I hate to be blunt, but I don't see any other way to get to the point, so I am hoping you'll answer a question for me."

Cheryl shrugged and stared at Mel as if she found her to be the most tedious person alive. Fine then.

"Is the reason Diane stopped speaking to you because she found out that you slept with her fiancé, Mike?"

THIRTEEN

Cheryl's expression didn't change, but Mel saw her pupils dilate. Since she had learned from her uncle Stan that dilation of the pupils is a good indicator of lying as it signified that the brain was working hard, usually in a panic to come up with a convincing lie, she didn't feel that she needed Cheryl to confirm or deny the accusation.

Still, she waited to see what Cheryl would say. Maybe it would give her a clue as to whether Cheryl had a reason to whack Mike. Perhaps he had threatened to tell Diane about their fling and Cheryl had panicked and killed him. Although Mel didn't sense that Cheryl cared enough about Diane to do that, it was still a possibility.

"Diane is very high-strung," Cheryl said. "I have no idea why she's not speaking to me."

Mel stared at her. Hard. "Yes, you do."

Cheryl huffed out a breath and pressed a

hand to her chest in a protestation of innocence that Mel believed about as much as she did that Cheryl was a natural blonde. Not.

"Save it," Mel said. "I already know that you were sleeping with Mike."

"Is that what Diane told you?" Cheryl asked.

The look she sent Mel was sly, as if she knew Diane would never admit such a thing. The expression made Mel want to slap her. What sort of a mother was she? Mel shook her head. That was a no-brainer. She was an odious one.

"No, someone else did," Mel said. She studied Cheryl. The woman was clinging so hard to her youth, she was leaving claw marks on her twenties. Vanity was her weakness. All Mel had to do was hit her right where she lived. "But you know, now that I've seen you, I really don't see how it's possible."

Mel gave a scoffing laugh that said in no uncertain terms that she didn't think Cheryl was capable of snagging Mike. She rose to her feet, signifying that she was done here.

Cheryl's eyes went wide. She looked at Mel in frustration, as if she didn't know how to play it. Obviously she had been planning to admit nothing and revel in everyone's suspicion that she had slept with her daughter's fiancé, but now Mel was throwing her a curve ball by not believing the gossip.

"It is more than possible," Cheryl said. She stood and assumed a red-carpet pose with her back straight and a hand on her hip. "Mike wanted me. In fact, he pursued me until I finally gave in just to get him to leave me alone."

"Yeah, right," Mel said. She giggled as if that was the funniest thing she'd ever heard, then she let her gaze run over Cheryl from her head to her feet. "Sorry to waste your time. I've got to go."

She turned on her heel and made for the front door. Cheryl scurried after her with Toots in the crook of her arm in a football hold. Mel was almost to the door when Cheryl grabbed her arm and spun her around.

"It's true," Cheryl said. She tossed her hair and looked at Mel from under her false eyelashes. "I slept with Mike, several times, and it was fantastic. He said he'd never been with anyone so good."

Mel looked at her. "Um, let me just say, ew."

"Ah!" Cheryl drew herself up and shifted Toots in front of her as if the toupee with teeth could protect her from Mel's scorn.

The little rodent must have felt her mama's rage, because she started to snarl with her little lip curling up on one side.

"So, that is why Diane isn't speaking to you," Mel said. She needed confirmation before she left. "She found out about you and Mike, didn't she?"

"Yes, she walked in on us the other day. It was quite the dramatic scene as she pitched a complete hissy fit. She vowed never to speak to me again," Cheryl said. "Like I haven't heard that before."

"Well, I imagine she will be speaking to you soon. Or maybe not so much her as the police," Mel said. "Mike Bordow was found dead this morning. Murdered."

"Oh my god," Cheryl said. Her jaw dropped open and she looked down at Toots as if she was checking to see how she was taking the news. "She did it."

"What?" Mel asked.

"Diane, she killed him," Cheryl said. "And all because of me."

Mel frowned. That wasn't really what she had been going for, so she asked, "How do you know she did?"

"Because in the middle of her hysterical tirade she said she was going to shank him with one of his party favors," Cheryl said.

"Shank him?" Mel asked. At least this was

162

a different method than the one actually used.

"Yeah, she was crazy mad and then her assistant, that Elliott guy, dragged her out of there, kicking and screaming," Cheryl said. "The next thing I knew I got a text that the wedding was off. Not a big surprise. I can see where having her mother steal her man could drive her to murder."

"Diane didn't murder him," Mel said.

Cheryl looked at her as if she was too stupid to live, and Mel turned away from her and opened the door to leave before she said or did something that she knew she would regret. Well, maybe not regret but something that would likely not help the situation.

"Melissa, wait," Cheryl said.

Mel paused. She didn't correct Cheryl's use of the wrong name because when Uncle Stan came by it would actually help if Cheryl didn't mention that she'd been here. And if she used the wrong name that might buy Mel some time.

"What?" Mel asked. She glanced over her shoulder, not bothering to turn all the way around.

"How high-profile of a case do you think this is?" she asked.

"What do you mean?"

163

"You know, a gorgeous young business-woman murdering her wealthy fiancé because he was sleeping with her mother. Do you think it'll be covered by the news? If I'm going to be on TV, I'll need a new wardrobe, a makeover — ah, I wonder if I have time for hair extensions and a Botox session."

Mel narrowed her eyes at Cheryl. Yep, a tiny dribble of drool glistened in the corner of Cheryl's mouth. The woman was actually salivating at the thought of being famous, never mind that it would come at the expense of her daughter's freedom and possibly her life. *What the hell?*

"No," Mel snapped. "I don't think anyone is going to give two hoots about this situation or about you. You are a truly horrible, disgusting human being."

Cheryl stepped back from Mel as if she'd tried to bite her. Even Toots must have registered the anger in Mel's voice, because she buried her head against her mama's chest and shivered.

Mel turned and strode away from the house. She was so furious, she was pulsing with it. Poor Diane. What a horror show her mother was. No wonder Diane was so driven and, frankly, socially defective. If that person had raised Mel, she shuddered to

164

think how she would have turned out.

She climbed into her car and turned it on. It was now midafternoon and the sun was reaching its peak baking point. Mel pulled away from the curb and drove down the street to park in the shade of a large mesquite tree. She left the car running and the air conditioning blasting while she took out her phone and called her mother.

"Hello," Joyce answered on the second ring.

"Hi, Mom," Mel said.

"Mel, you sound mad. Are you okay? Is everything all right with you and dear Joe? You didn't break up again, did you?" she asked.

Mel laughed. Her mother had been calling Joe "dear Joe" since the day Mel had started dating him. Joyce had known that Mel had sustained a crush on Joe since she was twelve years old and like any good mom, it had been her fondest wish that Mel get her Prince Charming. No one had suffered more than Joyce at Mel and Joe's on-and-off-again status over the past year and a half.

"No," Mel said. "Joe and I are fine. Better than ever, in fact. We even have a date tonight."

"Oh, good," Joyce said. "So what's up?"

165

"Nothing," Mel said. "I just . . ."

"Just what, honey?"

"I just wanted to thank you for being the best mom a girl could ever ask for," Mel said.

"Oh." Joyce's voice was soft as if she was too surprised to speak. "Well, thank you. I feel very lucky that I got to be your mom."

Mel felt her throat get tight. She knew tears were in the offing if she didn't get a grip, so she cleared her throat and said, "I'd better go. I'm driving."

"Melanie Cooper, you hang up right this second. You know how I feel about phone use in the car," Joyce said. And they were back to normal.

"Yes, Mom," Mel said. She smiled. "Talk to you later."

"Bye and be careful," Joyce said.

Mel ended the call and put her phone away. She needed to get back to the bakery and do some prep work for the next day before her date with Joe. As if she needed any more reasons to love him more than she did, in comparison to Diane's sleazy fiancé Joe was the greatest catch ever and that included his moments of overprotective dumbassery.

When Mel thought about their relationship, she realized that Joe had consistently put her well-being at the top of his priority list, even to the point of breaking up with her to keep her safe, the idiot. She hadn't always agreed with him, but given the fact that Diane had been about to marry a man who was fornicating with both her mother and her bridesmaid, Mel would take Joe's constant vigilance for her safety any day.

Sheesh, if Mel had been with a man like Mike Bordow, she suspected there wouldn't be enough left of her self-esteem to sop up with a sponge. It wasn't right. Diane was an intense person, yes, but she was also a good person. She didn't deserve to be treated so poorly.

The thought that Diane might have sought to inflict harm on Mike for his cheating crept up on Mel like a dark shadow. She didn't want to think it. She didn't want to acknowledge the possibility, but she couldn't help it. Could Diane have been angry enough to kill Mike or to have him killed? And what about Elliott? He was clearly besotted with Diane. How far would he go to prove his devotion to her?

Mel drove back to the bakery, feeling as if she'd aged a year since this morning when she'd found Mike's body. Parking in the lot across the alley behind the bakery, she glanced up at her apartment. The lure of climbing into her futon and pulling the covers up over her head was almost more than she could resist.

Unfortunately, she had a business to run and there was product to be made for tomorrow. Plus, if she curled up at home alone then she might fall asleep and would miss her date with Joe. That was unacceptable, mostly because she had a feeling the only thing that was going to make her feel better about the day was packing up Captain Jack and heading over to Joe's house.

Joe used to live in a townhouse in Phoenix, but last month he had purchased a house, a real house with a yard and everything, in the Arcadia neighborhood where they had both grown up. His parents lived three streets away while Mel's mother lived two. Three of his brothers had houses in the area as well.

They hadn't talked about it before he bought it. In fact, he didn't even mention it until he drove her there to show it to her. When Mel asked him why he bought it, he said it was because he knew she loved this type of house and he'd been watching the real estate in the area for a while and this one, a fixer-upper, had come onto the market at a greatly reduced price so he made an offer and literally owned it within hours. It helped that the sellers were friends with his parents.

The house was a mid-century modern marvel that needed to be stripped to the bones and restored. Mel was giddy by the prospect, as she loved all things retro and fifties, which was why her bakery was done in black-and-white tile and pink vinyl, but she was also nervous. After their aborted elopement a few months ago, they hadn't talked about marriage since and Mel wondered if Joe was rethinking the idea. Maybe now that things had calmed down, he didn't really want to tie the knot and was happy just to be dating. She knew they needed to talk but she wasn't really sure how to go about starting the conversation.

After so many false starts in their relationship, she was afraid that if she made one wrong move she might wreck the happy place they were in right now. With Tate and Angie's wedding taking center stage, she and Joe had been able to spend their time dating and just being together. Mel had loved every second of it.

She took a deep breath in, held it, and then let it out through her nose. She wasn't going to blow things with Joe. She wasn't. She was determined to live in the moment and be present. No pushing for outcomes, no overanalyzing his every move; she refused to do any of that. The future would be what it would be and she was 100 percent okay with that. Really, she was.

After several hours spent in her happy place, the bakery kitchen, Mel and Captain Jack arrived at Joe's house. She parked in the driveway and hefted her purse in one arm and Jack in the other as she strode up the walkway to the front door.

Joe opened the door before she had to knock, for which she was grateful. Captain Jack was a little over a year old but he had certainly packed on the pounds since she and Angie had found him abandoned in the Dumpster behind the bakery when he was just a wee kitty.

"Hey, buddy," Joe said as he took Jack from her arms and held him up so they could do their ritual head butt. Once Jack had greeted Joe, he yowled to be let loose. Joe put him down and he took off running across the hardwood floor.

"My men," Mel said. She put her hand over her heart as if overcome by the sight of Jack and his kitty daddy. She was only partially teasing. One of the many things she loved about Joe was his way with animals, particularly Captain Jack.

Joe pulled her into a hug and rested his cheek on the top of her head. "How did the rest of your day go? I was worried about you."

"It went well," Mel said. She didn't really feel the need to talk about her field trips to Nicole's and Cheryl's houses. "You know, cupcakes to bake, counters to clean, employees to pester."

"People to question about the murder of Mike Bordow," he added.

Uh-oh.

FOURTEEN

Mel pulled back to study his face. How much did he know? His warm chocolate-brown eyes were steady, as if he knew exactly how she had spent her day and he was waiting patiently for her to tell all.

"Would that be wild speculation on your part or do you have intel that I don't know about?" Mel asked.

Joe wiggled his eyebrows at her. It was ridiculously sexy and distracting so she kissed him, and much to her relief he kissed her back. Good. So, it had been wild speculation.

Joe broke off the kiss and stepped back. Then he shook his head as if trying to get his brain to function again. So charming.

"Stan called me about an hour ago right after a visit with Diane's mother," he said.

"Oh." Not wild speculation then.

Mel stepped away and then turned and walked away. She could feel Joe following her in that relentlessly patient way he had. The house only had the barest of furniture since it was three times bigger than Joe's old townhouse and he'd lived pretty sparsely even in the smaller space.

Captain Jack had bolted for the kitchen, where Joe kept a food and water dish for him. Sure enough, he had his face in his food bowl. Mel knew that once he had decimated his kitty kibble he was going to saunter out to the large screened-in porch and stalk the birds he could see in the large backyard. Joe had invested in one of those multi-level carpeted cat playhouses and it allowed Captain Jack a nice view where he could chatter his teeth and twitch his tail to his heart's content.

"Cupcake, you can't escape me," Joe said.

"Not trying," Mel said. She went right to the refrigerator and took out a bottle of wine. "I just feel the need for fortification."

Joe nodded in understanding. He took the bottle from her and began to open it while Mel foraged for glasses. They were going to have to discuss layout. The chef in her didn't understand why he didn't have the glasses to the right of the sink. Everyone knows glasses go to the right.

"The police department is inept, I tell you, totally useless! They don't care who murdered

my son. They botched the case and now they're trying to cover their asses!"

Mel turned, following the sound of the voice. Joe had the TV on the local news, which, given the house's open floor plan, meant the large-screen TV in the family room was visible from the kitchen. According to the caption on the bottom of the big screen, the voice coming from the television belonged to Butch Bordow. He looked like he was just warming up to his topic about how lame the local police were.

Mel glanced at Joe to see if he was catching this. He gave her a tired look and nodded. "Yeah, that guy has been blowing hard all day about how the police have already messed up the investigation. Note that he's standing in front of the Triple Fork Saloon, his favorite watering hole in Old Town."

"He certainly has the red nose of a drunk," Mel said.

"And the bloodshot eyes, slurred speech, and occasional belch," Joe said. "But that's the media for you. Don't vet the source, just toss him on the television, because ratings!"

Joe had a love-hate — no, more of a hate-hate — relationship with the media. Mostly because in today's divisive world there really was no one who just reported the facts;

174

every reporter was pandering to a bias of some sort and it had skewed far too many of Joe's cases for him to be forgiving.

He picked up the remote that was sitting on the counter and switched off the television. Mel held the glasses out to Joe and he gave them each a generous pour before putting the bottle down onto the counter.

"So, what did Diane's mother have to say?" he asked.

Mel picked up her glass, made a "just a second" gesture, and took a long sip. Then she closed her eyes as if the power of the grape could block out finding Mike Bordow's body, Nicole's meanness, and Cheryl's hideousness as a mother.

It helped, but Mel had a feeling nothing would ever truly erase this day from her mind. Ever.

"Let's discuss it all while we eat," she said.

"Good call. What do you want for dinner?" he asked. "I can fix anything you want so long as it's made from bacon, eggs, and bread."

Mel hadn't assessed the fridge when she took out the wine. She opened the door again. Sure enough there was a carton of eggs, a package of bacon, and a pink box from her bakery. She opened the freezer and found it empty. She moved to the pantry.

There was a loaf of bread. She went back to the fridge and took out the pink box from her bakery. She had brought Joe some of her latest experiments in cupcake baking yesterday. Half of them were history but she figured the others would do nicely with wine.

"How about dessert for dinner?" she asked.

"You're a terrible influence on me," he said. Then he took the cupcake box and his wine and led the way into the living room.

Mel followed with her wine, a handful of napkins, and two plates. Her mother would never approve of this clear violation of the food pyramid, but Joe's weakness was his sweet tooth, which was how Mel had gotten him to notice her in the first place.

Oh, sure, he had told her he'd noticed her years before that, but he hadn't made a move until after she opened her bakery, so she considered her culinary abilities responsible for sealing the deal between them and she wasn't above using her skill set to soften the lecture that she knew was coming.

The cupcakes would need to soften a bit as refrigeration sometimes made the cake dry and the frosting hard, but these were baked fresh yesterday so Mel wasn't worried. Plus, June in Arizona meant the cupcakes would be room temperature in about twenty minutes. Just enough time for her to duck and weave conversationally before stuffing a cupcake into her cake hole to avoid the conversation.

"Okay, so let her rip," Mel said. She sat beside Joe on the couch, dropping the napkins on the table beside the box.

"Let what rip?" he asked. He lifted his arm and she took her spot, tucked into his side, while they sipped their wine and stared at the pink box as if willing the cupcakes to soften up faster.

"The lecture that I know you are dying to unleash upon me," she said.

"Me?" Joe blinked his dark lashes in feigned innocence. "When do I ever lecture?"

Mel turned and their faces were just inches apart. The man was ridiculously handsome and for a moment she forgot what they were talking about. As his gaze moved over her face, he seemed to lose track of his thoughts as well and Mel took that as a compliment.

"This is nice," she said. She put her head on his shoulder.

He rested his cheek on the top of her head and Mel knew that this was what she'd longed for all day. To be here with her honey, where she felt safe and protected and loved.

"Mel, I want you to move in," he said.

Mel snapped her head up. She clocked his nose with the top of her head, and he let out a yelp and spilled his wine.

"I'm sorry," Mel cried. She took his glass out of his hand and put both of their glasses down on the table. "Oh, nuts, you just caught me by surprise."

"It's okay," he said. "I'm all right."

"Yeah, more believable if you didn't have blood streaming out your nose," she said. She snatched a napkin off of the table and held it to his face.

"I'm fine," he said. He put his hand on hers and looked at her over the napkin, which was beginning to bloom with a dark crimson stain. "Really."

Mel sighed. "And just when I thought this day was getting better, I clobber my boyfriend."

"Boyfriend?" He frowned.

"What?"

"I thought I was your fiancé."

"Oh, yeah, sorry. I forgot."

"Forgot?" he asked.

"It's been a rough day," she said.

His expression softened. "I'm sorry. You're right. I'm not trying to add to it. I just, I

178

really love having you and Captain Jack here, and I meant what I said. I'd really like for you to —"

Mel's heart was hammering in her chest. Was he asking her to move in, like permanently? To live with him, day in and day out? Share a home? It was everything she had ever hoped for and more. She opened her mouth to answer him when a voice interrupted.

"What did my idiot brother do that you felt the need to punch him in the nose?" Angie asked as she strode into the living room.

Both Mel and Joe glanced at her and then back at each other, each knowing that the moment between them was gone.

"Angie, I love you like a sister," he said.

"That's because I am your sister," she said.

"Which is the only reason I can forgive your spectacularly bad timing," he said. "Now, why are you walking into my house without knocking?"

"The door was unlocked," she said. "Besides, I need Mel. It's an emergency."

Mel let go of Joe's nose and hopped to her feet. "What happened? Is it the bakery? Is Tate okay? What about Marty and Oz?"

"Everyone is fine," Angie said. She held

up both hands in a gesture that was supposed to calm Mel down or stop traffic; it was unclear.

"Then what's the emergency?" Mel asked.

"I'm trying to plan the menu for my reception," Angie said. Then she huffed out a breath and looked completely overwhelmed. Mel had known her long enough to know that tears were incoming. As if to confirm her suspicion, Angie let out a wail and cried, "And I can't do it!"

There was a moment of silence as Mel and Joe both looked at Angie and then at each other. Mel shrugged and Joe gave her a slight nod. Their discussion was going to have to wait.

"I'm going to go order a pizza," Joe said. He left the room, still holding his nose, while moving at a clip as if he could outrun female tears. Silly man.

"Sit," Mel said to Angie. "I'll get you a glass so you can have some wine and then we can talk about your wedding menu, and by the time we're finished everything will be okay."

Angie made a hiccup noise as she sucked in a deep breath and sank onto the couch like a fifties movie siren. All she needed was a peignoir and some feathered mules.

Mel went into the kitchen, grabbed a

glass, and hurried back to Angie. She poured her pal a generous amount and handed it to her. By unspoken agreement, they waited until Angie had taken a long sip and let it mellow her for a moment before they addressed the situation at hand.

"Okay, now, what is freaking you out about the menu?" Mel asked. "Your cousin Judi knows the wedding industry, have you talked to her?"

"I think I've unloaded enough on her with wedding decorations and the favors she's making," Angie said. "I thought the menu would be a no-brainer. I met with the chef and she said she could do anything I wanted, so I got one of Martha Stewart's wedding books from the library and figured I'd just do what good ol' Martha said."

"And . . ." Mel encouraged her.

"And now I don't know whether to go with a whole locally sourced, go-green dinner or a family-style one, where each table passes around their own bowls of mashed potatoes and green beans or whatever, or is it all about color and I have to have food dyed to match our wedding colors, or do we want to go exotic and have it be stuff no one has ever heard of?" Angie said. "I mean who thinks up this stuff anyway?

"Should we have a buffet or a sit-down

181

meal? Should we have several courses or just two or three? And what about food stations? We could have a bacon station, a deviled egg station, and what if there are people who can't have nuts or only eat organic, vegetarian, or have to be gluten-free?"

"Stop!" Mel said. "Breathe."

"But —"

"Breathe," Mel ordered. When Angie looked calmer, she said, "A deviled egg station, really?"

"It's a thing," Angie said.

"Do you like deviled eggs that much?"

"Tate does."

"Yeah, his vote doesn't count right now," Mel said. "Since he's not the one having a nervous breakdown on the couch."

"Fair enough," Angie said. "Plus, he said he'd be okay if we grilled burgers in the backyard. He doesn't care so long as at the end of the day I'm his wife."

"Aw," Mel said. Good old Tate. He always knew exactly what to say. Angie made a slashing motion with her hand. Or not.

"No, not 'Aw.' Sheesh, it's like he doesn't even get that three hundred–plus of our nearest and dearest are expecting a well-catered, over-the-top, romantic day with the perfect food, music, setting, decorations, not to mention a gorgeous bride and groom. Ugh, I think I'm going to throw up."

"Whoa," Mel said. "Not on the couch. Joe just bought it."

Angie turned a sickly shade of green and Mel grew serious. Angie wasn't kidding. She was having a bridal meltdown of epic proportions. Mel frowned. This was Angie, the person who never cared what anyone thought of her, ever. What the heck was going on in her head that she suddenly cared now?

"Ange, what's up?" Mel asked. "What is making you so self-conscious about this wedding?"

"Nothing," Angie said. She glanced away, which was how Mel knew she was lying.

"Oh, please, I know you better than you know yourself and this is not how Angie Maria Lucia DeLaura handles things. Now spill it or I'm calling Tate and telling him that you're having a freak-out over bacon and deviled eggs."

"No!" Angie cried. She looked genuinely alarmed and Mel frowned even more deeply.

"Then tell me what's going on, right now," Mel said.

Tears poured out of Angie's eyes and she hugged herself as she rocked back and forth on her seat. Mel wanted to hug her friend

183

close, just like she did her nephews when they were hurt or scared, but she didn't. Instead, she forced herself to wait out Angie's crying jag. It almost killed her but she waited.

"I'm not good enough for him," Angie said. Her voice was raspy and gritty as if it hurt her throat to utter the words.

"Shut the fucupcake!" Mel cried.

Oz had come up with this particular expression when things in the bakery were particularly stressful or when someone was just plain talking crazy, like Angie right now. This was the first time Mel had cause to use it and, boy howdy, did it fit.

"That is the dumbest thing I have ever heard," Mel said.

A ghost of a smile flitted across Angie's lips but her eyes remained shadowed with sadness and self-doubt.

"But it's true," she said. "Tate is so far out of my league, it's not even funny. I thought love would be enough to make it equal, but it's not. I'm never going to fit into his world of wealth and privilege, of Ivy League educations and country club memberships. I'm just Angie; nothing special, a former teacher turned cupcake baker, and I'm not even that good at that."

"We've been friends since we were twelve,

right?" Mel asked.

Angie nodded. "Seventh grade in middle school."

"So almost twenty-two years now," Mel said.

Again, Angie nodded.

"Huh, and in those twenty-two years, I have to say I have never wanted to slap you like I do right now."

Angie's eyebrows lifted and she leaned away from Mel. "That's kind of harsh, don't you think?"

"Not really, no," she said. "Tate is crazy in love with you."

"It'll fade when he realizes I'm not going to fit into his world," Angie said. "Oh, it'll start out all right but slowly as his family and friends get to know me, he'll start to see me through their eyes and he'll see that I'm not up to scratch."

Mel closed her eyes. A moment's meditation was the only thing that was going to keep her from banging her head on the coffee table.

"I think you're right," Mel said.

"What?" Angie asked.

"This" — Mel paused to gesture at the pitiful heap that was presently Angie on the couch — "is not the woman Tate fell in love with, not even close."

185

Angie's chin dropped to her chest. She looked so defeated, it absolutely killed Mel to continue, but she knew her friend and she knew that compliments would do nothing for Angie. However, if she went the other way, Angie's ingrained obstinacy would kick into gear, or so she hoped.

"Tate fell in love with Angie DeLaura, a fiery, feisty, beautiful woman who would kick the butt of anyone who even thought to harm the people she cared about. That Angie is the one who spun Tate's head around and knocked him on his keister when he least expected it. And why?"

"I don't know, why?" Angie asked.

"Because that Angie loves Tate with her whole heart; that Angie is fiercely loyal, confident in who she is as a woman, and knows whose opinion matters: her own. She's beautiful and funny and smart, and she would never, ever let anyone make her feel unworthy, because she knows she is worthy, more than worthy, of marrying the love of her life and having the fairy-tale wedding of her dreams, no one else's, and living happily ever after. That is Tate's Angie, and I'd be willing to bet he's been missing her mightily these past few weeks."

The last of Mel's words were drowned out over Angie's big gulping sobs. Mel wrapped

186

her arm around Angie and let her friend cry it all out on her shoulder.

"Promise me you won't tell him how stupid I've been," Angie said.

"Of course I won't," Mel said.

A movement in the doorway caught her attention and she saw Joe, standing there watching them. The look in his eyes was full of affection and pride. While her gaze held his, he mouthed the words, *I love you,* and Mel knew exactly what her answer to his question was going to be.

FIFTEEN

By the time Angie left, looking more like her old self than she had in weeks, Mel went to find Joe so they could finish their conversation. When she did find him, after locking up the house, she didn't have the heart to wake him up.

He was lying on the bed in the master bedroom with his feet crossed, one arm behind his head, and one hand holding Captain Jack, who was snoring where he slept on Joe's chest. Mel felt her chest get tight at the sight of the two of them. A man snuggling his cat. She couldn't think of a more heartwarming sight.

She went into the bathroom and got ready for bed. She crawled in beside Joe and Captain Jack. Neither of them stirred but that was okay. She put her hand on Joe's arm, just wanting to feel his warmth beneath her fingers.

When she closed her eyes, she was afraid

that images of Mike Bordow and his mashed melon would be all that she would see, but it wasn't. Instead, she saw herself here in this house, cooking in the kitchen, lounging by the pool in the backyard, decorating one of the spare bedrooms as a nursery.

Instead of jolting her upright as the thought might have in the past, Mel felt a soul-deep contentment that she had never imagined existed before. She was going to move in with Joe; they were going to get married, she hoped; and they were going to have the life of which she'd always dreamed.

A cup of coffee appeared on the nightstand on Mel's side of the bed. Its aroma beckoned and she opened her eyes to find Joe, freshly showered and dressed for work, crouched beside the bed, watching her while she slept.

"Morning, cupcake," he said.

"Mrnuh," she replied. It was clear her verbal skills were not quite where they needed to be as yet.

"I have to go to work," he said. "Promise me you'll talk to Uncle Stan and let him know what you've discovered and then let him do his job. He's really a good detective, you know."

Mel sat up, dislodging Captain Jack from

her side, who gave her a sharp "Meow" before curling back up into a round white fur ball. She reached for her coffee, stalling for time, and took a sip. It was perfect; just the way she liked it.

"Mel?" Joe asked.

"I promise," she said. Before she could take a second sip, Joe took the cup away from her and yanked the sheet back. The hand she had kept under the covers was now clearly visible, showing her index and middle finger were crossed.

"Mel." Joe glowered.

"Dear Joe," Mel said. "If you don't want me to fib, then you shouldn't ask me to make promises that you know I am incapable of keeping."

He shoved his hands into his hair as if debating ripping it out in chunks. Thankfully, he let go and dropped his hands, as patchy bald spots would have been a terrible look on him.

"You're right," he said. "What was I thinking?"

"Are you mad?" Mel asked. "You look mad."

"I'm not mad, I'm worried," he said. "Which is infinitely worse."

"For who?" she asked. She took her coffee cup back and took a big gulp, fortifying herself for what she had to say next.

"For me, clearly," he said. He stood and put his hands on his hips. "I suppose since you're consumed with Angie's wedding and Diane's murdered fiancé, you haven't had time to think about what I asked you last night."

Mel put the coffee back on the nightstand. She clasped her hands in front of her and feigned a somber expression that was quite at odds with the butterflies doing the tango in her belly.

"Actually, yes, I have," she said. She looked away from him as if she was about to deliver the news that a loved one had passed and she couldn't bear to look at him.

Joe took her chin in his hand and forced her gaze up to meet his. He looked nervous and hopeful and she just didn't have it in her to torture him anymore. Well, too much more anyway.

"I think it's best if, well, if I move in with you as soon as possible," she said.

Joe had clearly expected a different answer. He stared at her for a second and then he snatched her close and hugged her until her ribs protested.

"You, me, and Captain Jack living here together?" he asked as if to be sure that he wasn't hearing her wrong.

"Yes," she said. She leaned back and smiled at him. "Let's make this a home."

Joe let her go for a moment and stepped back to give a huge fist pump. Seeing his joy made Mel laugh, which brought his attention back to her. The look in his gaze was wicked, and he used one finger to push her shoulder and Mel found herself falling backwards onto the bed.

"Hey!" she cried.

She gave him a "what was that for" look, and Joe wiggled his eyebrows at her and then started to yank off his tie.

"What are you . . . Oh," Mel said as it all came into focus. She smiled at him. "You're going to be late for work."

"Yeah, don't care," he said. Then he kissed her.

Captain Jack lifted his head and gave them a look of scorn that only a cat being forced to vacate his nap spot can manage. Then he shook himself, hopped off the bed, and strode out of the room with his tail in the air.

"Get used to it, buddy," Joe called after him.

Mel laughed and held her arms open to him. And yeah, Joe was late for work, and it was totally worth it.

■ ■ ■ ■

Mel left Captain Jack at Joe's since they had agreed to meet there after work and discuss the plan for moving Mel and Captain Jack into the house. Joe wanted to call his brothers and have the move done that weekend, but Mel knew she needed to run the new living arrangements by her mom, who would be ecstatic, and her uncle Stan, who would be less so.

It wasn't that Uncle Stan didn't love Joe. He did. But he had stepped into the father role in Mel's life when her father had passed away, which meant he tended to be a bit more reserved about her relationships than her mother. The living-together thing was not going to make him happy.

She knew she could argue that she and Joe had almost made it official a few months ago, and that they had been engaged before, but she had a feeling that neither of those arguments were going to help her police detective uncle embrace the new normal.

Maybe she would just check on his investigation of the Bordow homicide and leave the intel about her and Joe for another day. She was still pretty drained from yesterday and she wasn't sure she was up for a long lecture, especially since she had to get to the bakery and oversee the cupcakes for a fiftieth wedding anniversary party. She knew Oz was up to the challenge, but she wanted to make sure he wasn't overwhelmed by the details.

Mel strode into the station. Lisa Kelley, a uniform officer, smiled when she saw her.

"Hey, Mel," she said. "Long time, no see."

"Yeah, and no cupcakes, either," Juan Muñoz, another uniform, added.

"My bad," Mel said. She raised her hands in surrender. "Next week, I promise."

"So long as they're carrot cake, you're forgiven," Juan said.

She walked into the back where Uncle Stan's desk was shoved up against a wall. Luckily, Uncle Stan was there, leaning back in his swivel chair while he frowned at a sheaf of papers in his hand. He glanced up when she was just a few feet from his desk. His frown deepened. Okay, maybe not so lucky.

"We need to talk," he said.

"No conversation that starts with *we need to talk* is ever a good one," she said.

Mel moved in and hugged him, hoping it would soften him up. He hugged her back, so she took that as a hopeful sign. When she stepped back his frown was still ravine-deep.

Okay, so much for the hug.

"Where's your partner?" she asked. She figured she might as well jump in with both feet first.

"Out doing her job," Stan said. "Questioning people about yesterday's murder."

Mel cringed a bit at the word but there really was no other way to describe what had happened to Mike Bordow. It was most definitely not an accident.

"How's she working out?" Mel asked. "Tara, I mean."

"Fine, why?"

"She seems, I don't know." Mel paused and then said, "Annoyingly fixated on my boyfriend."

"You think she has a crush on Joe?"

"Seems like it, judging by the way she went all weak in the knees and fluttery at him at the crime scene yesterday," Mel said.

A tiny smile lifted the corner of Stan's mouth. "You jealous?"

"No," Mel snapped. "Joe and I are fine, better than ever, in fact."

"Then it really doesn't matter if Tara is crushing on him or not, does it?"

"No, it's just annoying," she said. Mel didn't like the sulky tone of her voice, but she was darned if she could stop it.

"Speaking of annoying," Stan said, paus-

195

ing to frown at her before he continued. "What were you doing talking to Nicole Butterfield and Cheryl Kelly yesterday?"

Mel studied the toes of her running shoes as if looking for a hole or a rock wedged into the treads. More accurately, she was stalling. What could she say? She had been asking questions for Diane, and Uncle Stan knew it. Was there even a point in lying?

"Diane asked me to break the news to them about Mike," Mel said, which was sort of the truth; okay, not really. "Apparently, they were both inordinately fond of him."

"Mel." Stan said her name on a puff of infuriated breath. It was quite plain that he just couldn't believe they had to have this conversation. "That was a job for the police. What if one of them knew something? Your telling them about Bordow's death ruined them for questioning."

"How do you figure?" Mel asked. "Bordow's father was already on the news spewing about how the police department screwed the pooch on the investigation. I'd bet dollars to donuts they would have known about his murder before you showed up anyway."

"Mel," he said. Just her name. Just the one word.

She knew the point he was trying to make,

but she didn't feel like being lectured right now and she didn't feel like conceding the argument, either.

Uncle Stan looked at her. His eyes, so much like her father's, were steady as they met hers. He wasn't allowing her any wiggle room here. Mel crossed her arms over her chest in what she knew was a defensive stance. Uncle Stan knew it, too.

"All right, I'm sorry," she said. She sat on the edge of his desk. "But when I was with Angie yesterday at the bridal salon, and I heard that Nicole Butterfield had tried to bust up Diane and Mike's wedding by sleeping with Mike, I felt the need to pay her a visit, especially since she and I went to college together."

"And you didn't call me when you heard this little tidbit?" Uncle Stan said.

"No, because Nicole and I have a history, plus she was the one who told me that she wasn't the only little bit on the side Mike was maintaining. There was another woman," Mel said.

Uncle Stan threw the papers he'd been holding onto the desk and rubbed his face with his hands. "Again, that might have been an excellent time to call me."

"Perhaps," Mel said.

"Who was the other woman?" he asked.

It was Mel's turn to look at him, as if to say the answer was obvious.

"No," he said.

"Yes," she said.

Mel was pleased that even Stan, who had been on the force forever and had heard every sort of low-life human-behavior story going, looked shocked by the news that Cheryl had been fornicating with her future son-in-law.

"Man, what did that guy eat for breakfast?" Stan asked. "Juggling three women, I'd be in traction for a month."

"And those are just the ones we know about," Mel said. "I'm guessing there were more."

"Small wonder he's dead," Stan said.

Mel nodded. If Mike treated Diane this badly, he had to have been treating the other women in his life equally so. It stood to reason that one of them got fed up and let him have it.

"Hey, Cooper, I've got something," Detective Tara shouted from across the room.

She power walked toward them and Mel felt her irritation rise. She never power walked anywhere and it irked her that this woman walked across a room like that. Of course, it could also be the other woman's clear interest in Joe that bugged her, but for the moment it was the walk.

"Let's hear it," Stan said.

Tara cast Mel a look that said she didn't think she could be trusted, but Stan waved his hand for her to spit it out. Tara cast one more dark look at Mel and then said, "I have it from a reliable source that Mike Bordow was sleeping with one of the bridesmaids, a Nicole Butterfield." She looked quite pleased with herself.

Stan looked at her. "Yeah, I already know about that."

"What? When? Who told you?" Tara snapped.

Mel smiled at her and gave her a little finger wave.

"You?" Tara looked at her with scorn.

"He also slept with his future mother-in-law, Cheryl Earnest, or Kelly, or whatever her last name is now," Mel said.

Tara's jaw dropped and she flapped her hands. "How do you know this?"

"I have my ways," Mel said with a shrug. She rose from where she had perched herself on the edge of Stan's desk. She was feeling quite full of herself, so she added, "Here's another news bulletin: Joe DeLaura and I are moving in together effective immediately."

199

Sixteen

If Mel had been hoping to see Tara's head explode, she was sorely disappointed, mostly because Stan erupted out of his seat and hauled her out of the office "to talk" about the situation before she had the satisfaction of seeing Tara's reaction. Darn it.

It took Mel a good twenty minutes to calm Stan down, assuring him that she and Joe were still going to get married and that he didn't have to worry about any of the bad guys in Joe's life coming after her. Although, it had happened before. By the time she left the station to go back to the bakery, she was exhausted.

On the drive, her phone rang and she glanced at the display, fearing it was Uncle Stan calling to hassle her some more with some concern that he had forgotten to mention. Fortunately, or unfortunately, it was not Uncle Stan; rather, it was Diane.

Mel parked the car in the lot behind the

bakery and answered her phone. She knew it was better to answer than not as Diane would just keep calling her, and calling her, and calling her. She could be relentless like that.

"Hi, Diane," Mel said.

"Mel, you have to help me," Diane said. "The police have let me go, but I know it's only temporary because I am still a person of interest."

"Could that be because your fiancé was sleeping with your mother and one of your bridesmaids?" Mel asked. She got out of her car and locked it.

Silence, the type that was weighted in truth, was the only non-sound Mel heard on the phone. She might have thought the call had been cut off, but she was sure she could hear Diane's brain whirring as she tried to think of what to say.

"Why didn't you tell me?" Mel asked.

Diane's voice when she spoke was faint. It sounded as if all of the fight had gone out of her and Mel felt terrible that she was the one who had brought her to such a low. Then again, better that it was Mel than the police.

"I was ashamed," Diane said.

Mel blew out a breath. Shame was a familiar feeling for her. She used to feel it every time she broke a diet or went on an eating bender or heard someone make fun of her weight. Given Diane's controlling nature, she could only imagine how much the information that her fiancé was cheating had destroyed her. Enough to kill him? Mel shook her head, refusing to think it.

"I'm sorry, Diane," Mel said. "That has to be rough."

Diane snorted. "What am I going to do, Mel? How am I going to get out of this?"

"You're going to sit tight," Mel said. She made her voice firm, hoping she sounded much more confident than she felt. "You've got Steve as an attorney. He won't steer you wrong. In the meantime, I'll figure out a plan and call you back."

"Are you sure?"

"Positive," Mel said. She hoped her voice sounded more certain than she felt. Honestly, the case against Diane was mounting and she didn't really know how she could help her friend.

"Hey," Diane said, with what sounded like a forced laugh, "after this I'm going to owe you one."

"Huh," Mel said. It was supposed to sound like a chuckle but it came out more like a grunt of pain. She hoped Diane didn't hear it that way.

She ended the call and thought about her next move. She could try and find more women who Mike had slept with but she didn't really think that would play in Diane's favor. Instead, she needed to find someone with a different take on the situation. Someone like Mike's father, Butch Bordow. If she could crack him and find someone with a better reason to kill Mike than Diane, well, then she'd be able to help her friend. And Mel knew just who she needed at her back to shake up Butch Bordow.

She spent the morning in the bakery, listening to Angie, who was so happy about her wedding menu that she didn't have one wedding meltdown, not one. When her cousin Judi dropped by with her daughters, Ciera and Arianna, to discuss the decorations for the church, Angie deferred to Judi's excellent suggestions and all was well with the world.

Marty, who'd been watching Angie laugh with her cousin with one bushy eyebrow raised in suspicion, looked at Mel and asked, "What happened to bridezilla? Did you put Xanax in one of her cupcakes?"

"No!" Mel protested. "First, I would never drug an unsuspecting friend, I'm pretty sure, and second, where would I even get that stuff?"

"I figured after your brush with another dead body, a doc might hook you up," he said.

"Yeah, no thanks," Mel said. "I'll stick to my mood elevator of choice. Frosting."

She unloaded the batch of freshly decorated Orange Dreamsicle Cupcakes into the display case then glanced at the clock. It was a little before noon and Oz should be here at any moment to take over the bakery so she could relieve Tate from his duties at the bridal expo in downtown Phoenix. If she was going to intercept Butch Bordow at his favorite drinking spot, she had to go now.

She put her tray on a rack under the counter and began to untie her apron.

"Marty, I need to go run an errand. I'll be back in an hour," she said.

She glanced at him to see if he was listening, and he nodded and said, "No."

Mel shook her head. The mixed signal, a nod with the word *no,* was throwing her off.

"What?" she asked. "What do you mean?"

"What do you not understand about the word *no*?" he asked.

"At the moment, you saying it to me," she said. "I'm the boss, remember?"

Marty shrugged. It was clear he didn't

really think that point had any weight in their discussion.

"Mel, I saw you when you came in yesterday. You were rattled. Finding that guy, sheesh, it had to be rough. I read the description in the paper this morning. They're saying it was murder. You have to stay away from this," he said. His bushy eyebrows lowered. "It could be dangerous."

"Marty, he was engaged to my friend. She hired me to deliver breakup cupcakes to him," Mel said. "I can't help thinking it's weird that I found him dead at the same time that I was there to end his relationship, which would naturally make his ex the prime suspect."

"Okay, I can see where that would bother you, but it really has nothing to do with you," Marty argued. "You were hired for a job, you did the job. It doesn't matter that you once lived with this woman. The job was done. The gig is over. Time to move on."

"It's not that simple," she said. "I owe Diane a favor, a big one, from our past."

"So buy her a fruit basket and call it even."

"That doesn't quite cover it."

"Neither does getting yourself killed in order to help her out," he said.

"I'm not going to —"

"You don't know that," Marty interrupted. "Someone whacked that guy, which means he had enemies. If those enemies don't like you poking your nose where it doesn't belong, they are going to come after you. Or have we not learned that over the past year and a half when bad people have tried to hurt us?"

Mel pressed her index finger to her right eyelid, which had begun to twitch.

"What's bugging her?" Oz asked as he joined them behind the display case.

At well over six feet tall, with an off-putting black fringe of hair that hung over his eyes, and an athletic build more suited to wielding a hammer than piping rosettes out of buttercream, Oz had been a welcome addition to the bakery crew last year. Aside from his talent as a pastry chef, Mel always enjoyed it when new customers came in and found him behind the counter and looked varying levels of shocked, stunned, and suspicious, right up until they tasted his cupcakes.

"She's going snooping and I'm trying to talk her out of it," Marty said. "You know how she is."

"Stubborn," Oz said.

"Yep, she's the only person I know who could argue with a wall and win."

"And I'm standing right here," Mel said. She glanced between them. "And now I'm leaving."

"Does Joe know what you're up to?" Marty asked.

"Sorry, I can't hear you," Mel said. She ducked through the swinging door into the kitchen.

"How about your uncle Stan, does he know?" Marty persisted. He was hot on her heels like a toddler chasing a snack. "I'll call him if I have to."

"Go ahead," Mel said. "He won't take the call. He's still mad at you for giving me away at my non-wedding, taking what he considers his place in my life."

"Really? Still mad?" Marty asked. "You didn't even get married. He needs to get over it."

"I'll be sure to tell him you said that," Mel said.

She hung up her apron and grabbed her handbag from her office. She slung it over her shoulder and headed out the back door.

"Don't forget that Tate is working the bridal expo in Phoenix," Oz said. "You promised T-man you'd take the afternoon shift with Marty."

"I know. I'll be back soon," she said with a wave. "I promise."

"You have one hour and if you're not back, I'm calling in the brothers," he said.

Mel waved at him as if it was no big deal, but as soon as she shut the door, she began to run. She did not — not — want to deal with the DeLaura brothers. No way, no how.

She hurried to the end of the street and was relieved to see the tattoo shop was open. She glanced through the window and saw Mick, the owner, sitting in one of the barbershop-type recliners while he perused the paper. Mel yanked the door open and hurried inside.

"Hey, Mick, are you busy?" she asked.

Mick lowered the paper. "You finally here to get some ink?"

"No," she said. "I have to go talk to someone, and I need backup, scary-looking backup."

Mick rubbed his big, blocky jaw with the back of his hand.

"You know I'm a pacifist, right?"

"Uh-huh," she said. "It's really more your look that I'm after."

"Mr. Donnelly, I found the discrepancy in your accounts," a woman's voice interrupted them.

Mel turned toward the back of the shop, where a petite woman in a navy blue suit stood in the doorway of Mick's office. She had a sheaf of papers in her hand and her dark-framed reading glasses were shoved up on top of her head, resting against her bun of honey-colored hair.

"Thanks, Frankie," Mick said. "I knew a smart girl like you could figure it out."

"It's Frances," she corrected him. She gave him a weary look, as if they had this conversation every day and he just wasn't getting it.

"I think Frankie suits you better," he said. He took the papers from her and began to look them over. "Just like a tiny little dragonfly tattoo right on your —"

"Stop right there," she said. Frances frowned at him but it was belied by the pink suffusing her face in an embarrassed shade of seriously crushing on Mick. Huh.

"It'd be smokin' hot, that's all I'm saying," he said.

Mel glanced between them. Frances was an accountant who rented the office above Mick's shop. She was a no-nonsense, prim and proper sort of girl, and while Mick had mentioned previously that he liked her, Mel had never thought his interest would be returned. Go figure.

"Hi, Frances," she said.

"Mel." Frances nodded. "I have to go now."

Frances strode toward the front door as if the hounds of hell were nipping at her heels. Mel shook her head. The woman was more socially awkward than a belch in church.

"Hey, Frankie," Mick called just before she disappeared out the door. "Don't forget, dinner is on me."

Frances's face flashed crimson. Mel would have laughed if she wasn't so worried that the poor thing was about to pass out.

Instead, she made a squeaky little noise and ran around the side of the building to the staircase that would take her back up to her office.

"So, you and Frances, huh?" Mel asked.

"Not yet, but I'm working on it," he said.

"Well, she's definitely not indifferent to you," Mel said.

Mick grinned. With his full lips, it would have been a devastating smile, but the multiple lip rings he was sporting along with the small horns coming out of his nose made it more terrifying than anything else. And for Mel's purposes, that was perfect.

"So, can I borrow you?"

He looked at her and frowned. "No quid pro quo?"

"I didn't have time, but I swear, I will bake you a dozen Moonlight Madness Coconut Cupcakes by the end of today," she said.

"Can you make half of those Tinkerbells?" he asked. A faint pink tinged his cheeks.

"Frances's favorite?" she guessed.

Mick shrugged. "What can I say? She gets to me."

"It's a deal." Mel grinned, then she grew serious. "But you have to look really scary. Like, terrifying."

"I have no appointments booked for the next half hour, so you're on and I will do my best to be intimidating. Lead on, fearless cupcake baker," he said. He gestured toward the door. "So, where are we going, anyway?"

Mel waited while he paused to lock up behind him.

"A bar," she said.

The silver ball stud pierced where Mick's right eyebrow used to be — he had shaved the entire thing off — lifted up in surprise. "Not what I expected."

"Nothing ever is," Mel said.

"Amen to that."

They strode in companionable silence to the Triple Fork Saloon, nestled amid the shops in Old Town Scottsdale. The small bar had been here since the fifties and retained its retro ambiance of days gone by.

Mel pushed through the swinging doors, of course they were, and stepped into the

211

dimly lit space, feeling the empty peanut shells crunch under her feet as she made her way to the bar that ran along the wall on the left. Tables were scattered around the narrow room. Several large-screen televisions were mounted on the wall and at the back a pool table was spotlighted under a stained glass lamp that was advertising beer.

Mel hadn't been in here in a year or more and the place hadn't changed a bit. It even maintained its pungent smell of fried food and stale beer. It only took a moment for her eyes to adjust to the gloom and then she saw him, perched on a stool, elbows resting on the bar, keeping his bloated face just inches above the pint of beer sitting in front of him. Butch Bordow, barfly.

"Hey, isn't that —" Mick began, but Mel cut him off.

"Yes," she hissed. "Now hush."

"But he's been all over the news," Mick protested. "His son was —"

"Murdered, yes, I know," Mel said.

"Oh, no." Mick shook his head. "You are not dragging me into one of your crazy dead-body situations. I was warned about you."

SEVENTEEN

"What dead body? There's no dead body here," Mel said. "And who warned you about me?"

"Frankie," he said. "She said you have the devil's own luck."

Mel blew out a breath. "Did she mean that in a good way or a bad way?"

Mick glowered.

"Okay, bad way, got it." Mel lowered her voice before continuing, "Listen, I know this is awkward, but my friend was engaged to the dead guy and she's being wrongfully accused of harming him, so I'm just going to talk to his father and see if there may have been someone else who might have had reason to kill his son Mike."

"Yeah, 'cause that's an easy conversational segue to work in from *how you doin'?*" he said. "You're going to have to up my payment to two dozen cupcakes or, depending upon how this goes, maybe three."

"Fine," Mel said.

She glanced over at Butch, who seemed unaware that they were there. She felt bad about interrupting a bereaved father and she wasn't exactly sure how she was going to play it. Still, she needed information. Judging by how Butch had filleted the police on the news last night, he wasn't going to be sharing with them anytime soon, so really she was doing a public service to try and get him to share any information he had with her. She couldn't help it if Uncle Stan did not view it in the same light.

Mel sat on the empty barstool next to Butch. With some muttering and grumbling Mick took the seat on the other side of her. Butch was so entranced with the bubbles floating up to the top of his pale ale, he didn't even turn to check them out. Mel wondered how blotto he was already and if this was going to be a complete waste of her time.

Ah, well, nothing ventured nothing gained, as they say, even if it meant a stern talking-to from Uncle Stan and Joe, as well as a whole lot of *I told you so*'s from Marty.

She swiveled on her stool so that she nudged Butch Bordow's knee. This was not hard to do as he was sitting on his stool with his knees splayed wide in a clear manspreading move to get as much of the bar real estate as he could manage. When Mel brushed by him, he didn't even glance her way, making it more challenging to engage him in conversation.

Mel decided to go for the direct approach. She leaned in close, hoping she smelled of vanilla and cinnamon, as she'd read in a fashion magazine that those are the scents that usually turned men's heads, although she suspected an Eau de Hops would be more Butch's jam.

"Hey, there," she said.

Butch didn't even glance her way. So much for the lure of baked goods that usually clung to her skin. This guy was oblivious. Of course, he had just lost his son. He was probably drowning his sorrows and too grief-stricken to register anything that was going on around him.

"Butch Bordow!" a voice boomed from the swinging doors. "I want to talk to you."

The man who entered the saloon had neatly trimmed gray hair with an equally well-maintained mustache. He stood almost as tall as Mick and a little wider, mostly in the gut. Despite the dress shirt and slacks that he wore, Mel didn't think she was imagining the feeling of menace that pulsed off of him like a growl coming from a scary dog.

Butch turned on his stool and took in the man with a bleary squint. Mel wondered how many of the man he was seeing, two or three, or maybe he was just near-sighted. Finally, the man registered and Butch nodded.

"Tyson," he said. He then turned back to his drink.

"Oh, this is not good," Mick whispered in Mel's ear. "Not good at all."

"Why? What do you know?" she whispered back. Mick opened his mouth to answer but Mel shushed him when Tyson began to speak.

"I want my money, Butch," Tyson said.

"It's not a good day," Butch said.

"It's never a good day with you," Tyson said.

He strode into the bar, looking like he owned it.

"Tyson Ballinger. He's a glorified loan shark," Mick whispered into Mel's ear. "He gets companies in deep, deep debt and then when they are on the brink of ruin, he swoops in and takes them."

"Uh-oh," she said. Maybe he did own the joint.

"Yeah," he agreed. "Big-time."

216

The bartender chose that moment to ask Mel and Mick what they would like. To Mel, it was still a bit early in the day to be drinking, so she went with a root beer. She was surprised when Mick did the same.

"What?" he asked at her surprised look. "I have fine art to produce. You can't do that wasted."

Mel smiled. Despite his outward scary appearance, Mick had a true artist's soul.

"When are you going to pay me?" Tyson asked Butch. "I mean, you don't think I gave you all that scratch for your gambling debts for nothing, do you? You know what I want."

Butch was curling into himself, obviously ignoring Tyson and looking like he wanted to take a dive right into his beer headfirst.

"Answer me, Butch," Tyson badgered him.

"Go away," Butch snapped over his shoulder.

"I will when you pay me," Tyson growled.

Butch let loose a string of expletives that made the bartender's eyes go round, and he looked as if he was trying to decide whether he needed to call someone for backup or not.

"What did you say to me?" Tyson asked. He leaned over the other man as if he was just spoiling for a fight.

217

Mel had a feeling that things were about to get ugly. Tyson was stroking his mustache as if he really wished he could wrap his fingers around Butch's throat instead. In fact, she got the feeling that he just might do it anyway.

"Hey!" she cried, looking wide-eyed at Butch. It was not entirely an act. "Didn't I see you on television last night?"

Butch turned toward her. There was a nervousness in his gaze that Mel knew meant he wasn't totally unaware that Tyson Ballinger was looking to do him some harm.

"I'm sorry, what?" Butch asked.

"You were on the news," she said. "Oh my goodness, the story was about your son, wasn't it?"

Butch nodded. "Yeah, he was murdered."

Mel looked at Tyson. "I don't know what it is you want from him but, clearly, he is struggling with grief right now. I suggest you save your discussion for another day."

Now Tyson looked like he wanted to have her neck under his fingers. Mick must have gotten the same vibe because he stood up behind Mel, looking like one big badass avenging angel.

Tyson looked Mel over. His lip curled with scorn. "You should be careful about ordering people about. Some might not like it."

The menace in his voice dripped over her like hot wax. Mel felt a shiver wiggle at the base of her spine, but then she remembered Mick had her back and she straightened up and stared Tyson down.

"The man lost his son," she said. She looked at the bartender to see if he was planning on doing anything. He nodded at her and showed her that he had his phone in hand, ready to call the police should the situation escalate. "Surely whatever problem you have with him can wait."

"For now," Tyson said. The look he sent Butch made Mel's heart turn cold. Then he strode out of the saloon, casting Mick a doubtful look as he went. He moved like a man who had all the time in the world.

"Oh, wow," Mel said. She sank back onto her stool.

"Two shots of Jack," Mick ordered, and the bartender nodded, poured three, and then downed one himself.

Mel took a sip of hers but then pushed it away. Mick downed his and she realized he really hadn't been kidding. He was a pacifist and this scene with Tyson had shaken him badly. She squeezed his forearm and then turned to Butch.

"What, no shot for me?" Butch asked. Mel pushed her half-full glass at him and he threw it back like it was a miracle cure for whatever ailed him.

"What was that all about?" Mel asked.

"No idea," Butch lied. "Obviously, the guy is crazy, coming in here and hassling me when I'm grieving for my son."

"Cut the crap, Bordow," Mick interrupted, the clenching of his jaw signaling that he was out of patience. "Tyson Ballinger eats guys like you for snack, so what are you into him for?"

Butch ran a hand over his eyes. He looked broken and Mel felt sorry for him. His son was dead, Tyson was after him, he clearly had a drinking problem — yeah, on the scale of bad days, his was off the chart.

Sympathy aside, however, Tyson struck Mel as a ruthless sort and it occurred to her that he might have gone to Mike Bordow about money owed to him by Mike's father, Butch. If Mike refused to pay, would Tyson have put a hurt on him or have hired thugs to do so? Could it have gone wrong and ended in Mike's death? It could be the first real lead in who might have killed Mike Bordow aside from his bitter fiancée.

"Everything," Butch muttered. "I'm into him for everything, which is why . . ." He began to sob. "He k— kill — killed my son."

EIGHTEEN

"Did he say that?" Mel asked. "Do you have proof? Have you told the police?"

"Pah, the police!" Butch picked up his beer and chugged it down in one long guzzle. If Mel had done that, she'd be sitting on the floor. "The police are useless. My daughter told me they had a suspect in custody right after his body was found and they just let her go, just like that. She was related to one of the detectives so they looked the other way."

Mel could feel Mick's eyes boring a hole in the side of her head, but she refused to look at him and risk giving anything away.

"I'm sure if the police had a person in custody, they wouldn't just let them go," she said. "Didn't I hear on the news that they were looking at your son's fiancée? What did you think of her?"

"She's evil, Satan in a dress, a total she-devil," he said. "I told Mike she wasn't good

221

enough for him, but would he listen to me? No. She probably hired the person the police had in custody."

Mick and Mel exchanged a look.

"I thought you said Tyson Ballinger killed your son because of the debt you owed him," Mick said.

"He did!" Butch bellowed.

Mel and Mick exchanged another look. It was clear that whatever brain cells Butch Bordow had were so pickled that they would never get a straight answer out of him. Still, Mel had to try.

"So who is it? Who killed your son, Tyson or Diane?" Mel knew she was pressing. She knew it was uncool but she couldn't seem to help it. She wanted someone other than herself to confirm her belief that Diane didn't kill Mike Bordow.

Butch wobbled on his stool. He leaned toward Mel, almost as if he was about to fall on her, and then he reared back as if yanked by an invisible string.

"How'd you know her name was Diane?" he asked. "I never said her name."

Okay, so not all of his brain cells were sotted. Mel felt herself start to sweat. What if he figured out she was the woman the police had found at the scene yesterday? She felt her heart pound hard in her chest as he regarded her with a suspicious look on his face.

"Yes, you did," she lied. She had no idea where it came from but it was out her mouth before she had the wherewithal to stop it. She slapped her hand down on the bar with more bravado than she felt, and said, "Duh, how could I know her name unless you said it?"

Butch looked from her to her hand on the bar and back to her. Mel held her breath.

"Good point," he said. "Well, one of them killed him."

He sagged against the bar, as if he needed it to hold him up, then a sob ripped out of him as if it had had to fight its way out of him. Behind the sob came a flurry of more sobs, a hiccup, a wail, and then the tears. They ran unchecked down his face as he blubbered.

Mel felt ill that she had caused the man to crack wide open but, truly, booze can only anesthetize a person for so long. Better Butch lose it here than out there alone in the world with no one to make sure he got home okay.

"Hey, man, is there someone I can call for you?" the bartender asked.

"He was my best friend," Butch cried and buried his face in his hands. "We did everything together. What am I going to do without him? Oh, god, and Suzanne. She'll never forgive me if I caused this to happen. She loved her brother. She'll hate me. She can never know." He looked desperately at all of them. "She can never find out that it might be my fault. She's all I have left."

Mel and Mick exchanged a look. Mick looked like he might cry with sympathy and Mel squeezed his tattooed forearm to steady him. She put an arm around Butch and gave his shoulders a gentle squeeze. It was a comforting gesture, sure, but it also gave her access to his shirt pocket, where she could see his cell phone.

As Butch dropped his head onto his forearms on the bar, Mel slipped his phone out of his pocket and checked to see if she could get in. It had no blocks on it. She could. She scrolled through his contacts until she saw the name *Suzanne Bordow.*

"His daughter," she said to the bartender as she handed him the phone. Then she fished her money out of her purse and paid for their drinks and for one more beer for Butch. It would keep him busy until his daughter got here and, maybe, help ease his pain if only for a little while.

She stepped back from the bar, looked at Mick, and said, "Let's go."

"Now?" he asked. His voice sounded tight, as if he was talking around a lump in his throat. "Are you sure there aren't some puppies you want to kick or butterflies whose wings you want to pull off?"

Mel frowned and pushed past him toward the swinging half doors. Once they were outside she stomped to the corner before stopping. She crossed her arms over her chest and frowned at him.

"Was that nice?" she asked.

Mick mimicked her stance. "I don't know, you tell me."

"Oh, come on," she protested. "Don't put this on me. He is a horrible father, just look at him. He's in there getting wasted when his son was just murdered."

"Maybe that's why he's in there getting smashed," Mick said.

"No, he's a regular barfly," Mel said. "And what about that situation with Tyson Ballinger? He even said he thought Tyson might have killed his son because of his gambling debts."

"All right." Mick uncrossed his arms and matched his stride to Mel's as she continued back to their part of Old Town. "He does seem to be a lousy father but you have to feel sorry for him."

"Do I?"

Mick looked at her as if he didn't recognize her. "Melanie Cooper, I had no idea you could be so cold."

"Yeah, well, when it comes to keeping my friend from being accused of a crime she didn't commit, I'm solid ice, baby."

Mick shivered as they hurried on their way. Mel left Mick at his shop with a promise to deliver his cupcakes later. He told her she didn't have to, but Mel insisted. A deal was a deal and she didn't want to be a swindler. She paid her debts fair and square. Besides, she never knew when she might need him again.

"I'm in hell, aren't I?" Mel asked Marty an hour later as they sat beside each other in the Fairy Tale Cupcakes booth at the bridal expo.

"Only if hell is full of crazed brides and their mothers and is swathed in organza and taffeta and reeks of cheap perfume and dead flowers," he said.

Mel glanced at the florist booth beside theirs. She wondered if they heard Marty's commentary on their flowers. Then again, their booth did smell of rotting blossoms, so he wasn't wrong.

As for their setup, they had opted to keep it simple, mostly because the Phoenix Bridal

Expo had been a complete surprise to everyone except Angie, who had booked it without telling anyone. Apparently Angie wanted to wallow in her bridal-ness at the expo and had figured that if she was a vendor, she might rate some special deal from the other vendors. She was off working the room, which Mel hoped did not undo her pep talk of the evening before. If Angie changed one more thing on her wedding, Mel was pretty sure she was going to have an aneurysm.

Mercifully, it was only a one-day event and they spent it handing out brochures and coupons for free cupcakes to any brides who wanted to stop by the shop and try out some samples.

"Can I offer you a coupon for a free cupcake?" Mel called out to a group of women all surrounding one cute young thing who was clearly the bride since she had a veil on her head and was working the I'm-getting-married strut.

"Puleeze," the bride scoffed. "Cupcakes are so over. No, I'd rather have an ombré cake, you know, something really on trend."

Marty looked like he was about to launch one of their cupcake samples at the unsuspecting diva. Mel grabbed his arm just in time. They'd been in food fights before and it never ended well for them.

"Where's your main squeeze?" Mel asked him. She didn't really care where Marty's girlfriend, Olivia, was but she'd use anything to distract him from glaring at possible customers.

"She's not speaking to me at the moment," he said.

"Oh, why not?"

"Because someone is a complete and utter slob," a voice answered from behind them.

Mel spun around to see Olivia there. She was glaring at Marty, and Mel wondered if they were going to start arguing, which would not be great for business at a bridal expo.

"I am not," Marty protested. "If you weren't such a neat freak —"

"I am not," Olivia protested. "I just believe there is a place for everything and everything should go in its place, you know, as opposed to being left on the counter or dropped on the floor."

"See?" Marty raised his hands in the air. "She is completely unreasonable."

"I'm unreasonable?" Olivia gaped at him. "You, who can't be in the house for three seconds without switching on the TV? That

228

thing is on twenty-four-seven. It's maddening!"

"It's company!"

"I'm supposed to be your company!"

Mel frowned at Marty. She'd known him
for well over a year now and she knew for a
fact that he wasn't a slob nor was he the
sort who kept the television on all the time.
So why was he doing these things now that
he lived with Olivia?

"That doesn't sound like —" she began,
but Marty interrupted.

"Listen, Queen of Clean," he said. "You're
the one who wanted to move in together."

"Yes, when I thought you had at least a
tentative relationship with a hamper," Olivia
snapped.

Mel glanced at Marty for his rebuttal
when a movement behind him from several
booths away caught her attention. It was
Suzanne Bordow, looking like she was trying to hand out brochures for the business.
Judging by how wide a berth most of the
prospective brides gave her, the news was
out about her brother's death and people
were responding as they generally do when
something is uncomfortable: They avoid it
and ignore it almost as if they thought to
acknowledge it made it contagious.

"Excuse me," Mel said to Marty and

Olivia. She was several feet away when it occurred to her that leaving them alone was a bad idea. Still, she needed to speak with Suzanne. She turned around and added, "I'll be right over there. Behave yourselves."

"What's that supposed to mean?" Marty snapped. "What did you think we were going to do here?"

"Brawl," Mel said.

Marty looked horrified while Olivia was intrigued and said, "That could be fun."

"On that note," Mel said. "I have an errand to run."

She felt bad about lying to them. Well, not super bad. Not enough to tell them the truth and technically, it was an errand, sort of, in a totally sticking-her-nose-where-it-didn't-belong kind of way.

Suzanne looked tired. Her face was pale, making her makeup stand out a bit too boldly. Her long brown curly hair was arranged in a pile of messy curls on her head and she was dressed in casual professional, meaning nice jeans with a tank top and blazer.

Mel approached her, not really knowing what she was going to say. The last time she had seen Suzanne, the woman had been a potent cocktail of shock and grief with a splash of anger, all of which had been directed at Mel.

"Hi, Party On! party rental supplies for all of your party needs," Suzanne chirped at Mel as she shoved a brochure at her.

Mel took the brochure. Obviously, Suzanne didn't recognize her out of the context of a murder scene. Weird. She wondered if she should introduce herself or play like they'd never met. Probably, Suzanne would recognize her eventually, so it was best to —

"You!" Suzanne snapped and snatched the brochure out of Mel's hands. "What are you doing here? What do you want from me?"

"Nothing!" Mel raised her hands in the air in a show of innocence. "I just saw you from my booth and I wanted to come over and, I don't know, see how you're doing."

Suzanne gave Mel a suspicious glance as if trying to determine her trustworthiness.

"Listen, I was just hired to bake and deliver cupcakes. I had nothing to do with what happened to your brother," Mel said. "Believe me, no one was more horrified than me to find him like that."

Suzanne stared at her for another few seconds and Mel could see the resemblance between Suzanne and her father, despite his drunkenness, in the shape and color of their eyes as well as the stubborn tip to their jaw.

Suzanne finally glanced away. She looked

231

around the packed convention center and her shoulders drooped. They were surrounded by hundreds of brides and not one of them was going near her booth.

"I'm sorry," Suzanne said. "I can't imagine what that must have been like. Well, I can, but I'm sure it doesn't compare to the reality of being alone with the dead body of a stranger."

"Yeah." Mel let out a shaky breath. Good. Suzanne was talking to her. This was very good.

"I'm sorry I thought you killed my brother," Suzanne said. "I was out of my head, and you were there with bloody hands . . ."

Mel swallowed hard. That was not one of her favorite memories.

"I was just making a delivery for a customer," Mel said. She did not feel the need to add that Diane was her former college roommate. She knew it would only make Suzanne suspicious of her again. "Talk about your right place, wrong time."

"So, you bake cupcakes?" Suzanne asked.

"I co-own Fairy Tale Cupcakes with some friends," Mel said.

She gestured to the booth where Marty and Olivia seemed to have forged a truce judging by the passionate clinch they were now engaged in. Ew!

"And you? You run Party On! I've seen your stuff at some of the venues I've worked," Mel said.

"Yes," Suzanne said. "We are . . . were . . . the go-to place for all your party needs. Oh, man, what am I going to do without Mike? This was his sort of thing, meeting and greeting potential customers, working his shmoozy magic on them. I can't do this. I suck at this. And Troy, who usually works these events with my brother, well, he's apparently got a concussion from his fall."

She looked depressed and on the verge of tears. Mel wondered what the heck she was doing here when she was obviously grieving. Her thoughts must have been apparent because Suzanne shrugged.

"I don't know what to do. I don't know where to put everything that I'm feeling. It's like I'm drowning in pain and I can't breathe."

Mel looked at her grief-ravaged face. She knew exactly how Suzanne felt. When her father had died, it was Mel's first brush with true loss. She had frequently thought the pain would consume her. Before she thought it through, she opened her arms and hugged Suzanne.

She said the words she had heard a million times, words that didn't hurt and didn't help, either, but were simply true.

"I am so sorry for your loss," she said.

To her surprise, Suzanne hugged her back. The woman had not really struck Mel as a hugger, so she had to assume the pain she was feeling was significant.

When Suzanne released her and stepped back, surreptitiously wiping tears from her face, Mel looked at her and gestured to the crush of bodies around them.

"Maybe this is too much," Mel said.

"I don't know what else to do, and I'm terrified that if I don't do something, I'm going to lose the business," she said. "We booked this event months ago. It's always been great for boosting our presence in the marketplace, but now I'm a pariah. No one will come near me. I can't even get them to take my brochure."

"Do you have any swag to give out?" Mel asked.

"I'm sorry?"

"Swag? Free stuff?" Mel asked. "We're giving out bite-sized samples of our cupcakes at our booth. Did your brother ever give out pens, pencils, stress balls, anything, when he did these events?"

Suzanne shrugged and then went back to her booth. Under a table were several gray packing bins. She popped open the lid and Mel saw a ton of bright colorful notepads, key chains, water bottles, and markers, all emblazoned with the Party On! floating balloon logo on them.

"Come on," Mel said. She hefted one side of the bin and Suzanne scrambled to lift the other. Together they dumped the contents out on her table. Mel didn't even bother with careful arrangement. She simply spread the stuff out with her hands in a happy scatter of swag.

Like locusts, people abruptly veered toward the table. Mel pushed Suzanne into place behind it and helped her hand out the brochures while she chatted up the business. After a few minutes it was clear that Suzanne was going to be okay and whatever taint the crowd had felt toward her was overcome by the lure of free stuff.

When there was a lull, Suzanne turned to Mel and said, "Thanks, and I'm sorry about, well, you know. I was wrong about you."

"It's cool," Mel said. "Listen, I know it's none of my business but I did find your brother, so I'm just wondering, do you have any idea who would have done this to him?"

"Oh, yeah, I know who did it," Suzanne said. Her eyes turned hard and brittle. "His fiancée, Diane Earnest, did it. She found out he was two-timing her. Hello, he two-timed everyone — did she really think she was going to be different? She killed him. I'm sure of it, and I am going to make very sure she pays for it."

Oh, boy.

On that happy note, Mel said she'd better get back to her own booth. She waved at Suzanne as she left, hoping with all that she had that Suzanne was wrong. She didn't want to believe that her friend could be responsible for a man's death, and she couldn't believe that she would be so selfish as to put Mel right in the middle of it.

Mel got back to her booth to find Marty and Olivia making goo-goo eyes at each other. Gag! She sent them away to go look at competing bakeries, one of which was Olivia's, and sat down to ponder all of the information she'd gathered.

There was no denying that the most likely suspect was Diane. The police thought so, Suzanne thought so, even Butch had a lucid moment where he believed it was her. Mel knew her friend was ruthless, but as far as she was concerned the fact that Butch was in debt to Tyson meant someone else had a motive.

Butch had said Mike was his best friend.

Maybe he told Mike what sort of trouble he was in with his debt to Tyson, and Mike had confronted Tyson. Tyson could have had him killed to remove him as a problem. Mel thought back to Tyson's slick suit and pushy manner. He was a man who was used to getting his way. No doubt about it.

If that was the case then Mel knew exactly where she needed to look next. She glanced up when she caught a glimpse of someone walking into her booth. Thinking it was a prospective client, Mel put her please-the-customer smile on. When recognition finally hit, the smile relaxed and then turned into a look of incredulity. Whoa!

Angie stood before her with her long, dark brown hair shellacked into an enormous bow, made out of her own hair, on the top of her head.

"Spectacular, right?" Angie asked. She spread her arms wide to encompass the ginormous hair bow.

"That's one word," Mel agreed.

"I'm thinking I could attach my veil to the base of the bow, back here." Angie pointed to the back of her head and Mel tried not to visibly flinch.

Anything that was happening with Diane was now going to have to be shelved, as Angie, aka bridezilla, was back!

NINETEEN

The bridal show ended at five and it took almost no time for Mel and the crew to pack up what little was left from their display. Oz arrived to pick them up in their cupcake van and Angie hustled them all out the door. She couldn't wait to show Tate her new hairdo.

To Oz's credit, when Marty had opened his mouth to yelp at the sight of Angie, Oz had caught him with an arm around his neck and a knuckle noogie to his bald head, which sufficiently diverted Marty's attention from Angie's outrageous hair to the knot on top of his noggin.

Mel split off from the group, as she was being picked up by Joe. They had a date to celebrate their decision to move in together and she was looking forward to being away from all of the drama that seemed to be swirling around her. For one evening she didn't want to think about Diane and her situation or Angie and her wedding. Freedom beckoned.

She stood outside the Phoenix Civic Center, looking at her phone to see exactly how hot it was at six o'clock on a June evening in Phoenix. One hundred and seven degrees Fahrenheit. Lovely. Just as she began to feel the sweat gather in her boobage, Joe's car zipped up to her side. He reached across the front seat and popped her door open. Mel scurried in before the car behind him started honking and gesturing as only Phoenix drivers can do.

Joe flashed her a grin and squeezed her hand in his before he pulled away. As always, just the sight of him made Mel's heart lift in her chest and suddenly the troubles that had been nipping her heels all day were left behind on the curb.

"Hungry?" Joe asked. He loosened his tie as he drove.

"Always," Mel said.

"Great. I was thinking we could have a picnic," Joe said.

"In Phoenix in June?" Mel was incredulous.

"No, I thought we could drive north, get out of town a ways," he said. "It's a little over an hour to Prescott."

"Can we stop for pie at Rock Springs?"

she asked.

"Is that a real question?"

Mel laughed and leaned across the console to kiss his cheek. It felt as if she and Joe had been working their way back to each other for so long. Even though their wedding had been a bust, they were going to move in together, and Mel felt that if they survived Angie's wedding then their own happy ever after might be just around the corner.

Joe asked her about her day and she told him about Angie's hair. He laughed and asked if she'd managed to get a picture of it. She gave him a dark look and he feigned innocence, as if he really wasn't mocking the bridezilla his sister had become.

She asked Joe about his latest case and he gave her an overview of how it was going. He never gave her specifics, just a general idea of what the prosecutor's office had on deck. Mel, per usual, was impressed with his quest for justice in a world where it frequently felt lacking. She wondered if that was a part of their connection, this longing to see justice served.

"It seems like you and I are both committed to seeing innocence win out," she said.

"Speaking of which, how goes the situation with Diane?" he asked.

Mel shrugged. "Hard to say. It seems everyone I meet thinks Diane did it, but I just can't believe it. Diane is a lot of things, but I don't think killer is one of them."

"A lot of people aren't what they seem," he said.

"I know."

"Mel, tell me why you're helping Diane," he said. "I know you think you owe her a debt, but you've been very vague about it."

"I know. I'm not trying to shut you out on purpose."

"Then tell me what it is," he said. "Help me to understand why you are so sure she's innocent when both Stan and Tara think otherwise."

"Been in touch with them, have you?"

"It's my job," he said. "When I called Stan's desk, Tara answered."

"Uh-huh," Mel said. "How convenient."

"She is his partner," he said. "Are you telling me when you called him when Manny was his partner, Manny never picked up?"

Mel glanced out the window. She refused to answer the prosecutor on the grounds that she'd lose the argument.

"I just know Diane is innocent," she said.

It sounded lame even to her, but what else could she say? Yes, Diane came across as abrasive and pushy and frequently with no

241

filter but she really was a good, decent woman because she saved Mel's bacon before. But if she said that, then he'd want to know how. Should she tell him? Would he understand then that Diane was more than she seemed to be, or at least she had been when Mel had known her?

She glanced at Joe. She was going to move in with him. Did she want to start that chapter of their life together with secrets? No.

"Back when Diane and I were room-mates," Mel began but then paused. She wanted to tell this story in just the right tone so that Joe didn't freak out.

"Yes?" he encouraged her.

"Diane saved my butt," she said.

"You've mentioned that, repeatedly," he said. "I take it it was a pretty big save."

"Huge," Mel said. "Because when I say she saved my butt, I'm speaking literally."

Joe turned to look at her. He had that expression he wore when she was about to tell him something he didn't want to hear but knew that he had to listen anyway. She thought of it as his pained but stoic expression.

"All right, hit me," he said.

"We were at a college party," Mel said.

"Frat party?" he asked.

"No, nerd party," she said.

"Really? Nerds have parties? Did you have to dress as Princess Leia?"

"No, that would have been cool," Mel said. "Anyway, there was this guy —"

"Stop right there," Joe said.

"What? Why?" Mel asked.

"Because as far as I'm concerned, you never dated anyone before you dated me," he said.

Mel looked at him. He was not joking.

"Is that a guy thing?" she asked.

"It's a me-not-wanting-to-picture-you-naked-with-anyone-else-ever thing," he said. When Mel was quiet, he added, "Yeah, probably a guy thing."

"Good to know," she said. "But you don't have to worry. Things didn't go that far."

"Oh," Joe said. He looked relieved. "Continue then."

"So, college party, my social anxiety spiked, I used very poor judgment and accepted a beverage from a guy I didn't know," Mel said.

Joe was staring at the road ahead. He looked perfectly calm except Mel could see the muscle in his jaw clench and unclench and his knuckles were white where he gripped the steering wheel.

"You got roofied," he guessed.

"Yep," Mel said. "Being the niece of a police detective, you'd think I'd know better, but I was nervous. I didn't really do the party scene, even the nerd party scene, so I was in way over my head."

"Where were your friends?" he asked.

"Diane was the only person I knew at the party and she had gone to the bathroom," Mel said. "Looking back, I'm sure the guy waited until I was alone. I probably looked completely freaked out. I might as well have had a target painted on my back."

"What happened?" Joe asked. His voice was steady but Mel could tell he was agitated.

"The guy handed me a drink, challenged me to chug it, the next thing I knew I was in a bedroom with him and he was doing his best to make moves on me while I was fighting to stay conscious. Diane came busting through the door, knocked some expensive camera equipment to the floor, kicked the guy in the privates, and hauled me out of there."

The words came out in a rush, mostly because it was one of Mel's more painful personal memories, but also because she was dreading Joe's reaction. Not that he would get mad at her but that he might think as poorly of her young naïve self as she did.

"Huh," Joe said.

Mel waited but he said nothing more.

"Um, thoughts?" she asked.

"A few," he said.

"Care to share?"

"Sorry, I'm just taking it all in and prioritizing," he said. "Okay, first, did the son of a bitch touch you?"

"No," Mel said. She squeezed his arm, feeling the need to reassure him. "I was fully clothed when Diane got me out of there."

"Good, that's good," he said. "Otherwise I was going to need a name, and me and the brothers were going to go on a road trip to find the ass —"

"Breathe," Mel said.

Joe sucked in a huge gulp of air and held it. Then he let it out slowly and shook himself like a dog shaking water off his fur. "I'm good now, really. Unless of course you want to give me his name . . ."

"No, I don't think so," Mel said. "Last I heard he had given up big girl porn —"

"Stop," Joe said. "Let's be clear, what he was doing was a litany of multiple felonies. Drugging, kidnapping, oh man, I can't even finish this sentence or I *will* hunt him down and hurt him, slowly and painfully."

"Okay, keep breathing," she said. She was

aware that her inner girly girl was swooning at Joe's thirst for revenge on her behalf, but she squashed her flat, knowing that she needed to get a handle on this pronto. "I heard he became an IT guy and was living in Palo Alto, where all the rich nerds go to die, with his wife and two kids."

"I like the die part," Joe said.

"The point is that Diane pulled me out of there and kept me from being the unwilling star of a college nerd boy sex tape," Mel said. "For that, I will owe her for the rest of my life."

Joe was silent and Mel studied his profile for an inkling of what he was feeling. She didn't want to press him, but since she had never told anyone about this incident in her life, not even her closest friends Tate and Angie, she was concerned that he might think less of her for the whole sordid mess.

When she couldn't take it anymore, she asked, "You're starting to freak me out. What are you thinking?"

"I'm trying to make a decision," he said.

Mel felt her heart pound hard in her chest. Of course he was. He was in the public eye. He had to keep his life above reproach. Having a girlfriend who could get herself into a situation like that was probably making him rethink their whole relationship. He probably felt he had no choice but to dump her, or, at the very least, rescind his offer for her to move in with him.

Mel thought she might cry. She knew she should have kept her mouth shut, but what sort of relationship was that? If she couldn't tell him everything, even the bad stuff, what was the point of being together?

"Yeah, I can't decide," Joe said. "Maybe you can help."

"Okay," Mel said. Her voice was small but she didn't know how else to react to being asked to weigh in on the possible end of their relationship.

"So, I'm debating, do I send her a long-overdue cookie bouquet or regular flowers?" he asked.

"Who? What? Huh?"

"Diane," he said. "As a very belated thank-you for saving my girl, should I send her cookies or flowers?"

Mel thought the smile on her face might split her wide open. Joe glanced at her in surprise.

"What are you grinning at?"

"You," she said. "Always you."

Joe took his right hand off of the steering wheel and took her hand in his. He laced their fingers together and kissed the back of her hand.

"I'm so very grateful nothing worse happened to you that night," he said. His voice sounded a little shaky. "I promise that as long as I'm in your life nothing like that will ever happen to you again. Mostly because I'm never going to let you out of my sight."

"Promises, promises," Mel teased him, but her heart felt as if it were going to burst out of her chest, it was so full of love for Joe.

"And I understand completely why you feel you owe Diane your support, and I'll do everything I can to help you."

"Thanks," she said. "That means a lot to me."

She rested her head on his shoulder. She hadn't realized that keeping her story to herself had been such a weighty burden until now. Her spirits felt lighter than they had in weeks. She was glad she had told him. She didn't want any secrets between them as they started this new life of cohabiting.

They left the city behind and Mel sank into her seat. She didn't mean to nod off but the hum of the engine combined with the cool air blowing across her skin along with the fact that for the first time all day, she was not running around in circles, caused her to drop into a dreamless slumber.

When she woke up, the car was stopped and Joe was stretched out in the seat beside hers, fully reclined with his eyes shut. Not realizing that they had pulled over, she panicked.

"Joe!" she cried. She shook him awake. "Are you okay? Were we in an accident?"

"Huh . . . What?" Joe blinked and sat up quickly, grabbing her hand in his.

"Where are we?" she asked. "What happened? Did we run off the road?"

Joe smiled at her. "No, actually we arrived at our destination a while ago, but you were asleep and I didn't want to wake you so I decided to rest, too." He glanced at his watch. "A half-hour power nap. Not bad."

It was still light out as the sun was just beginning to sink toward the mountains to the west. They had driven far enough north that they were in the high country and the heat was nothing compared to what they'd left behind in the valley.

"Come on," Joe said. He opened his door and climbed out of the car. Mel followed, pausing to stretch her legs and back when she stood up.

Joe opened the back of his car and took out a blanket, a cooler, and a basket. Mel was impressed with the thought he'd put into their date night and was determined that when it was her turn to plan one, she'd make it just as special.

"Come on," Joe said. "Our spot is just up ahead."

Mel followed him. She glanced around the desert, admiring the vista. Red rocks, scrubby bushes, and cacti of varying types dotted the landscape. The desert certainly had its own stark sort of beauty. Having been born and raised in Arizona, she really couldn't imagine living anywhere else.

Joe spread the blanket and put the basket down in the center. He held up his hand to assist Mel when she sat beside him. Once she was settled, Mel looked at the landscape again. There was something familiar about it. She felt as if she'd been here before, but she couldn't place it.

She scanned the area, looking for familiar landmarks while Joe flipped the lid on the basket. Then it hit her. This was the spot, the exact spot, where Joe had proposed to her the year before. Did he know? Did he realize it?

When she turned back to him, all excited to share her discovery, it was to find him kneeling beside her, holding a small box with the lid popped up, where a sparkler of a ring was nestled inside, winking at her.

TWENTY

"Oh, Joe," she said. "Yes!"

A surprised laugh burst out of him and he said, "Well, that takes the pressure off."

Mel rolled to her knees and kissed him and hugged him hard. "Yes, yes, yes!"

Joe hugged her back, but Mel's momentum was a bit much for him and they went down in a heap, with Joe on the bottom and Mel sprawled across him. He leaned up and returned her kiss, and then he lay back down so he could look her in the eyes.

"I had a whole speech prepared," he said. "I worked really hard on it, too, even more than one of my closing arguments in front of a jury."

"So, you thought I needed convincing?"

"Maybe," he said. "We haven't had the most conventional relationship. I mean, you're my little sister's best friend. For years, I thought of you as another little sister."

251

"Hmm, and then you didn't," she said.

"Yeah, once I noticed you *that* way there was no putting the genie back in the bottle," he said.

"All right, well, I think I've earned a pretty speech. Lay it on me," she said. She pillowed her arms on his chest and propped her chin on them like a kid watching her favorite TV show.

Joe trailed one finger down her cheek, pausing when he reached her chin. His gaze moved up to meet hers and a small, shy smile tipped the corner of his mouth.

"Do you know what you remind me of?" he asked.

Mel shook her head. She was afraid to speak, as she didn't want to break the spell he was weaving around them with his low voice and his sweet words.

"A shooting star," he said. "There's something purely magical about you, and whenever I catch sight of you, dashing through my orbit in a trail of sparkling light, I catch my breath because I feel so lucky to bear witness to the wonder that is you, Melanie Cooper."

Her throat closed up. Mel couldn't speak if she tried. Tears leaked out of the corners of her eyes and she swallowed. It went down hard.

"I have never met anyone who gives so freely of herself, who loves her people so fiercely, or who always does what's right even when it's the hardest thing to do. You are the best person I know, and I would be deeply honored and humbled to call you my wife."

A sob bubbled up but Mel didn't want to cry, so she tried to stop it and it came out as a hiccup instead. Joe smiled and then he scooted out from under her and moved so that he was kneeling in front of her.

"Melanie Cooper, we have tried this a couple of times now, but this time I am doing everything by the book. We are on a romantic picnic in the same spot I proposed to you before. I even have a ring this time, although it doesn't shine quite as brightly as you."

Mel glanced at the ring in the box. A square diamond surrounded by smaller ones — it was dazzling.

"But I don't really think anything ever could," Joe said. He took her hand in his. He looked at her from under his ridiculously long eyelashes — such a waste on a guy — as if he was nervous. "Cupcake, when I am with you, I am the best version of me, and I want to be that guy married to you for the rest of our days. Will you marry me?"

Mel moved so that she was kneeling in front of him. She cupped his face in her hands and then she said, "Joe DeLaura, I have been in love with you from the first moment you smiled at me when I was in seventh grade and you came by my home-room class, looking for your little sister. Everything in my world changed that day, and I knew nothing would be right until you were mine. I have been waiting a very long time to call you mine. Yes, I'll marry you and make it official once and for all."

"Now and forever," he said. He kissed her, got distracted, and kissed her some more, then he let her go so he could slide the ring onto her finger.

Mel loved that his hands were as shaky as hers.

"Mrs. Joseph DeLaura," he said. "I like it. It suits you."

"I think so, too," Mel said as she admired her ring in the light of the setting sun. "There is only one person who will be even happier about this announcement than the two of us."

"Your mom?" he asked.

"You are her 'dear Joe,' " she said.

"I am, especially after I called her this morning and asked her permission to pro-pose to you," he said.

"You didn't."

"I did. And Uncle Stan, too."

Mel looked at him in wonder. "What did he say?"

"No," Joe said. He laughed and added, "An emphatic no, in fact."

"He was kidding," she said.

Joe shook his head. "No, I don't think he was. I told him I was going to marry you anyway, and he said that was pretty much what he figured."

They looked at each other and laughed.

"I love you," she said.

"I love you, too."

It was a long time before the picnic was finished and they headed home to share the good news with Captain Jack. Mel spent the ride admiring her ring. The unfamiliar weight felt reassuring on her left hand. She found herself studying Joe's profile in the light of the dashboard and feeling over-whelmed that this man was going to be her husband.

She couldn't help but wonder if Diane had ever felt this way about Mike. If she had, his cheating would have been devastating. Once again, Mel was swamped with doubt about her friend. She shook her head. She wasn't going to think about it. Not now. Not when everything in her life was perfect.

Instead, she rested her head on Joe's shoulder and enjoyed the happy feeling of looking forward to their future together. When they were a half hour away from home, Joe took his phone out of his pocket and placed a call.

Mel could hear the voice on the other end. It sounded like her favorite cranky octogenarian.

"Well?"

"She said yes," Joe said.

"She said yes," the voice repeated, and a riot of cheers sounded in the background. "See you in a few."

Joe put his phone away and grinned at her.

"Who was that?" Mel asked.

"Marty," Joe confirmed. "Come on, they're waiting for us."

When they arrived at the bakery, it was to find the entire place decked out for a party. Balloons, streamers, a huge glittery banner that read Congratulations!

Mel's mother was there, crying happy tears; Uncle Stan was there, looking disapproving but resigned; Mel's brother, Charlie, and his wife and kids had driven down from Flagstaff; all of the DeLaura brothers were in attendance with their families or significant others; and Joe's parents were there, too.

When Mel walked through the door, both Tate and Angie were there to greet Mel and Joe with hugs and high fives. Marty and Oz were next in line. With the way the menfolk shook Joe's hand and slapped him on the back, Mel got the feeling they'd all been in on it.

"Who knew that you were going to propose tonight?" Mel asked.

"Everyone but you," he said. "And Angie."

"You left her out?" Mel asked.

"I thought it was for the best given that she's somewhat unstable right now."

Mel couldn't argue with that. She just hoped Angie never found out or she might never forgive Joe.

"Dear Joe," Joyce said as she wrapped him in another hug. "Welcome to the family."

"Thanks, Joyce, er, Mom. Can I call you Mom?" he asked. In that very moment Mel thought her heart would melt. Two of the people she loved most in the world were becoming family.

Joyce watered up and waved her tissue at him. "Of course you can." Then she started to cry for real. Uncle Stan came to collect her and he gave Joe a dirty look.

"You may not call me Uncle," he said.

"Whatever you say, Uncle Stan," Joe said

with a grin.

"Really?" Stan looked at Mel with his eyebrows knitting into each other in the middle of his forehead. "All the guys in the world and you picked him?"

"Sorry." She shrugged. "He's the one I love."

Uncle Stan let out a beleaguered sigh and slapped Joe on the back, a bit harder than necessary, before he ushered Joyce over to a table where she could compose herself.

Joe slipped his arm around Mel and pulled her close to his side as they greeted the rest of the crowd. Mel leaned into him, memorizing the feel of his body beside hers. She wanted to remember this perfect moment for the rest of her life.

The problem with having a party in her place of work was that the party barely ended when Mel was back at work the next morning, baking up a storm to replace all that was eaten by the party guests last night. The younger DeLaura brothers, Tony and Al, in particular managed to decimate all of the Death by Chocolate Cupcakes. Mel wondered if they were suffering from cupcake hangovers this morning. She knew from experience that overindulging on cupcakes was a lot like a booze hangover in that it came with the same nausea and self-loathing, but not the bad headache.

She dipped the chocolate cupcakes into the ganache icing and with a swift turn of her wrist created a perfect swoosh of icing on top. She glanced again at her ring. It sparkled at her and she found herself grinning like an idiot. She and Joe were getting married; they were cohabiting; they were starting a life together. It was everything Mel had ever hoped for and she found herself tempted to pinch herself repeatedly to make sure she wasn't hallucinating the whole thing.

The first person to appear in the bakery that morning was Tate. Usually he and Angie came in together as he had unofficially moved into her house. Truly, there was nothing unofficial about it except that they hadn't told any of the brothers with the exception of Joe, since the brothers had made it pretty clear that Tate was to stay at arm's length until the vows were said.

Mel thought it was sweetly protective of them, but it drove Angie batty and Mel knew if she were in Angie's position, she'd feel the same.

"Well, well, well, another bride-to-be," Tate said as he slipped through the back door into the kitchen. He stopped by the coffeepot that Mel had already started and poured himself a mug. He lifted it toward her and said, " 'A toast before we go into battle. True love. In whatever shape or form it may come. May we all in our dotage be proud to say, 'I was adored once, too.' "

"Four Weddings and a Funeral," Mel said with a sigh. "I've always loved that movie."

"Seemed appropriate," Tate said. "You know, I was beginning to think you and Joe were going to go the way of the two leads in that film and *not* get married."

"I know." Mel glanced down at her ring. "I was beginning to feel as if we were doomed, but maybe it just had to be the right time."

Tate moved to stand beside her. He admired her ring and then kissed her cheek. "If anyone deserves a happy ever after, it's you."

"Thanks," she said. She glanced at him with suspicion. "Speaking of happy ever after, are you early in an attempt to hide from your future spouse?"

"I'm hurt, Mel, truly, that you could think such a thing of me." Tate gave her a shocked look but Mel knew him too well.

"What was on her agenda for today?"

"Music," he said. "Her brother Sal has a DJ guy he wanted her to talk to. Have I

260

mentioned how much I hate DJs?"

"Lately or within the history of our friendship?"

"Lately will work," he said.

"Pretty much every time we go out and there is a DJ instead of live music," Mel said. "So, why are you letting Angie do this on her own? If you don't say something, you're going to end up with a DJ."

Tate looked pained. "I'll die."

"No, you won't. What you will do, however, is get involved in the planning of your own wedding," Mel said. "Look, I've talked her down, her cousin Judi has taken on as much as she can. It's time to man up."

"But I'm scared of her like this," he said. "I'm starting to have nightmares where she's this Frankenstein-looking monster under a veil, yelling at me about roses versus daisies. Frankly, it's terrifying."

Mel puffed out her lower lip, blowing out a breath that made her bangs stir across her forehead. She put down the newly dipped cupcake she was holding and turned to face her friend. She had promised Angie she wouldn't tell Tate about how insecure she was feeling, but that didn't mean she couldn't guide him at least a little bit.

"Tate, I didn't want to say anything because this is between the two of you, but

261

I have to tell you that as a woman, a wedding can be a hugely stressful thing, especially if you approach it like Angie is and try to live up to some impossible ideal," Mel said. "You know, it's like she's trying to prove she's worthy of it."

"What?" Tate cried. He looked at her as if she'd just spoken in Klingon. "That's crazy. Angie's the greatest thing to ever happen to me. She's worth all of it."

"Uh-huh," Mel agreed. "We all know you're the one who traded up in this relationship, but Angie is superstitious and I think she believes that if she doesn't nail this wedding, your marriage is doomed."

"That's . . . I . . . Of all the . . . I have to go," he said. "I need to go fire a DJ and find a band."

"Yes, you do," Mel said.

Tate downed the hot coffee while Mel picked up the next cupcake. He turned and strode toward the door, looking more determined than Mel had seen him since they opened their first franchise in Vegas.

"Oh, hey." Tate paused by the back door. "I forgot to tell you, I did some digging and discovered that I have a friend who works at the accounting firm that does Party On!'s books. We had an interesting conversation as he said that everything Diane told you

262

was true — the company's tax returns do look pretty bad — but that it's not necessarily an accurate picture of the situation."

"I don't understand," she said.

"Party On! maintains the business practice of keeping two sets of books," he said.

"I thought that was Al Capone–type stuff," Mel said.

"Not really. There's the tax return set of books where businesses are really trying to minimize the net income so they can pay less taxes — you know, make it look like you're a loser," Tate said.

"And the second set of books is for what then?"

"That's what's known as the GAAP, generally accepted accounting principle, statements that are really more focused on the gains a company is making, for example, the business's net income, profit, equity, collateral. The stuff investors and bankers use to judge the business. Your eyes are glazing over."

"Sorry," Mel said. "You lost me at accounting principle."

"Okay, I'll keep it simple," Tate said. "The books Diane was judging the company by are the loss statements. I know Diane said that Mike was marrying her for her money, which would seem likely by the tax returns,

263

but it's not true. According to the GAAP, the company is solid, more than solid. If they pull off the maneuver the business community is talking about, to expand nationally, it looks like they'll make bazillions."

Mel blinked. That did not at all jibe with what Diane had told her. "Are you sure?"

"Positive," he said. "I sort of pretended that I was getting back into the investment game and my friend shared Party On!'s financials with me. Since Party On! looks to have other players in the game — a few small private companies own portions of the business, RR Ty, Hannity Investments, and Plus One — my friend figured it was okay to give me a look-see as a potential investor. We have to keep this on the down low, but it's all in a file on my hard drive in the office. Take a look."

"I will," Mel said. She waved as he disappeared through the door and then hurriedly finished up the cupcakes and stored them in the walk-in cooler in the kitchen.

As soon as she washed up and poured herself a third cup of coffee, Mel sat down with Tate's computer. He had named the file *Party On!,* so it was easy to spot. He'd also highlighted the parts that he thought were of interest. Even to a non-number-cruncher like Mel, it was easy to see from the GAAP statements that the business was successful — more than successful. They were looking to turn a substantial profit from expanding their business, so why did Diane think that Mike was just marrying her for her money?

This belied everything Diane had told her about breaking up with Mike. Mel had tried so hard to believe in her friend. Diane had saved her from public humiliation on a scale that Mel still couldn't quite wrap her head around. She owed her friend the same sort of loyalty Diane had shown her, but this, this made it look as if the reason Diane had given her for breaking up with her fiancé was bogus, meaning that Diane might have been dumping him for his philandering, which was understandable except for that little bit about him being dead instead of just dumped.

Mel went back out into the kitchen to finish up two other flavors of cupcakes, the first being Bananas Foster, a banana rum cake with banana frosting and a rum caramel drizzle on top, and the second one a Mandarin Orange Cupcake, an orange zest angel food cake with mandarin orange buttercream, while she thought about what Tate had discovered and how she wanted to handle it. When Marty came in to work the front counter and Oz arrived to take over the kitchen, Mel figured she'd better get over to Diane's office and have a little chat with her old college buddy.

The Earnest Design offices were slick. Located on a big piece of property off of Scottsdale Road and Lincoln Drive, Diane had set up shop in a mid-century modern building that was all glass windows and sharp angles. Mel parked her Mini Cooper in the small parking lot that was barren of cars.

She strode up the shallow concrete steps and pulled on the front door. It was locked. Huh. It hadn't occurred to her that Diane would not be at work. The woman was a workaholic. It was her therapy, her stress relief, the validation of her existence; heck, Mel was pretty sure it was the air she breathed. Would she really not show up to work? Especially when she had so much damage control to do?

There was no doorbell beside the door. Why would you need one when your walls were mostly glass? You could see everyone coming and going. Mel wasn't sure she liked that. She thought about knocking but given the empty parking spots and the locked door, it didn't appear that anyone was here. Mel supposed that Diane could be working from home. She was probably getting more peace and quiet that way.

Mel suspected that the local reporters had been hounding Diane since the story broke. It had to be horrifying, having everyone think the worst of you. Maybe Diane just hadn't been able to face it yet.

Mel pressed her face up to the glass, cupping her hands around her eyes so she could peer in past the glare. The office looked dark. It was an open floor plan in front of a large wooden wall, so there really weren't any places where a person could hide. Under a desk, maybe, or possibly behind some of the decorative statuary that filled the space. Mel's gaze swept the space, wondering if Diane was in her office, which she assumed was behind the big wall, and just didn't hear her knocking.

Mel knocked again just to be sure. There was no movement from inside. She opened her purse and searched for her phone. She had Diane's home number, as well as her office and cell. If she had gone home or never opened shop, Mel could catch her there.

As the phone rang, Mel held it up to her ear. She paced along the stoop. She glanced at the road, surreptitiously looking to see if any paparazzi were going to jump out at her and ask her about Diane. She knew that wouldn't go well, mostly because she was a panicker when it came to public speaking. She started to sweat and she'd clear her throat repeatedly, whether it needed it or not.

She had seen a video of a woman in Florida who had a tiff with her boyfriend — in the woman's defense it appeared she had just found out he was married when she walked into an anniversary party he was hosting for his wife — and the poor woman was caught on film hurling cake at him. The video had gone viral and they'd dubbed her "the party crasher." Since seeing it, Mel lived in fear of such a thing happening to her.

The phone rang and rang and then an automated voice came on and told her that the person she was calling had a voice mailbox that was full. Mel ended the call. She glanced back at the office one more time and that's when she saw it. A shoe was poking out from under a desk. Someone was in there, hiding from her.

TWENTY-ONE

Mel rapped on the glass. She saw the shoe start as if the person attached to the shoe hadn't been expecting that. Still they didn't come out from under the desk. Mel rapped again. Nothing. And again. Nothing.

"Oh, come on," Mel cried. "I know you're in there. I can see your shoe."

The shoe in question was abruptly yanked back under the desk.

"Puhleeze, how dumb do you think I am?" Mel cried. "I just saw you move. You might as well open the door, because I am not leaving."

She waited two seconds, then four. When she was about to shout again, a person popped out from under the desk and she yelped in surprise.

Elliott Peters appeared. He stood, adjusted his dark-framed glasses, brushed off his clothes, and strode toward the door where Mel was standing. She had an uneasy feeling about this. Cheryl had said Elliott had a thing for Diane; now Mel wondered: If everyone else was gone, what was Elliott doing here?

He was halfway to the door and waving at Mel to wait a second when another person popped up from behind the desk. It was Diane Earnest and she looked quite rumpled. And not in a "grief-struck, I'm too depressed to manage my appearance" but rather an "I just let my IT guy kiss the lipstick off of me" sort of way. Interesting.

Mel stood waiting while Elliott unlatched the door and ushered her inside.

"Hurry, hurry," he said. "The paparazzi have been circling like buzzards."

"So, you thought fornicating in front of the windows would distract them?" Mel asked.

As Diane joined them, Mel glanced between them and noticed Diane's face went red hot while Elliott straightened up with a bit of a swagger. He was clearly pleased with whatever had taken place. Hmm.

"Do you have news?" Diane asked. "Have the police found the killer?"

"No," Mel said. The strap on her handbag was digging into her shoulder and she reached up to adjust it. "At least not that I've heard."

Diane gasped. "What. Is. That?"

Mel froze. Was there a bug on her? She held her hands out in the bug slapping position and glanced down at her white cotton shirt and khaki capri pants. She didn't see anything. Before she could question her, Diane grabbed Mel's left hand and examined her ring finger.

"That!" Diane said. She pointed to Mel's engagement ring. "What the hell is that?"

Mel relaxed. "The ring? You're freaking me out over an engagement ring?"

"Aha!" Diane stepped back and pointed at her.

Mel looked at Elliott. He shrugged.

"It's no big deal, Diane," Mel said. "Joe asked me to marry him and I said yes. You don't really have a problem with that, do you?"

"Problem?" Diane sputtered. "Why would I have a problem with it? Just because you're supposed to be figuring out who killed my fiancé so that I don't rot in jail for the rest of my life, why would I have any problem with you spending your time on romantic engagement proposals?"

"What makes you think it was romantic?"

"Because they all are," Diane snapped. "It was, wasn't it?"

"Well, yeah," Mel said. "But just because

I got engaged doesn't mean I stopped trying to figure out who murdered your fiancé. Speaking of which, where were you, Elliott, the morning Mike Bordow was murdered?"

Elliott blinked at her from behind his glasses, as if he couldn't quite get her into focus. Mel snapped her fingers in front of his face.

"Elliott, you in there?" she asked.

"Well . . . I . . . You can't think . . . I would never . . ." he stammered and then stopped.

Diane and Mel watched him as he swallowed convulsively. Mel thought he might be sick. Would a man who bludgeoned another man to death get throw-uppy at the mere suggestion of his guilt? She wasn't sure.

"Elliott was with me that morning working on the Blanchard account," Diane said. "We had a presentation scheduled for later that day. Of course, I canceled it after you found Mike, but Elliott and I pulled an all-nighter the night before Mike's death."

"Can any other staff members verify this?" Mel asked.

"Why?" Diane looked hurt. "Don't you believe me?"

"I do," Mel said. She meant it, mostly. "But the police are going to want it verified, especially if they get wind of the two of you

272

getting busy."

"This just happened," Diane said, gesturing between her and Elliott. "We aren't — That is to say, things have been very stressful around here and Elliott was kind enough to comfort me when I was feeling very upset. And as for our alibis, the police have already grilled us and know we were here together."

"That's good. And the comforting thing is totally understandable," Mel said. As an aside to Elliott, she whispered, "FYI, you might want to zip up your fly."

Elliott glanced down and then spun away from them. He looked mortified as he hopped up and down while pulling up his zipper.

Mel glanced at Diane, who was looking at Elliott in mild confusion, as if she wasn't quite sure what to make of him. In all the years Mel had known Diane, she had never gone for guys like Elliott. Diane went for the über rich, very handsome, very powerful, arm-candy sort of guys.

Elliott was none of those things. Oh, he was a successful IT guy, and he was nerdy cute, but he was the sort of guy Diane used to get where she wanted to go, not the sort of guy she wanted when she arrived at her destination. Perhaps Elliott was just what she needed.

"Listen," Mel said to Diane. "I need to talk to you. Do you have an office or a meeting room where we can go?"

"Sure, follow me," Diane said. "Elliott, we can . . . um . . . finish our conversation later."

Elliott's eyes lit up behind his glasses and Mel had no doubt what conversation he thought they'd be finishing. Judging by the small smile on Diane's lips, she appeared happy to continue where they had left off as well.

The back half of the office space was one large wooden wall with Diane's corporate logo, sculpted out of brushed steel, hanging dead center and lit up with track lighting suspended above it. Diane led Mel toward the wall and through a door that blended so seamlessly into the wood, it was almost invisible to the naked eye. They entered a narrow hallway done in the same pale wood, past several offices with clear glass walls, to the last office, the corner office. On the door, engraved on a burnished steel plate, was the name *Diane Earnest, CEO*.

It made Mel pause. She knew how driven Diane had been in college. She knew that running her own marketing firm with clients firmly established in the Fortune 500 was

Diane's lifelong dream. Would she really give it all up, put it at risk, and jeopardize her future because her fiancé was cheating?

The answer was as clear as the glass that housed her office. Diane would never put her business in harm's way. She was the mother of this company and just like a mama duck protected her duckling, Diane would safeguard this company from all harm, and she would never do something like kill Mike Bordow — not because she didn't want to but because she would never put her baby at risk.

"Have a seat," Diane said. "Can I get you anything?"

"No, thanks," Mel said. She waited until Diane sat down behind her desk and then said, "Nicole Butterfield? Really?"

To her credit, Diane didn't pretend not to understand. Instead, she leaned back in her seat and put her hands over her face.

"I don't know what I was thinking," she said. "It should have been you."

"Well, weddings haven't really been my thing, so I'm okay to have been left out of your wedding party, truly, but to put Nicole in — for what possible reason?"

"I am an idiot," Diane said. "She's so well connected in town, thanks to her many ex-husbands, that I thought it would be good for the business if I had a socialite in the wedding party."

"Plus, you were worried I'd be fat," Mel said. Diane opened her mouth to argue but Mel waved her off. "Nicole told me."

"That miserable cow," Diane said. "First she tries to steal my fiancé and now she's ruining my friendships."

"Nothing is ruined," Mel said. "I wouldn't be here if it was."

"You always were the best of us," Diane said. She gave Mel a small smile. "I'm sorry, Mel, truly, really, all the way down to my soul, sorry. I don't know what got into me. I got so swept up in the planning of the wedding. It was like I lost myself."

"It's okay," Mel said. She thought about Angie morphing into a bridezilla and made a mental note that she would avoid this at all costs when planning her own wedding, even if it required electroshock therapy. Although she was enjoying the heck out of Diane's groveling, she needed to get to the point. "Honestly, I was just curious about that. I'm here about something else."

"Okay, shoot," Diane said. She looked relieved.

"You told me that Mike's business was in trouble. That's why he was marrying you, correct?"

"Yes, apparently he needed me to work my marketing magic to save them with big sales, or convince the bank president, also my client, to give them some extra time to come up with the capital they needed to repay their loan, which he said they were about to default on."

"How did you find out that he was using you for that?" Mel asked.

Diane looked wary, as if she hadn't expected Mel to go there.

"I need to know the truth," Mel said. "It's important."

"Mike told me," she said.

"He *told* you?" Mel asked. "How did that come up in conversation? Was he an idiot? Did you tell anyone? Have you told the police?"

Diane glanced away. She looked upset. More than that, she looked guilty.

"The truth, Diane, I mean it," Mel said. "Lying is only going to make things worse."

Diane blew out a breath. "Fine. I suspected that Mike was cheating but I wanted proof. I had Elliott set up surveillance on Mike and Nicole. I heard him tell her that I was his 'cash cow,' so technically he told me even if he didn't know he was telling me at the time."

"When did this happen?" Mel asked.

"A few days after my bachelorette party," Diane said. "I was upset. The party had been a disaster. Nicole got trashed. She started to talk about Mike in ways that made it clear she knew him better than she should."

Diane leaned forward, clasped her hands on her desk, and rubbed the pale patch of skin on her left ring finger, where her engagement ring used to be.

"I was so humiliated." She gave a humorless laugh. "But that was nothing compared to the moment my mother corrected one of Nicole's anecdotes about Mike's favorite naked role-playing game. It was clear my mother had had her own turn at dressing up like a French maid — such a cliché — for my husband-to-be."

"I'm so sorry," Mel said. She couldn't even imagine such a horrifying moment. Not for the first time she was fervently glad Diane had excluded her from this train wreck of a wedding.

"Yeah, well, I came back here and told Elliott and he offered to punch Mike right in the nose," Diane said. She glanced toward the door with a small smile. "When I turned down his offer, he asked me if Mike was just that sort of guy, a cheater, or if there might be something more going on.

"That hadn't occurred to me, so he suggested we tail Mike to Nicole's and listen in on their rendezvous; maybe we would learn more. That's when I got to listen to their barnyard-style lovemaking, and in the afterglow when she asked him when he was going to leave me for her, he said he couldn't because he needed my marketing skills to save his business, which was in trouble."

"How did Nicole handle that?" Mel asked.

"Not very well," Diane said. "She cursed him out and threw some breakables at him — we heard them smash — and then she screamed at him for sleeping with my mother, at which point he mentioned five other women he was banging and then he broke up with her."

Mel stared at her. "And you didn't share this with the police?"

"Well, I didn't want to get in trouble for stalking or whatever," Diane said.

"What if it wasn't true?" Mel asked. She thought about the GAAP statements versus the tax returns that Tate had shared with her.

"What do you mean?" Diane asked. "I heard them doing the wild thing with my own ears. It was true."

"No, not that," Mel said. "The company.

What if it wasn't failing?"

"You mean he lied to Nicole?" Diane asked. She looked thoughtful. "I hadn't really thought of that. I just assumed — ha — I assumed the lying rat bastard was telling her the truth." They shared a look that said, *Oh, the irony.*

"Did Elliott tape these conversations?" Mel asked.

"No, we just listened and then we hurried out of there before we got caught."

"Pity."

"Why? How would that help?"

"Because Mike broke up with Nicole, which is not what she said to me, meaning we have a woman-scorned situation, and wouldn't that give her a motive to kill him?"

Diane's mouth slid open in surprise. "I hadn't even thought of that."

"It gives her a stronger motive than you," Mel said. "She was rejected, whereas you were doing the rejecting, which makes her more likely to want to see him dead in a crime-of-passion sort of way."

"You know, I actually thought about going through with the wedding," Diane said. "I thought to myself, he's just sowing his wild oats while he can, he'll settle down once we're married and have a family. But then Elliott pointed out that if Mike was marrying me for my money then he might think I'd be okay with his taking my modest fortune and investing it into his failing company. That ripped it."

"Let me see if I understand this. You found his marrying you for business more offensive than his cheating on you with a bridesmaid and your mother and five other women," Mel said. There was absolutely no way she could keep the disbelief out of her voice.

"I know it sounds crazy," Diane said. "But in this business, as you know, it's all who you know, who you're connected to, and what favors you can call in for your clients. I thought a party planning company would be an asset. Besides, I really did convince myself that the cheating would stop once we were married."

"What if it hadn't?" Mel asked. "What would you have done if you discovered he was still pawing at every young thing that came onto his radar after you were married and probably would for the rest of your lives?"

Diane blew out a breath. "Don't think less of me for this, but I would have learned to live with it."

Mel felt her eyebrows shoot up. "Why would you do that?"

"Because I'm thirty-three years old," Diane cried. "Because I want more than this." She gestured to the office around them. "I love this, don't mistake me, but I want kids and a house in the burbs and a good-looking, wealthy husband who wants those things, too. And my biological clock is frigging ticking so loud I can barely sleep at night."

"So, you would settle?" Mel asked. "You would settle for a guy who treats you badly because you want the status of wealthy wife and mother with the picture postcard family?"

"Don't judge me, Miss Just-got-engaged-to-an-assistant-district-attorney," Diane snapped.

"Joe loves me for me. He'd never cheat and he'd never use me for my connections — if, you know, I had any," Mel argued.

"Well, bravo for you," Diane said. Her face was pinched with bitterness, and Mel would have felt sorry for her but Diane was too furious to elicit any pity. "I guess some of us just aren't lucky enough to keep our men from straying."

"But that's just it! It's not your job to keep him from straying," Mel said. "There's nothing wrong with *you* if your man is a two-timing jerk. It's *him,* his issues, not yours. Bottom line, he was not the man you thought he was and he was the one with the problem — the problem being that he was never worthy of you to begin with and clearly had a malfunctioning zipper on his pants."

A tear ran down Diane's cheek and she brushed it away with the back of her hand. Mel would have hugged her but she suspected it wouldn't be welcome at the moment.

"Look, I think I've taken this as far as I can go," Mel said. "I'm going to drop by the station and tell my uncle everything I've learned, and I think the police can handle it from here."

"No!" Diane cried. "You can't abandon me now. You've discovered more than the police have and I know you can figure out who really killed Mike. I need you, Mel. Besides, you owe me."

"You know, I'm getting really tired of you reminding me about that," Mel said.

"I know and I'm sorry," Diane said. She didn't look sorry at all. "But I'm desperate. I don't want to go to jail for a crime I didn't commit."

Mel hesitated. She really didn't want to do any more digging into the death of Mike Bordow. The whole situation was seedy and gross, and she felt like she needed a shower because it made her feel so grubby.

"Your life would have been ruined by that big-girl sex tape," Diane said. "Think about the humiliation that I saved you from."

Mel closed her eyes for a second. Why did some friendships seem to cost so much and others so little? She could never imagine Angie or Tate holding a situation where they had saved her over her head while demanding payback.

"Fine," Mel said. "I'll keep trying to find out who murdered Mike, but once I do I don't ever want to hear about the sex-tape fiasco ever again. We are square. Agreed?"

Diane nodded. "Absolutely."

Mel rose to her feet. She was done here except for one more thing.

"You know," Mel began, "outside this office is a man who is very much in love with you. I knew it from the first day you walked into the bakery together. Maybe he doesn't look like the cover of *GQ*, but his heart is sure in the right place, and doesn't that count for so much more?"

Diane's gaze flitted to the glass, where Elliott was clearly visible in his office across from hers. He was hunched over his computer, frowning at the screen while he pushed his glasses up on his nose.

"I'll be in touch if I find anything out," Mel said. "In the meantime, steer clear of the press, Nicole Butterfield, anyone in the Bordow family, and for pity's sake, if you decide to go full-monty badonkadonk with your IT guy, do it away from the windows."

"I will," Diane promised. Her gaze never met Mel's, however, as she was too busy staring at the man across the hall as if seeing him for the first time.

TWENTY-TWO

Mel knew that given how Elliott felt about Diane, he should be at the top of her suspect list. Diane's insistence that he was with her working on an account was the lamest alibi ever. Because who better than the guy who was in love with the dead guy's fiancée to be the one who helped the dead guy get that way? But Mel just couldn't see it.

Elliott was with Diane when she came into Fairy Tale Cupcakes and ordered the breakup cupcakes. He had no reason to whack the fiancé, since he knew Diane was going to be free of him in a matter of days. Unfortunately, this led right back to Diane. Now at least Mel could offer up Nicole as an alternative to Diane as the prime suspect, but the theory of Nicole as a scorned-woman killer, well, it was going to be a tougher sell than Diane as the cheated-on fiancée. Still, it was a start.

Mel was stopped at a light when her phone started to buzz. She glanced at the display. It was Angie. Guilt twisted inside as she knew she had been an absentee maid of honor lately. She had to take this call.

Mel checked her side and rearview mirrors. The road was clear, and she flipped on her signal and pulled into a parking lot. She parked under a shady tree and answered her phone.

"Hey, Angie, what's up?" She made her voice sound extra cheerful, hoping to defuse any tension.

"My . . . eh . . . wedding . . . eh . . . is . . . eh . . . ruined . . ." Angie sobbed.

Oh, boy, bridal meltdown number fifty-two was clearly happening right now. Mel pinched the bridge of her nose. She needed to be there for Angie; that was what good maids of honor did. She let go of her nose and blew out a breath.

"What's happened?"

"I . . . eh . . . can't . . . eh . . . talk . . . about . . . eh . . . it," she sobbed.

"Okay," Mel said. She wasn't sure what Angie wanted her to do if she couldn't talk about it. "Where are you?"

"At the bakery."

"I'll be there in five minutes," Mel said. "Don't fret. We'll figure this out."

"We can't," Angie wailed. "It's all ruined. Ruined!"

Mel ended the call and drove at light speed back to the bakery. What could have happened? Did the venue cancel, the photographer, the baker — oh, wait, that was her. The wedding was three months away. What could have happened to make Angie so hysterical?

She parked in the back lot and hurried across the alley and into the kitchen of the bakery. Oz was there, with both mixers running, and the Hobart convection oven was full of cupcakes being baked. Mel paused to breathe in the smell. Was there anything more soothing than the smell of freshly baked cake? No, she was sure there was not.

Feeling calmer, she asked Oz, "Where's Angie?"

"Locked in there," he said. "She got that package, let out a scream, grabbed a tray of Cherry Bomb Cupcakes, and bolted for the bathroom. She hasn't come out since." He lowered his voice as if he was sharing a deep, dark secret, and said, "I think she's crying."

He pointed first at a big brown box on the side table and then at the door of the staff bathroom. He was wearing his chef's hat and his hair was pulled off of his face and

288

tucked under the brim. She could see his brown eyes were wide with concern.

"Freaked you out, didn't she?" Mel asked.

"Why do you say that?" Oz asked. He crossed his arms over his chest, trying to look cool, which he clearly was not.

"Because you have every piece of equipment going in the kitchen at the same time," Mel said. "Typical chef's way of coping with uncomfortable situations. Bake."

"It is?"

"Definitely," Mel said. Then she punched him lightly on the arm. "See? You're a natural. You even respond to a crisis like a chef. There is no problem that can't be cured with food."

"Well, there isn't," Oz said as if he was stating a universal truth. "Which is why I didn't stop Angie when she took all of my cupcakes."

Mel nodded. She'd have done the same.

"So, are you going to see what's in the box that set her off?" Oz asked.

"You didn't look?"

"Hell, no." He shook his head.

"I'm afraid."

Oz gave her a stern look.

"I know, I know," she said. "It's my job as best friend and maid of honor. Fine."

Mel approached the box and carefully

289

flipped the top, which had been cut open, as if she expected a snake to pop out. Nothing happened. She leaned over the box and peered inside. Nestled in pretty silver tissue paper and packaged in individual boxes were Angie and Tate's wedding invitations.

The thick pearly cardstock caught the light from the window and Mel caught her breath. They looked beautiful. The letterpress — a style of relief printing using a printing press, which Angie had gone on and on about as the only acceptable way to have her invitations done — really did look fantastic against the thick glossy paper.

They were done in two colors: pewter for the fine print, and a pretty aqua blue for the script, which was Tate and Angie's names, and for the graphic in the bottom right corner of a bicycle built for two, which looked to be riding off the card and into a happy life. Mel grinned.

They were perfect. They were so Tate and Angie. The colors looked terrific, everything was centered, and the matching RSVP cards were in the box along with all of the envelopes for both. Hmm. What could have made Angie have a bridal episode? Mel looked at the card again. She reread the text.

"Oh," she gasped. "Oh, no."

"What is it?" Oz asked. He looked

alarmed, as if Mel might scream and wail and lock herself in the bathroom, too.

She gave him a grimace. "There's a typo on the invitation."

"How bad?"

"Pretty bad," Mel said.

Oz joined her and peered over her shoulder. He read the card. He frowned.

"I'm not seeing it," he said.

"Read it from right to left," Mel said. "Proofreader's tip."

"Oh!" His eyebrows went up. "Oh, crap."

"Yeah, somehow they put in *request the honor of your presents* instead of *presence*," Mel said. "It makes them sound like they're schilling for stuff."

"Oh, poor Angie. It's even worse because she used to be a teacher," he said. "You can't have typos when you used to teach. Bad form."

"Okay, there's no need to panic. We need to focus on damage control," Mel said. She went over to the bathroom door and knocked. "Angie, honey, are you okay?"

A sob was the only response. Mel glanced at Oz, who cringed and hurried back to his mixers.

"Angie, I can see why you're upset, but maybe the company that made these can do a rush order of new ones."

"It's no use," Angie cried. "These invites have to go out in three weeks. We're doomed. The wedding is doomed." Mel heard her sobbing and it hurt her heart. "Tell Tate I'm sorry, but I can't marry him."

"Angie —"

"No, just leave me alone, Mel, please."

Mel knew that tone in Angie's voice. There was no talking her out of her self-imposed bathroom exile. She was going to have to call in the big guns.

She took out her phone and began to search her contacts.

"Are you calling T-man?" Oz asked.

"Nope," Mel said. "It's time for the real deal: the Moms."

Both Mrs. DeLaura and Mrs. Harper arrived twenty minutes later. Maria DeLaura, a mature version of Angie, was in her usual jean capris with her gray hair styled in casual waves framing her heart-shaped face. Emily Harper was also dressed in her standard knit sleeveless top and pearls over a matching knee-length skirt. Mel met them in the front of the bakery so she could talk to them before ambushing Angie in the bathroom.

"Wow, that was quick," Mel said.

The moms exchanged glances and then Maria said, "We took an Uber."

Mel glanced from Maria DeLaura to Emily Harper and back. "An Uber? Wow, um, you two were hanging out?"

The women exchanged a look, and then Maria snorted and Emily grabbed her arm and started laughing. They looked like they were in on some sort of private joke, and Mel noticed that Maria was tilting to one side and Emily was going with her.

"Oh my god, are you two drunk?" she cried.

"Whoop, drunk ladies in da house!" Marty popped up from behind the counter, where he'd been stocking the paper supplies. When he caught sight of who was on the other side of the counter, his mouth formed a little O. "Sorry! Afternoon, Mrs. D, Mrs. H."

"Isn't he just the cutest thing?" Maria asked Emily.

Emily squinted at Marty. "I don't know, turn it around." She made a twirly gesture with her hand. "So we can check out the back door."

Marty clapped his hands to his bald head, clearly not used to being sexually harassed in the bakery. Maria cackled and Emily hooted, and Mel felt her temples compress into what she suspected was going to be a doozy of a headache.

"Marty, go put some coffee on," she said. "Ladies, if you could take a seat?"

"Hang on," Maria said. Then as Marty walked away, she sang, "Bow chicka wah wah."

Emily draped her arm over Maria's shoulder and the two of them doubled up with laughter.

Mel pulled out her phone and found Tate and Joe's contact information. She texted them both.

Bakery. Now. Your mother is drunk.

Mel's phone immediately lit up in response but she ignored it. Someone had to rein these women in and she had her hands full with the hysterical bride.

"What were you two doing before you got my message, vodka shooters?" Mel asked.

"No," Maria said. She slid into a booth, dragging Emily with her. "We were gardening, and I was teaching Emily how to make mimosas."

"Make them or drink them?" Mel asked.

"It turns out we share a love of gardening and mimosas," Emily said. Her eyes lit up and she clapped her hands. "Since we're going to be family, we've been getting to know each other. I love Maria."

"And I love you," Maria said. "Emily has a lovely rose garden. You should see her

Michelangelo rose bush. The blooms are big and buttery yellow with a lemony scent. Simply gorgeous."

"I will have my gardener get some cuttings for you," Emily said.

"You will?" Maria looked delighted.

"Of course," Emily said. She patted Maria's arm. "You're my very best friend in the whole wide world."

Then she slumped forward and passed out on the table.

"Nap time?" Maria asked. "Yay."

Then she, too, passed out in the booth. Mel checked to see that both ladies were breathing. They were. In fact, Emily was even snoring.

Marty came back with a tray of coffee. He stopped beside Mel and regarded the two ladies.

"Are we letting them sleep it off now?"

"I think that might be for the best," she said. "What do you think?"

"I think I feel violated since they were checking out my booty," he said. "I'm going to hide in the kitchen."

"A solid plan," Mel said. "See if you can talk Angie out of the bathroom while you're back there, would you?"

Marty set down the tray on a nearby table and disappeared in back. Mel sat down in the booth across from the moms. She didn't want to leave them unattended while they drunk-slept.

The front door to the bakery burst open and a disheveled Tate hurried inside.

"Mel, I got your message — what the he —"

"Cupcake, if you wanted to see me, you could have just — Oh, you weren't kidding," Joe said as he came in right behind Tate.

They both tipped their heads to the side as they considered their mothers.

"Drunk?" Tate asked.

"Snookered," Mel confirmed. "Apparently, they have discovered they have a shared love of gardening and mimosas."

"Mom?" Angie's voice interrupted, and they all turned around to see Angie enter from the kitchen. "Marty said, but I didn't believe — Are they blitzed?"

"Completely," Mel said. "Gassed, juiced, hammered, pissed, plastered, take your pick."

Angie sank into a chair. She had a smear of chocolate frosting on her cheek and there was a blot of cherry on her shirt as well as some chocolate cake crumbs. Her long curly hair was in disarray and her eyes were puffy and red-rimmed.

"Hey, sweetheart, are you okay?" Tate

knelt down in front of her, studying her face. "Have you been crying?"

"No," Angie said. But her voice quavered, giving her away.

Tate lifted her out of the chair and hugged her. "Come on, tell me what's wrong."

Joe sidled over to Mel and whispered, "Shall we leave them alone?"

"I don't know," she said. "I don't want Tate to bungle it."

"Retreat to the shadows then?"

Mel nodded, and she and Joe slipped back into a corner of the bakery. He pulled her back against his front and looped his arms around her waist. He propped his chin on her shoulder as they watched the moment between Angie and Tate unfold.

"So, what happened?" Joe whispered in Mel's ear.

"Typo on the invites — bad one. I called the moms for backup, they showed up drunk, I texted you and Tate," she whispered back.

"Rough morning."

"Hmm." Mel thought about her time at Diane's office and decided not to dump that on him as well. "Promise me something?"

"Sure," he said.

"Let's not get crazy like this when we plan our wedding," she said. "I just want to be

Mrs. Joseph DeLaura."

Joe didn't answer, so Mel turned to face him. The look of love and affection in his warm brown eyes made Mel's insides go all aflutter.

"How did I get so lucky to win your heart, Melanie Cooper?"

He sounded genuinely in awe at what he considered his good fortune. Mel wanted to correct him and tell him she was the lucky one; she knew she was, but instead she kissed him. It was supposed to be a chaste I-love-you sort of kiss but it did not maintain its PG rating for long.

Joe pulled her right up against him, cupped the back of her head, and kissed her as if his life depended upon it. Hot. Hot Hot.

"Joseph DeLaura, what on earth are you doing?" Maria's voice broke through Mel's lusty haze and she pushed away from Joe.

Her face was hot, and she was panting like she'd just run, well, across the room, because she was not a runner and panting pretty much happened at the fifty-foot mark.

"I'm kissing my girl," Joe said, not looking the least bit embarrassed. "And what have you been up to, Mom?"

Maria looked at Emily still snoring beside her. She fluffed her gray curls and said,

"Nothing. Not a thing." Then she nudged her friend. "Emily, Em, wake up. We have a situation."

"Huh." Emily lifted her head off of the table and glanced at Maria with one eye open. She took in the bakery and then glanced at Tate and Angie. She smiled. "Aren't they just perfect together?"

Mel left Joe to bring the tray of coffee over to the two moms. She had a feeling they were going to need it.

"What's going on?" Maria asked. "Why do Tate and Angie look so tense?"

"We had a small — okay, that's a lie — we had a huge bridal meltdown," Mel said. "Angie locked herself in the bathroom with a dozen cupcakes because of a typo on the wedding invitation. That's why I texted you. I thought we might need an intervention."

"Oh, my poor girl," Maria said. "We've been so worried about her but she won't let us help with the wedding. She just pushes us away whenever we try."

"Mom, I do not," Angie protested.

Maria rose from the booth and took Angie's hands in hers. She looked at her daughter and cupped her face in her hands, and then gave her a steely-eyes look and snapped, *Basta, mia bambina!*

299

TWENTY-THREE

"Uh-oh," Joe whispered in Mel's ear. "She's busting out the Italian. Mom only does that when she is really unhappy."

"What does it mean?"

" 'Stop, baby girl,' " Joe said. "I think she's finally calling Angie on her crazy."

"Amen," Mel said.

"But —" Angie protested, but her mother cut her off.

"No more," Maria said. "Emily and I have been beside ourselves because you won't let us help you with anything. Well, look at you. You're covered in cupcake crumbs and are clearly having a nervous breakdown. No more."

She glanced over her shoulder and motioned for Emily to join her. The two mothers stood united.

"And you," Emily said to Tate. "Why is your bride a mess and you look fine? How could you let her get into such a state? Have you been acting like your father and hiding?"

"No. Maybe. Okay, yes," Tate admitted. He looked at Angie. "I'm sorry, baby, I love you more than life itself but you have been straight-up terrifying these past few months."

"Finally, the boy is talking sense," Marty said from behind the counter. They all turned to look at him and he ducked his head. "Sorry. I'll just . . ."

His voice trailed off as he disappeared back into the kitchen.

Angie looked at everyone in the room. "Have I been that bad, really?"

"Worse," Joe said. Mel elbowed him in the middle and he grunted. "Ow."

"Shh," she hushed him.

"Angie, what is it that's bothering you?" Tate asked. "I've tried to figure it out but you just duck and weave and give me that fake smile and say, 'I'm fine.' I've been trying to stay out of your way and let you work through it but I have to tell you, you don't seem to be getting there. Every time I turn around, you're freaking out about flowers, colors, cardstock, the photographer — truly, the list is endless."

"But —" Angie began, but Tate shook his head. He had the floor and he was not giving it up.

"I have to be honest. I don't care about any of this stuff. I just want to have a party to celebrate the fact that I have somehow, miraculously, convinced the hottest, funniest, most loving girl in the world to be my wife. And I don't care if we make our vows with parachutes strapped to our backs as we jump out of a plane or if it's in a castle with a three-hundred-piece orchestra. I just want you to be Mrs. Tate Harper and the sooner we can make this happen, the happier I am going to be."

"Oh, Tate." Angie began to cry again. "See? That's what's wrong."

Mel and Joe exchanged a confused look. On the scale of awesome I-love-you speeches, Tate had just laid down one of the best — truly, even Mel had felt her throat get tight — but instead of making Angie happy it made her cry.

"What's wrong?" Tate asked. He looked like he wanted to hit his head on something hard.

"Don't you see?" Angie asked. "I don't know how to throw a wedding fit for society. I'm a backyard-shindig, come-as-you-are, wildflower type of girl. I don't know how to do any of this. I'm not good enough for you."

Maria and Emily both drew in sharp breaths. Then they looked at each other. Maria opened her mouth, looking like she was gearing up to give Angie a blistering speech, but Emily held up her hand.

"I got this," she said. "Angie, I am shocked and more than a little hurt."

Angie turned from Tate, who handed her a napkin to blow her nose with, to Emily.

"I'm sorry," Angie said. She sounded so meek, Mel wanted to hug her friend hard until she was back to being her usual feisty self.

"No, I'm the one who is sorry," Emily said. "It is quite obvious to me that I have failed as a future mother-in-law."

"What?" Angie cried. "No!"

"Oh, yes," Emily said.

"No, it's me," Angie said. She dropped her chin to her chest. "I don't know how to do any of this. I'm the failure."

Emily gently took Angie's chin in her hand and lifted her face until her gaze met hers.

"Tell me the truth," Emily said. "If you weren't marrying Tate —"

"Mom!" Tate cried in protest. Emily gave him a look and he clamped his lips together.

"If you were marrying someone from a less privileged background, would you have made yourself this crazy over the wedding?"

Angie blew out a breath. "No."

"Then why are you doing it now?" Emily asked. "It hurts me that you think we are such shallow snobs that we would judge you on your special day."

"But I don't, I just . . . I wanted to fit into Tate's world," Angie said. Her voice cracked and again Mel had to force herself not to cross the room and hug her friend.

"But, Angie, *you* are my world." Tate's voice was so soft, Mel could barely hear him, but Angie did. She spun around and threw herself at him, and Tate caught her in a hug that crushed.

Then he kissed her.

"Look at the T-man," Oz said from the kitchen door. "Getting the priorities straight."

He walked across the room to join the group and held up a fist to Joe. Joe tapped his knuckles with Oz's but then frowned as the clinch between Tate and Angie continued.

"Yeah, she's still my baby sister, Tate," Joe said. His voice was low with warning, and Mel laughed when Tate pulled back from Angie and raised his hands in the air as if Joe had a gun on him.

"Sorry, man," he said.

"I'm not." Angie hugged him hard around

304

the middle.

"My dear," Emily said as she took Angie's hands in hers. "You must plan the wedding you've always dreamed of, not the one you think the rest of the world wants. It's your day and I am so sorry that you ever felt like you had to meet some unspoken ideal."

"Thank you," Angie said. She turned to her mother with a shy smile. "Do you think the Italian-American Club might have an opening?"

Maria DeLaura beamed at her daughter. "Your brother Ray has some connections. He'll make it happen. You just tell him the day."

Mel felt Joe heave a sigh beside her. Ray was the black sheep of the family, the one who thought the law was flexible when it suited his purposes. He was also the one Joe lost the most sleep worrying about.

"Not Ray, Mom," he said. "You know his contacts are sketchy at best."

"I know nothing of the sort," she said. "Come on, let's sit and have some coffee. I bet we get this wedding nailed down within the hour."

Maria pushed Emily back into their booth, and Tate and Angie took the seats across from them. It was the first time Mel heard Angie laugh while planning her wedding.

One glance at Angie's face and Mel saw the radiant bride her friend would be now that she was planning the day for her and Tate and no one else.

Oz drifted back into the kitchen and Mel walked Joe to the door. He wrapped his arm around her and kissed the top of her head.

"Crisis averted," he said.

"Yeah, and now maybe we can get back to normal around here," she said.

Joe glanced past Mel at Tate and Angie, then he looked down at Mel. He traced her cheek with his thumb while he met her gaze.

"Is it bad that I'm really wishing our Vegas elopement had worked out for us?" he asked.

"Nope," she said. "I feel the exact same way."

He planted a quick kiss on her and then lifted her hand to examine the ring he'd so recently put on her finger. A small smile parted his lips. "See you at home, my future wife."

A ridiculous thrill rocketed through Mel at his words and she grinned at him.

"Yes, you will, my future husband," she said.

Joe hit her with his brain-frying, patent-worthy grin, and Mel slumped against the doorjamb and watched as he walked away.

She was going to marry that man.

Ray sauntered into the cupcake bakery an hour later wearing his usual leather jacket and overdose of cologne.

"Leather in June. Seriously, Ray?" Angie asked. She was sequestered in a booth with all of her bridal magazines, going over what she planned to keep and what she planned to scrap in the wedding she had planned so far.

"Hey, no cracks about the leather if you want my help," he said.

"Oh my god, it's like I have the Fonz for a brother," Angie said to Mel.

Mel turned away so Ray wouldn't see her smile. Marty was behind the counter helping a short line of customers. When the door opened and a passel of school kids arrived, Mel got out of the booth and gestured for Ray to take her place.

"Ray, can I talk to you before you leave?" she asked.

"Sure thing, doll," he said.

Mel nodded to keep from laughing. Ray was the only one of the DeLauras whose New York accent had gotten thicker in the twenty years since they'd moved from New York to Arizona.

Ray hunkered into the booth with Angie,

and Mel went back into the kitchen to help contain the ridiculous amount of cupcakes Oz had baked. She had finished frosting several dozen when Ray peeked around the door.

"You have any of those Mocha Latte Cupcakes laying around?" he asked.

Mel smiled at him. "After you went on a bender a few weeks ago, I didn't think you'd ever want another again."

"I worked through it," he said with a shrug.

Mel looked at Oz, who was sweaty and rumpled-looking from working by the oven.

"Oz, why don't you go help Marty out front so you can cool off," she said. She gestured to the rows and rows of cooling cupcakes. "I'll take care of this."

"Thanks, boss," Oz said. He passed by Ray with a nod. "Hey."

"Hey back atcha, kid." Ray nodded in return.

Mel went to the cooler and plated two Mocha Latte Cupcakes for Ray. She also poured him a cup of coffee. Ray was known for the immense amount of coffee he drank.

She set the cupcakes and coffee down on the table and gestured for him to sit while she finished frosting the Key Lime Cupcakes Oz had baked. It was a lime-flavored

308

cake that was topped off with a vanilla-lime icing, so it packed a double whammy of sweet, tart goodness.

Ray took a bite of his cupcake and then washed it down with the hot coffee. The look of happiness on his face captured perfectly the reason Mel loved what she did for a living. A good cupcake with the right frosting-to-cake ratio never failed to hit a person right in the feels. Mel never felt better than when she saw that first look of joy pass over a person's face when they were eating one of her cupcakes.

"So, I'm guessing now that you've got that dazzler on your finger, you're wanting my help with your wedding to Joe," he said.

Mel opened her mouth to answer but Ray kept talking, cutting her off.

"I know some people who might be able to help out," he said. "What do you need? Venue? Photos? Music? How about a dress? Do you have a dress? I'm thinking you're going to want something that shows off the female assets without showing off the ass —"

"Stop!" Mel interrupted.

Ray blinked at her.

"That's not why I wanted to talk to you," she said. "I need your help with another matter."

Ray took a bite of his cupcake and then looked thoughtfully at her while he chewed. Mel continued frosting the cupcakes in front of her, allowing him a chance to mull over her request. He took a sip of his coffee, still considering her.

"Does Joe know about this?"

"No," she said.

"Would Joe be okay with this?"

"Probably not," she admitted.

A slow smile spread across Ray's face. He really did live for making his brother crazy.

"Explain."

"I need someone to hook me up with Tyson Ballinger," she said.

Ray let out a low whistle. "And by *hook up* you mean what, exactly?"

He looked disapproving. He might enjoy yanking Joe's chain but Mel knew he would protect his brother from harm, even of the heartache kind, with his dying breath.

"I think he has information that I need," Mel said. "I need to talk to him."

Ray nodded. He reached for the second cupcake and polished it off along with the coffee. Mel continued decorating.

"Be straight with me," he said. "Is the business in trouble?"

"No," Mel said. "It's nothing like that."

"Personal gambling problem?" he asked.

She shook her head. He looked dubious.

"You can tell me," he said. "I won't judge you."

"I think Tyson might have some information about who murdered Mike Bordow, the owner of Party On!, and I want to ask him some questions," she said.

"Mel," Ray groaned. "You don't ask Tyson Ballinger questions — ever. In fact, you don't even enter a room that he's in unless you want him to clean out your pockets so thoroughly, there isn't even lint left in them."

"I need to talk to him," Mel said. "I saw him threatening Butch Bordow. It sounded like he planned to take his company, but here's the thing: The company financials check out. I had Tate look into it. There is no way with the profit they are making that Tyson stands a chance of taking away the company, so why was he threatening Butch?"

Ray looked at her. "And your plan is to what? Just ask him this? You really think he's going to tell you jack?"

"That's why I wanted your help," Mel said. She looked at him from under her lashes and gave him her best coquettish look.

"Yeah, I'm not my brother, that so doesn't

work on me," he said.

"Fine," Mel said. "Look, I have to find out who murdered Mike Bordow — it's a long story — and I need to talk to Tyson. Can you make this happen or not?"

Ray pushed the empty plate toward her. "Good thing I have plenty of time to hear the whole story. Now if I just had some more cupcakes and coffee to go with it."

Mel met his gaze. She knew he was going to help her, but she was going to have to tell him everything about Diane, the favor from college that she owed her, the breakup cupcakes, and finding the dead guy. The brown eyes that met hers were so like Joe's. Mel knew that despite his thug-like appearance, Ray was a good man. She trusted him. She could live with telling him everything.

"Deal," she said. She took the empty plate and headed back into the cooler.

TWENTY-FOUR

"Why are we meeting here?" Mel asked Ray. "Shouldn't we be in a parking garage somewhere?"

"Nah," Ray said. "Ballinger has a train fetish. Weirdo."

Mel sat on a picnic table in the middle of the McCormick-Stillman Railroad Park. Hordes of children ran back and forth across the field, which sat in the center of a one-mile train track. Two different miniature locomotives, used for taking people on rides, with several passenger cars attached chugged around the park.

At mid-afternoon, it was busy and loud and full of parents and children, riding the trains, playing on the playgrounds, looking at the displays of model trains in the building that housed them, touring the parked historic engine, and riding on the carousel.

Mel had taken her nephews here when they were little and at the height of their

Thomas the Tank Engine obsession. It was a beautiful park. She glanced at the ring on her finger. She couldn't help but wonder if she would be returning here if she and Joe had children of their own. The thought made her break out into a sweat.

"Steady there," Ray said. He jerked his head to the right. "Here comes Ballinger."

Mel glanced in that direction, trying not to be obvious, but then her head swiveled of its own accord as she took in the man in the grubby denim overalls with a red bandana tied around his neck and a striped train engineer's cap on his head. He looked nothing like the man who had threatened Butch Bordow at the Triple Fork Saloon when she was with Mick, and yet it was undeniably him with his carefully trimmed mustache and substantial girth.

"Wow, just wow," she said.

"Right?" Ray asked. "Has he no sense of style? Who dresses in a getup like that?"

It was scorching hot even though they were under the shade of a large tree. Ray had sweat trickling down the sides of his face and he still wore his thick leather jacket.

"I can't imagine," Mel said.

"DeLaura, I heard you wanted to talk," Tyson said.

He was a grizzly of a man and Mel felt

314

the same sense of caution that she had the last time they'd met up.

"You sure you have time?" Ray asked. "Aren't you engineers on a schedule?"

"Hilarious," Tyson snapped. "Never heard that one before. I'll have you know I do this for my kid, so shut up."

Ray raised his hands in surrender. "Whatever."

Tyson looked at Mel. "I know you."

She felt like hiding behind Ray, sweaty leather jacket and all, but she didn't. Instead, she stood up and held out her hand.

"I'm Melanie Cooper," she said. He frowned, trying to place her. "I'm friends with Diane Earnest."

His gray eyebrows shot up, so he knew the name. He looked at Ray. "What's this all about?"

"Word is Butch Bordow owed you money for gambling debts," Ray said. "Now his son is dead. Coincidence?"

Tyson leaned in close to Ray. A vein was throbbing in his temple just beneath his engineer's hat. Ray met his furious face with a bored look. Mel had to give it to him, the one time she had faced down Tyson at the saloon, she'd almost peed her pants.

"What are you trying to say, DeLaura?" Tyson snarled.

Instead of backing up like any sane person would, Ray leaned forward. He looked like a junkyard dog, all bared teeth and bristling with hostility.

"What do you think I'm trying to say?" Ray asked. "Did you kill Mike Bordow?"

Mel glanced between them. It was a lot like the staring contests she used to have with Tate and Angie when they were kids, except these two looked like they wanted to punch each other for the win. She figured she'd best step in before there was a brawl.

"I'm sorry, Mr. Ballinger," Mel said. "I think we are off to a bad start here."

She gave Ray a look and he eased back just a little. Tyson did, too, and Mel took a steadying breath.

"You and I have met before," she said. "I was in the Triple Fork the other day and I saw you talk to Butch Bordow."

Tyson ran his finger over his mustache. "Oh, yeah, that's where I know you from. You've got some balls standing up to me."

Mel nodded. This felt like very high praise coming from Tyson, so she went with it.

"It's clear Butch owes you some money and, well, after you left the bar, Butch did say that he thought you might have had Mike killed to get even."

"What?" Tyson roared. "Butch Bordow is

a lying sack of sh—"

"Hey, lady present," Ray interrupted.

Tyson growled at him but Ray didn't back down.

"I didn't have anyone killed," Tyson said. "I don't need to do that. I use other people's weakness and stupidity to ruin them financially and their company becomes mine. It doesn't get any easier than that. Sheesh, I'm not the mob."

"So then your plan is to take away Party On!?" Mel asked.

Tyson stepped back. "What's this to you, anyway?"

"I told you, I'm friends with Diane Earnest," she said.

"The fiancée who probably killed him," Tyson said.

"She didn't," Mel said.

"Yeah," Tyson snorted.

"Look, it's important," Mel said. She was feeling desperate. She could feel Ray watching her intently, and she could only imagine what he was thinking. "I owe Diane Earnest a debt. The only way I can repay her is to find out who killed her fiancé."

Tyson studied her. "If it's money you owe this Diane, we could talk about what collateral you've got and do a deal."

"No, Mel," Ray said. He sounded fierce.

Mel reached over and squeezed his forearm with her hand. She appreciated the support but she had to get some sort of information out of Tyson before this meeting ended.

"It's not money," Mel said. "I wish it was that simple."

Tyson's expression softened as if he understood that there were much worse things to be in debt for besides cold hard cash.

"I can't help you then," he said not unkindly.

Mel nodded. This had been a long shot at best. "Thanks anyway."

"Sure." Tyson jerked his head at Ray. "DeLaura."

"Ballinger." Ray returned the nod.

Tyson turned to leave, took two steps, but then turned back around, his gaze meeting Mel's. "Word of advice?"

"Okay."

"Stay away from this situation," he said. "There's stuff . . . Well . . . a pretty girl like you should steer clear is all."

Mel and Ray watched silently as he crossed the park and disappeared into the building that housed the clubs that maintained elaborate model train displays.

"Did you get anything out of that?" Ray asked. He wiped the sweat off his face with his forearm.

"Only the feeling that Tyson Ballinger knows more than he's saying," she said.

"What's our next play?" Ray asked.

He pushed off of the table and led the way through the park to the parking lot. They had to stop at the train tracks and wait while one of the trains passed with several families all jammed onto the ride. Mel smiled when Ray waved back at the kids who waved at him as they passed.

"Don't have one," Mel admitted. "I think I am forever going to be in debt to Diane. She'll be doing time in prison for a crime she didn't commit and asking me to bake cupcakes with metal files in them."

Ray laughed and Mel gave him a look letting him know she didn't think it was funny. He laughed harder.

"I can see why Joe is smitten with you," he said. "You're a kick in the pants, Melanie Cooper."

"Thanks, I think," she said.

They crossed the hot pavement and climbed into Mel's car. She turned on the engine and blasted the air conditioner. Ray turned his vents so they blasted right onto his face and chest.

"What if . . ." Mel paused. The thought was only half formed and she wasn't sure how to say it so that it sounded as plausible out loud as it did in her head.

"Yeah?"

"What if Tyson is telling the truth and he didn't kill Mike to punish Butch?" she asked.

"Then your friend is in a whole lot of trouble because who had a motive to kill him besides the woman he was cheating on?"

"Exactly," Mel said. "This whole thing has been aimed at Diane from the start, but it doesn't make sense. She was having breakup cupcakes delivered. Clearly, she was moving on. She had no reason to kill him. In fact, it really ruined the amount of gloating she was planning to do."

"So, who else had a motive? Tyson's MO is to take people's companies, not kill anyone."

"But that's weird, too." Mel chewed her lip in thought. "Tate checked the financials for Party On! and they're doing fine. In fact, they are on the brink of breaking out, so how could Tyson have a financial investment in the company unless someone sold him a chunk?"

"Meaning Mike Bordow could have just paid Tyson to make Butch's gambling debts go away," Ray said. "In which case, why is Mike dead? Why didn't he pay Tyson?"

"Exactly," Mel said. "Unless, Mike chose not to pay Tyson to bail out his father but rather planned to expand the company, like he told his girlfriend Nicole, using Diane's money and marketing ability. Maybe Butch wanted Diane's money for himself and when Mike blocked his father from taking her money, there was a fight between father and son."

Ray nodded. "Dear old dad might be the killer then."

The thought made Mel queasy, but who else could have crushed Mike's skull? That was the act of a person who was desperate. Butch was desperate to pay Tyson before Tyson ruined him and left him penniless. Mike could move on with the company with Diane's money and not be hampered by his father's debt if he cut him loose. Could Butch have murdered his own son to get his hands on the money? It was all wild speculation but she felt like she was getting closer to the truth.

"I need to talk to Butch again," Mel said.

"He's not going to tell you jack," Ray said.

"You have a better idea?"

"Yep, blackmail," Ray said.

"Oh, I don't think blackmail is in my wheelhouse," Mel said. "I'm better off just asking him what's what."

"And he'll shut down and you'll get nowhere." Ray cracked his knuckles and then stretched his fingers. "Good thing you have the help of a master."

He turned to look at her and grinned. It was a smile rife with that deadly DeLaura charm and Mel knew without a shadow of a doubt that if Joe found out about this, he would be livid.

Knowing this, she said, "Explain."

"Simple," he said. "We call Butch, we tell him we know what he did, and then we have him meet us at Party On! for a payout so we don't rat him out. If he shows, we know he did it."

"That easy?"

"Of course," Ray said. "All the best plans are."

Mel was racked with indecision, but her desire to prove Diane innocent and be free of her control was too strong to resist.

"All right." She glanced at him, and knowing full well she shouldn't trust the gleam in his eye, she said, "Let's do it."

Ray and Mel sat in his black Porsche Carrera, of course, in the adjacent lot from the Party On! warehouse store and waited. Ray had instructed Butch to meet them at nine o'clock. No cars were in the lot and the lights were off. Thankfully the area was well lit, so Mel knew they'd be able to see Butch if he used either the front door or the side entrance.

"What time is it?" she asked Ray for the fifth time in as many minutes.

"A minute after the last time you asked me, making it seven minutes until nine," he said. To his credit, he sounded more amused than irritated.

"Why isn't he here yet?" Mel asked. "If you were being blackmailed, wouldn't you get to the designated meeting place early?"

"Depends upon how scared I was of the blackmail," Ray said.

"Do you think you scared him?" Mel asked.

"No idea," he said. "I sent a text."

Mel turned and looked at him. "You sent a what?"

"A text," Ray said. He gestured with his thumbs as if the concept of texting had to be acted out for Mel.

"I thought you were going to call him," Mel said. "You know, make with the scary voice and freak him out. A text, really? What sort of emoji do you use for that? Why not send him a candy-gram? I mean, would you do what a blackmail text told you to?"

"Depends upon the text," Ray said.

Mel dropped her head into her hands. They were doomed. This whole thing was doomed. She was going to be an indentured servant to Diane forever.

"Hold up," Ray said. "Someone is creeping along the outside of the building."

Mel glanced up to where he pointed. Sure enough, she could just see someone easing around the side of the building. A wedge of light appeared and Mel saw the silhouette of the person as they slipped inside. It definitely looked like a man.

Mel opened her door and Ray grabbed her arm. He pulled her back inside and reached past her to close the door.

"Where do you think you're going?" he asked.

"Inside," Mel said. "We have to confront him and get him to admit what he did."

"No, no, no," Ray said. "Now we call the police and tell them that a big, fat mouse is in our trap."

"But we have no proof," Mel said. "We need a confession. Heck, we're not even sure that's Butch."

"The police can figure that out," he said. He took out his phone and opened his contacts.

His voice had a *that's final* note to it. Mel gave him a look of disbelief. Ray DeLaura had known her for more than twenty years. Surely he knew better than to try that tone with her.

"Why don't you want to go in there?" she demanded.

"Because that's a job for the police," he said.

"And you are so respectful of the boundaries of the men and women in blue," Mel said. The note of disbelief in her voice could not be missed.

"Mel, there was a dead guy in there," Ray said. He said it as if it was the most obvious reason in the world not to go in there.

"I know," she said. "I'm the one who found him."

He gave her a horrified look and all of a sudden it clicked.

"Oh, wow," she said with a sharp laugh. "You're afraid to go in there."

"No, I'm . . . I just think it would be best —"

"You're afraid," Mel said. "I forgot how terrified of ghosts you are."

"No, I'm not," he argued. "Because there is no such thing as ghosts."

It sounded like an oft-repeated affirmation and Mel wondered how that was working out for him. She couldn't see his face in the dark, but his hands had felt clammy when he grabbed her arm and his breathing was quick, as if he was nervous.

"No, there isn't," she agreed.

Mel knew Ray was going to be her brother-in-law and she didn't want to have any tension in the family, but honestly the urge to slap him was overriding her naturally nice disposition. Butch Bordow was right there! Within confessing distance! All they had to do was play this right.

"Yeah, Stan, how you doing?" Ray said.

Mel knew it was her uncle on the phone. He and Ray shared a respectful distrust for each other that they had maintained ever since Uncle Stan arrested Ray for the first time when he was sixteen. It was a vandalism charge, not a big deal, but it had set the tone for their ongoing relationship.

"Yeah, I'm behaving, I guess," Ray said. "Here's the thing; I'm with Mel."

There was a pause and Mel could hear Uncle Stan speaking harshly, but she couldn't make out what he said.

"No!" Ray denied. He gave Mel an apologetic look and then turned to look out the window. "She's Joe's girl. What kind of an amoral bastard do you think I am?"

There was another pause.

"Now is that nice?" Ray asked. "I could have left you out of the loop on this, big

326

man, but I didn't and you know how I feel about the Five-O."

While he was trash talking with Uncle Stan, Mel saw her chance. She bolted out of the car and ran for the warehouse. She was going to talk to Butch Bordow if it was the last thing she did.

TWENTY-FIVE

"Mel!"

She heard Ray's shout. She ignored it. She dashed across the dark parking lot and ducked up against the building, clinging to the shadows in case there were security cameras watching her approach.

She heard a car door slam and knew that Ray was following her. She suspected Uncle Stan would now be on his way as well, probably calling Joe en route. If she was going to talk to Butch, it had to be now.

She reached for the side door Butch had slipped through, fully expecting it to be locked. It wasn't. She eased it open and slipped inside.

The darkness slammed up against her as if it had been dropped over her head like a thick blanket. She knew she was in the warehouse but it was so dark, she couldn't make out any shapes and her sense of spatial relations was gone, baby, gone.

She reached out with her hands, trying to feel her way along the wall, hoping her eyes would adjust to the dark before something popped out of the shadows to clobber her. She shuffled her feet. Her fingers tapped metal shelves and she used them to guide herself farther into the room.

She wondered if she should call out Butch's name. After all, he was expecting to meet someone, wasn't he?

She figured she could wait until her eyes adjusted and she could see where she was. In the meantime, she'd just keep moving steadily across the floor until she arrived at the offices. Mel pressed forward, hoping she hadn't gotten it wrong and was headed in the right direction.

She moved down two more shelves and into a small alcove, when a hand clamped over her mouth while another grabbed her arm. She immediately began to thrash and kick.

"Ow, damn it, Mel, it's me, Ray," a voice hissed. "I'm letting go, don't scream."

"Why are you grabbing me?" she snapped as soon as his hand lifted off of her mouth.

"To drag you out of here," he said. "The police are on their way. We've done all we can do here."

"Are you kidding me?" she asked. "We've

done nothing. We need a confession at the very least."

Bang! Bang! Bang!

Ray grabbed Mel's arm and dragged her to the ground. He covered both of their heads with his arms and Mel had to shove him off so she could get enough air to breathe.

Ray let loose a string of curses and then began to rant under his breath. "Great, now Bordow is shooting at us! I knew we shouldn't have come in here. I knew it. Didn't I tell you, didn't I?"

"Shh," Mel hushed him. "We don't know where he is and if he is shooting at us, he sure has a crappy aim."

"Let's just go out the way we came in," Ray said. "We can meet the police outside."

"Okay," Mel whispered. The gunfire was a game changer. Her voice was shaky and she had the feeling that coming into the warehouse had not been one of her better ideas. "Lead the way."

Ray turned and stayed crouched down as he moved through the dark warehouse. Mel followed him. They'd only gone a few feet when bullets blasted over their heads, exploding into the concrete above them, spraying them with chunks of cement.

"Run for it!" Ray shouted.

She heard him take off running and she tried to follow as he twisted and turned through the big metal shelves, but Mel miscalculated and slammed into a shelving unit. The impact knocked her to her knees. She braced to hit the hard floor but instead she landed on something soft.

She went to push up with her hands and felt the solid warmth of a body beneath her hands. Mel clamped her lips together to keep from screaming. She quickly ran her hands over the body. The person wasn't wearing leather, so it wasn't Ray.

She felt the rise and fall of the chest. No boobs, definitely male, and he was breathing. She felt something hard in his shirt pocket, and she reached in and pulled out his phone.

Excellent! She didn't dare turn it on for fear that if Butch Bordow saw any light, he might shoot his gun in her direction. Instead, she scurried forward away from the body. If she could find some cover, she'd be able to check the phone and see who the unconscious person was.

On hands and knees, she made her way down one aisle and then turned into another. She paused, listening. She didn't hear Ray. There were no more gunshots. She hit the button to turn on the phone.

The home display picture was an old one of a beautiful woman who had the same features and dark hair as Suzanne Bordow. Mel had seen this picture on a phone before at the Triple Fork when she'd taken it off Butch so the bartender could call his daughter to pick him up. Her heart hammered in her chest. This was Butch Bordow's phone.

Hot damn. That meant the body she had just fallen on had been Butch Bordow. Had he been shooting at them and knocked himself out? There was no privacy block on the phone and Mel went right to his texts. She saw that the one from Ray to meet them hadn't been read yet, but the one before that, sent from his daughter Suzanne, had, and it asked him to meet her here to talk this evening.

Mel felt her heart thump hard in her chest. Had Suzanne been the one to fire the gun just now? And if so, had she been aiming at Mel and Ray or her father?

A door slammed at the end of the warehouse, and Mel jumped and dropped the phone with a clatter. She quickly snatched it up from the floor, pressing it against her stomach to hide its glow. She pressed herself back into the shelves, trying to hide. The sound of voices, agitated voices, reached her and she held her breath.

Were they looking for her? Was it the police, coming to help? Or was it Suzanne, looking for her father?

Mel knew a bit of police protocol from her uncle. There was no way they were going to just enter a building where shots had been fired. They'd be outside, waiting to see what unfolded and trying to strategize how best to enter without turning it into a bloodbath or a hostage situation.

Oh, man, had Ray gotten out, or was he hiding somewhere else in the warehouse? Mel fervently hoped he'd gotten out. She could never live with herself if something happened to Ray because he'd been coming in to save her.

"This was not part of the deal."

It was a man's voice. The level of agitation was high but even so, Mel knew that voice. It was Tyson Ballinger and he sounded furious. She glanced at the phone and even though she couldn't see where Tyson was, she hit the video record button, hoping to get audio on their conversation.

"Don't be stupid." Now it was a woman's voice. She didn't sound agitated; she sounded furious. "The deal is for you to do whatever I tell you to do and right now I'm telling you to find my father and finish him off."

Suzanne! Mel blocked her mouth with her fist to keep from crying out. Suzanne was berating Tyson for not killing her father.

"No, I'm not a killer," Tyson said.

"Oh, stop it!" Suzanne said. She sounded irritated. "Don't even think you're on a higher moral ground than me. You straight-up rob people of their businesses and then shrug when they commit suicide. If that's not murder, I don't know what is."

"At least I didn't bash my brother's skull in," he said.

Mel's ears began to buzz and she could barely hear their next words over the thudding of her heart, which seemed to echo through her body like the beat of a bass drum keeping time to her terror. She had no doubt that if Suzanne found her, she was dead.

"He was a worthless womanizing son of a bitch," she said. "I did that fiancée of his a favor by getting rid of him. Instead of bitching about jail time, she should be thanking me."

"For getting her sent to prison? Not likely," he said.

"When this company goes public, your investment is going to be worth a hundred times what you put in," Suzanne said. "Surely one man's sad, drunken life is worth less than that. Shoot him and I'll know you're on board with me."

"I'm not a killer," he said. He sounded like he was having a hard time standing up to her.

Mel inched forward, trying to see around the shelves. If she could just get some video of them, she'd have all she needed as proof. In the darkness, she had no idea how she was going to pull that off.

"Help me find him," Suzanne's voice said. "Then we can decide who gets to pull the trigger."

"Hold up," Tyson said. "I have an idea."

Mel strained to hear what he said next but he wasn't talking. She could hear him tapping on his phone and Suzanne let out an impatient huff of breath. She tried to guess how far away they were and figured they were several shelves over from her. That meant they weren't sure where Butch was. She hoped he came to and got the heck out of there before they found him, because she had no idea how she was going to save them both.

All of a sudden the phone in her hand lit up and started to blare the ringtone "Love Will Keep Us Together," by Captain and Tennille.

"Ah!" Mel jumped up, smacked her head

on the shelf above her, and doubled over as she frantically tried to mute the phone.

"Over there!" Suzanne shouted.

The sound of running feet headed in her direction forced Mel out of her hiding spot and back into the aisle. She dashed around the shelving unit, not knowing which way to turn, when all of a sudden the lights in the warehouse snapped on.

She was standing directly in front of the same portable ball pit where all of this had begun. She couldn't help but stare at it. It only relaxed her a smidge to realize it was a different ball pit, all clean and shiny with no dead body. At least, for a moment she felt better, then her heart dropped into her stomach when she saw that standing on the other side was Suzanne, and she had a gun pointed right at Mel.

"Stop," Suzanne said.

Mel held her hands up as if in surrender, but instead the video camera on Butch's phone was still going. So long as Suzanne didn't shoot her right away, Mel might be able to verify the information she'd over-heard. With any luck, Ray was out there and would save her before Suzanne started blasting holes in her.

"What are *you* doing here?" Tyson asked. He looked at her as if she was too stupid to live — not the first person to do that — and then said, "I told you to butt out of this."

"Butch and I were supposed to have a meeting," Mel said. "He knows. He knows everything."

Suzanne threw her head back and guffawed as if Mel had said the funniest thing she had ever heard.

"Please, the only thing my father knows is how to maintain his buzz for days at a time," she said. "He's been like that ever since my mother died — a complete waste of space just like my brother. I'm the one who runs this company, not them. It thrives on my blood, sweat, and tears, and how do you think they wanted to repay me? They thought this would be a great time to sell it."

Mel didn't move, afraid that if she drew too deep of a breath, Suzanne might just shoot for the heck of it. Still, there were questions that needed answers.

"You keep two sets of books, don't you?"

Suzanne tipped her head to the side. Mel swallowed, wondering if that knowledge was going to get her shot.

"How do you know that?"

"I own a business, I get it," Mel said. She got nothing. If it weren't for Tate she'd be clueless, but Suzanne didn't know that.

"One set is for losses — that's what your brother and father got to see, right? The other is for investors — that's what Tyson here got to see. Correct?"

Tyson glared at her, but Suzanne looked impressed. "You're not as dumb as the blond hair would lead one to believe."

"Low blow," Mel said.

"Yeah, I let Mike and Dad think the business was in trouble," she said. "I didn't think they'd care. When Mike said he was going to marry Diane as she had money and we could use her marketing savvy to bolster the business, I figured shacking up with her would keep him out of my way, and it did for a while, but then Mike got wind of Dad's gambling and wanted to sell the business to bail him out. I couldn't tell him we were doing well. He'd want a cut of it and I'd worked too hard to make it successful to let him just swoop in and take it."

"Shut up, Suzanne," Tyson growled.

"So you had Tyson kill him," Mel said. She ignored the furious look Tyson sent her.

"No, I didn't. I brought Tyson in for business, not killing." Suzanne jerked her head at him.

That's when it clicked in Mel's head. "RR Ty, one of the private companies that bought in." She looked at Tyson. "That's

338

you. RR Ty. Railroad Ty."

He shrugged. She had seen him at the train park; there wasn't much use denying that the small company was his.

"Ty let my father rack up gambling debts, which, unbeknownst to Dad and Mike, I paid off to Tyson in ownership percentages of the company. I figured if Tyson owned a bigger stake in the company than the two of them but not as much as me, my brother and father wouldn't be able to sell it. I didn't expect my father to panic and convince my brother to try and sell it out from under me so quickly, however."

She gave Tyson an irritated look. "You were too scary and you freaked my dad out."

He raised his hands in the air as if to ask, *What do you want from me?*

"They made their move before Tyson owned a larger portion of the company than they did, making their combined ownership greater than ours." She gestured between her and Tyson. "That's why they both had to go. Given that my brother was a lying, cheating dirtbag, it was natural that suspicion would fall on his fiancée."

"So if Tyson was just the money, then it was you. You killed your brother," Mel said. She tried to make it sound as if she was just trying to understand; meanwhile, she was freaking out. Where was Ray? Uncle Stan? Heck, she'd even take grumpy, after-her-man Detective Tara.

"Duh," Suzanne said. "I didn't plan it. He had a hissy fit about the business and insisted we were selling. He didn't care because he was marrying moneybags. I lost my temper and the next thing I knew I'd crushed his head with one of those cheesy faux pedestals. Luckily we were next to the ball pit, and I could roll him right in. I thought I could make it look like an accident, but then you showed up with those stupid cupcakes and ruined everything."

Mel was breathing through her nose, trying to keep her sudden bout of nausea at bay.

"But what's done is done. His fiancée is still the prime suspect, and I just have a few loose ends to tie up. So where did you get my father's phone?" Suzanne demanded.

"I found it," Mel said. She had no doubt she was one of those loose ends. It was not a comforting realization.

"Where?" Suzanne said.

Mel tilted her chin up. If she told them where Bordow was, they'd kill her and then him. She had to lie.

"On the floor, back there. He must have dropped it." Mel gestured toward the back

340

of the warehouse. Then she gave Suzanne a hard stare. "It has a nice record feature on it."

"Give it to me," Suzanne said. Her eyes went wide and she sounded nervous.

Mel glanced at Tyson. The phone proved he had nothing to do with the murder. If Mel lost that evidence, if Suzanne destroyed it, he was screwed. Mel wondered if he could read this on her face or if he was in too deep to care.

"I said, give it to me," Suzanne demanded.

"You want it?" Mel asked. "Go get it."

With that she whipped it into the ball pit as hard as she could.

"No!" Suzanne cried.

She turned toward the pit, and Mel ran. First she dashed past the faux pedestals, knocking them over behind her as she went. If Suzanne or Tyson followed, she was not going to make it easy for them.

Behind her, Mel heard a yelp and a scream. She ducked down and scurried across two rows until she was able to see the ball pit from a shielded vantage point. Both Tyson and Suzanne were in the pit searching for the phone. Suzanne had dropped her gun in the process, and just as she dove down into the balls to look for the phone, five Scottsdale police officers appeared around the edge of the pit, all pointing their weapons at Tyson and Suzanne. When she surfaced it was to find Detective Tara Martinez waiting with a pair of handcuffs, which she snapped around Suzanne's wrists before Suzanne could dive away from her.

"Mel!" Mel turned around to see Joe and Ray hurrying toward her. "Are you all right?"

She threw herself into Joe's arms and squeezed him as hard as she could without cutting off his air supply.

"I'm fine," she said. Ray was smiling at them like a big dope and she reached over to punch him on the shoulder. "Nice timing with the cavalry."

"I do what I can," he said with a shrug, but he looked pleased.

"Joe, I got it all on video on Butch's phone, but I had to throw it in the ball pit. We have to get it before someone steps on it."

"On it," Joe said. He released her and grabbed her hand, leading her toward the area where Uncle Stan was reading Suzanne and Tyson their rights.

"He just called Butch's phone," Mel said to Joe. He nodded in complete understanding.

Joe took Tyson's phone out of his pocket and then grabbed Tyson's hand and pressed his thumb on the home button to unlock it. The display lit up and Joe opened his recent activity and called the number last called.

Captain and Tennille began to chime out of the ball pit and Joe looked at Mel.

" 'Love Will Keep Us Together'?" he asked.

" 'Think of me, babe, whenever,' " Mel sang. She tipped her head in Tara's direction and continued, " 'Some sweet talking girl comes along —' "

"Stop!" Joe ordered and then sang, " ' 'Cause I really love you.' "

Mel laughed, and he drew her close and kissed her.

"Ugh, I think I'm going to vomit," Tara said. She waved for a couple of uniforms to enter the ball pit and retrieve the phone as she joined their group with a frown marring her features.

"What?" Ray turned to look at her as if she had just committed sacrilege. "You don't like Captain and Tennille? Who doesn't like Captain and Tennille?"

"Anyone with any taste in music," Tara said. She rolled her eyes and began to walk away from him, but Ray was not to be deterred.

"So, are you a cop? You don't look like a cop. I have to say I'd let you frisk me anytime you wanted. You're utterly adorable minus the questionable taste in music and career," he said.

"Oh. My. God." Tara picked up her pace but Ray was hot on her heels.

"That could be fun to watch," Mel said.

"Oh, yes, Ray might have finally met his match," Joe agreed. He turned to Mel and wrapped her in his arms. "Just like I met mine."

"Ready to go home?" she asked.

"Always," he said.

TWENTY-SIX

Butch Bordow was taken to the hospital. It seemed that when Suzanne shot at him, he threw himself to the ground and knocked himself out cold. He was going to live but with his drinking problem it was anyone's guess for how long.

Mel and Joe spent most of the evening at the station while Mel gave her statement. It became clear fairly quickly that Ray had been playing secret double agent on her. She wasn't sure how she felt about that but given that it had undoubtedly kept them from being killed, it was hard to hold a grudge.

Ray had kept Uncle Stan and Joe in the loop from the moment Mel had sat him down for coffee and mocha cupcakes in the kitchen of the bakery. They'd had undercover officers in the train park the day that Mel and Ray had met Tyson Ballinger, and Ray had worn a wire during that meeting, which included the conversation where they decided to blackmail Butch.

As it turned out, the idea was actually Uncle Stan's, thinking that Ray and Mel could set Butch up for a takedown. No one had ever thought that Mel would go dashing into the warehouse. Luckily, they'd all been in the neighborhood, staking out the place while they waited for Butch to show up.

"I should have known you'd throw us a curveball," Joe said. "You always do."

He held Mel close and kissed the top of her head, so she knew there were no hard feelings, which was a nice change for the two of them after another dramatic episode in their lives.

"So you're not going to break up with me?" Mel asked.

Joe tapped the engagement ring on her finger. "Never."

Once in custody, Tyson Ballinger cut a deal with the district attorney. He rolled over on Suzanne, confirming the information Mel had recorded, that she killed her brother to keep him from selling off the company when he thought it was going under.

Suzanne, of course, had a whole different agenda in operation. Having positioned the company for great success, if her brother sold it out from under her she stood to lose millions, millions that she'd had no intention of sharing with her brother or her father. So in a fit of frustration and rage she'd killed Mike, and framing Diane for the murder of her cheating brother was too easy to resist. Diane breaking up with Mike, however, didn't jibe with his murder — not when she was having breakup cupcakes delivered to him. Ultimately, Suzanne's plans had been crushed by a batch of caramel cupcakes.

Joe left bright and early the next morning to get started on the case against Suzanne. The news media hadn't gotten wind of the story yet, so he was hoping to get as much done as he could before the office became a media circus.

Mel watched him go, knowing that she needed to meet up with Diane and tell her what had happened so that she could make it clear that she was the one who caught Suzanne and that her debt was now officially paid.

She took a quick shower, fed Captain Jack, and dashed out the door after only one cup of coffee, which was a small miracle given that after last night's adrenaline-fueled moments of sheer terror, she was pretty sure she could have slept for a month and one cup of coffee was really not enough of a hit of go-juice to convince her body otherwise.

She stifled a yawn as she parked in front of Diane's office. This time when she approached the doors, they were unlocked. In fact, sitting in the front reception area on some squashy chairs were Diane and her mother, Cheryl.

Cheryl was thumbing through a fashion magazine while Diane was furiously typing a message on her phone. There was no sign of Elliott. In fact, other than the two women the office appeared empty.

"Hi, Diane," Mel said.

She glanced between her and her mother, wondering what could have happened that the two women seemed to have made up. If Joyce had slept with Joe — Okay, yeah, Mel couldn't imagine anything like that happening ever, since her mother had a fully functional moral compass and Cheryl did not.

Diane raised one finger in a gesture for Mel to wait while she finished typing. Cheryl did not even glance up from her magazine to acknowledge Mel.

There was a pitcher of orange juice and a plate of donuts on the table between the two women, but neither of them offered Mel a drink, a donut, or a seat. She shifted from foot to foot, feeling more and more like the invisible hired help.

After several more moments, Diane put her phone down and glanced at Mel.

"What brings you here so early?" she asked.

"I have news," Mel said.

"About who really killed Mike?" Diane asked. She looked like she was bracing for disappointment.

"Yes," Mel said. "The police have a suspect in custody."

"Well, don't just stand there, tell me everything," Diane ordered. She turned to her mother and said, "Did you hear that? The real killer's been caught."

Cheryl put down her magazine and sighed, "Well, it's about time. Who did it?"

Mel glanced from her to Diane. The confusion at their reconciliation must have shown on her face because Diane shrugged and said, "She's my mom."

Mel knew better than to argue that point. If Cheryl was here, Diane had obviously forgiven her, which was really none of Mel's business.

She shook her head to get her focus back and said, "Well, it turns out that Suzanne

Bordow is the one who killed her brother over his plans to sell the business."

Diane gasped. "Little Suzanne?"

Mel nodded. "And last night she tried to kill her father, too. Apparently she has built the company up and has it on the brink of making millions, but she hadn't planned to share the profits with her brother or her father. Mike thought the company was failing and was looking to sell it. Suzanne couldn't let him do that. They had a fight and she crushed his head with one of the faux pedestals they rent out. Then she tossed him into the ball pit, hoping to make it look like you did it, but when you broke up with Mike via cupcake that story didn't work so well."

Diane stared at the ground as if trying to take it all in. She didn't look sad — not even a little bit. She looked relieved, giddy in fact, that she was now cleared of Mike's murder.

"So," Mel said. "I am going to assume that my debt to you is paid in full and I don't ever want to hear that I owe you ever again."

"Owe her?" Cheryl said. "Whatever for?"

"Nothing, Mom," Diane said quickly, too quickly.

Diane had a guilty look on her face and Mel frowned. Something felt wrong, really wrong. She looked at Cheryl.

"Diane saved me from being the unknowing star of a frat boy sex tape back when we were in college," Mel said.

"Oh, those," Cheryl said. She nodded and looked at Diane. "You made a fortune off of those back in the day. Why did you give it up? That was a solid income stream."

Diane closed her eyes as if praying for patience. Mel turned to look at her, feeling as if her body had just been hit with a blast of icy cold air. She didn't have to ask to know if it was true; the answer was written all over Diane's face.

"You were in on it?" she asked. "You made money off of the sex tapes?"

"In on it?" Cheryl snorted. "She was the mastermind behind it. How else do you think she paid for college? I didn't have that kind of money."

"I can explain —" Diane began, but Mel cut her off.

"This whole time I thought I owed you a favor, and it turns out it was your fault I was in that position to begin with," Mel snapped. "My god, I could have died trying to repay a debt that is just one more big, fat lie."

Diane went on the defensive. "You can't prove anything. Besides, I got you out of

351

there. I didn't let them film you. It was only supposed to be willing participants, but you were so uptight back then, one of the guys really wanted to get you to loosen up."

"So you let him roofie me?" Mel cried.

"No!" Diane protested. "He wasn't supposed to go after you and no one was supposed to be drugged. That guy crossed the line, which is why I smashed his equipment. It was only supposed to be drunken party-girl coeds who didn't care if we filmed their wild nights. What are you so mad about? I didn't let them film you. I didn't have to stop it, you know."

"No, you didn't," Mel said. She was so angry, she was visibly shaking. The urge to put a hurt on Diane was almost more than she could resist. Instead, she picked up the pitcher of orange juice and dumped it over Diane's head. "Just like I didn't have to do that, but I did. Do not come near me ever again."

When Mel got back to the bakery, she was in a foul mood. She went right to the kitchen and began baking. It was the only thing she could think of to do that would channel all of her hurt and anger in a productive way.

She was frosting her third set of cupcakes

— more Mocha Latte ones to replace all that Ray had eaten — when the kitchen door banged open and Angie appeared looking pasty pale and wild-eyed.

"What's wrong?" Mel asked. "Are your wedding flowers not in season, was there another misprint on the invites, did the band fall through, what?"

"No." Angie shook her head. "It's Marty."

"What about him?" Mel asked.

Angie jerked her head in the direction of the bakery, her sense of panic palpable. Mel dropped her pastry bag on the steel worktable and strode across the kitchen, pushing through the swinging doors into the bakery.

When she entered the room, she stopped short. Facing Marty across one of the bakery tables in a combative stance were two middle-aged women and one very sharply dressed man in a suit.

"Enough is enough," one of the women said.

At a glance, she looked to be in her late forties but upon closer inspection, it was easy to see she had a well-maintained veneer that shaved off about a decade until you got up close and could see she was really in her late fifties.

"We have given you plenty of time to get this whole working-in-a-bakery thing out of your system, but since you won't end it on your own we're going to end it for you," the woman said. "You need to come home to Chicago, Dad."

Dad? She was Marty's daughter? He never really talked about his life before, and Mel had just assumed he was alone in the world since his wife had died. She gave him a surprised look, but he was too busy glaring at the two women to pay Mel any mind.

"It's time, Dad," the other woman said. Like her sister, she was immaculately dressed in a silk blouse and slacks with her hair scrupulously maintained a lovely shade of honey.

"I'm sorry, can I help you?" Mel asked. She rounded the counter and stood beside Marty. Angie moved forward and flanked him on the other side.

"Yes, you can," the man in the suit spoke. "I am Pierce Henry, legal representative for his daughters, Nora and Julie" — he gestured to the two women — "and the rest of the Zelaznik family. I am here to express their concerns about the recent behavior of Martin Zelaznik and to see that the appropriate action is taken."

"What? Why?" Mel asked.

The lawyer popped open the briefcase on the table in front of him. "There is a considerable fortune at stake here and my clients are concerned that their father has become incapable of managing his affairs."

"Marty, you're loaded?" Angie asked.

"I do okay."

"Okay?" Mr. Henry cleared his throat as he pulled a large manila envelope out of his briefcase. "Excuse me, but at the end of the day you are worth well over seven million dollars, Mr. Zelaznik, which is to say significantly better than *okay*."

Marty shrugged. "It's just money."

"Did you hear that?" Nora asked Julie. "He never talked like that before."

"He really has gone mental," Julie agreed.

"I don't understand," Mel said.

"They think I'm one taco short of a fiesta platter," Marty explained.

"But why?" Mel asked. "Is there something you haven't told us?"

"Yeah, aside from the whole being-a-millionaire thing?" Angie said.

"His behavior has been erratic, unpredictable —" Nora began.

"He's left his home in the senior center to move in with *that* woman," Julie added.

It was pretty clear to see how they felt about Olivia. Mel couldn't really argue the point with them.

"Okay, questionable taste in girlfriends

aside, I don't really think there is any cause to question Marty's mental state. He runs the counter here like a champ," Angie said. She punched Marty on the shoulder and he gave her a half grimace, half smile.

Mr. Henry opened the envelope and tossed a picture onto the table. It was a blurry shot of Marty, covered in garbage, linguine hanging out of the back of his pants and a tomato slice on his shoe.

"Oh, hey, that's when you and I jumped into a Dumpster to hide from Olivia," Mel said with a laugh. "We stunk so bad."

"Hiding from Olivia?" Nora said.

"Yeah, that was before we were a thing," Marty said. "I lost my hair in that Dumpster dive."

"You did!" Mel laughed. "You look so much better without it."

Mr. Henry tossed another photo on the table. This one was of Marty in full cowboy gear. The photo was grainy but it was obvious he was helping to corral a bull into a trailer.

"Hey, that was last summer when we ran the cupcake truck at the rodeo," Angie said. "I remember that day. Oz almost got stomped by that runaway bull. You boys were so brave."

Julie and Nora exchanged horrified looks.

356

"Stop talking," Marty said out of the side of his mouth.

Another picture landed on the table. It was Marty wearing a helmet, knee pads, and elbow pads, skateboarding with Oz and his girlfriend, Lupe, on a big glittery ramp. No one said a word. Another photo hit the pile and it was Marty dressed as a zombie in a casket. Not his best look to date.

Mel wanted to say that the pictures looked worse than they were. That Marty had been perfectly safe in every instance, but that would have been a lie.

"You're going to get yourself killed, Dad, is that what you want?" Julie asked. Her lips were pressed into a tight thin line.

"We've been watching the news; we know what happens around this bakery," Nora insisted. "Dead bodies, murder attempts, it's like a vortex of evil."

"Hey, now," Angie said. Mel could see her temper was beginning to heat, which would be no help in this situation and would probably get Marty in deeper hot water than he already was.

"There have been some unfortunate events," Mel said. "But for the most part, we are a perfectly safe place and provide a wonderfully supportive work environment for all of our employees."

Both Nora and Julie crossed their arms over their chests and made a *phftht* noise.

"Be that as it may, we are here to have Mr. Zelaznik temporarily put into the custody of a physician for a full psychological evaluation," Mr. Henry said. He took a thick sheaf of papers out of his briefcase and dumped them on the table.

Marty turned to Mel. His watery gaze met hers and he said, "Don't let them take me. This is the happiest I've ever been in my life since my wife, Jeanie, died, and I don't want to go."

Mel glanced past him at Angie and they exchanged a nod. They linked their arms through Marty's, forming a small but no less meaningful human chain.

"Over our dead bodies," Mel said.

"Really?" Marty said. "That's your word choice at the moment?"

She patted his arm. "Don't you worry. We got this."

"Oh, boy," Marty said.

RECIPES

CARAMEL BREAKUP CUPCAKES

1/2 cup butter, softened
1/2 cup packed dark brown sugar
1/2 cup granulated sugar
2 eggs
1 teaspoon vanilla extract
1 3/4 cups all-purpose flour
1 1/4 teaspoons baking powder
1/4 teaspoon salt
3/4 cup milk

Preheat oven to 350 degrees. Line cupcake pan with paper liners. In a large bowl, cream butter and sugars until light and fluffy. Add eggs, one at a time, beating well after each addition. Beat in vanilla. In a medium bowl, combine flour, baking powder, and salt; add to creamed mixture alternately with milk, beating well after each addition. Fill paper-lined muffin cups two-thirds full. Bake 18 to 22 minutes or until a toothpick inserted in center comes out clean. Cool completely. Makes 12 cupcakes.

Dulce De Leche Icing
1/2 cup cream cheese (4-ounce package)
1/2 cup unsalted butter, room temperature
4 cups powdered sugar
1/2 cup dulce de leche (found with sweet-ened condensed milk)

In a medium-sized mixing bowl, beat cream cheese and butter on high speed for three minutes, until light and fluffy. Alternately, mix in powdered sugar and dulce de leche until fully combined. Spread or pipe on cooled cupcakes. Garnish with drizzled caramel, or, you know, a candy button that says, *It's not me, it's you,* if desired.

MOCHA LATTE CUPCAKES
Chocolate coffee cupcake with chocolate coffee icing.

1 1/3 cups all-purpose flour
1/4 teaspoon baking soda
2 teaspoons baking powder
1/2 cup unsweetened cocoa powder
1/8 teaspoon salt
3 tablespoons butter, softened

1 cup white sugar
2 eggs
3/4 teaspoon vanilla extract
1/2 cup milk
1/2 cup cold coffee

Preheat oven to 350 degrees. Sift together the flour, baking soda, baking powder, cocoa, and salt. Set aside. In a large bowl, cream together the butter and sugar until well blended. Add the eggs one at a time, beating well with each addition, then stir in the vanilla. Add the flour mixture alternately with the milk and coffee; beat well. Bake for 15 to 18 minutes. Makes 12.

Mocha Latte Icing
1/2 cup butter, softened
1/2 cup cream cheese (4 ounces), softened
1 1/2 tablespoons instant espresso (powdered)
2 teaspoons vanilla extract
4 cups powdered sugar
3 tablespoons milk

In a medium-sized mixing bowl, beat butter and cream cheese on high speed for three minutes, until light and fluffy. Mix in instant espresso, vanilla extract, powdered sugar, and milk until it reaches desired consistency. Spread or pipe on cooled cupcakes. Garnish with a chocolate-covered espresso bean, if desired.

KEY LIME CUPCAKES

A golden cupcake flavored with lime zest and topped with a key lime buttercream.

3/4 cup sugar
1 1/2 cups flour
1/4 teaspoon salt
2 teaspoons baking powder
1/4 cup melted butter
1 beaten egg
1 cup milk
1 tablespoon key lime zest
2 tablespoons key lime juice

Preheat the oven to 350 degrees. Sift the dry ingredients together in a big bowl. Melt the butter and add the beaten egg to it. Add that to the dry ingredients, then stir in the milk until smooth. Zest half of a lime, and add it to the bowl. Squeeze in the juice of half the lime, mixing well. Bake for 15 to 18 minutes or until golden brown. Makes 12.

Key Lime Buttercream
1/2 cup salted butter, softened
1/2 cup unsalted butter, softened
2 tablespoons key lime juice

1 tablespoon key lime zest
1/2 teaspoon vanilla extract
4 cups powdered sugar

In a medium-sized mixing bowl, beat butter on high speed, until light and fluffy. Mix in key lime juice, zest, and vanilla extract. Add in powdered sugar, mixing until it reaches desired consistency. Spread or pipe on cooled cupcakes. Garnish with a candied lime peel, if desired.

CHERRY BOMB CUPCAKES
A cherry chocolate cupcake with
cherry cream cheese frosting.

1 1/2 cups all-purpose flour
1/4 teaspoon baking soda
2 teaspoons baking powder
3/4 cup unsweetened cocoa powder
1/8 teaspoon salt
1/2 cup (1 stick) butter, softened
1 cup sugar
2 eggs
1/3 cup Maraschino cherry juice
1 cup milk

Preheat oven to 350 degrees. Put liners in muffin tin and set aside. Sift together the flour, baking soda, baking powder, cocoa, and salt. Set aside. In a large bowl, cream together the butter and sugar until well blended. Add the eggs one at a time, beating well with each addition, then stir in the cherry juice. Add the flour mixture alternately with the milk; beat well. Fill the cupcake liners evenly and bake for 18 to 20 minutes. Makes 12.

Cherry Cream Cheese Frosting
1/2 cup cream cheese (4 ounces), softened
1/2 cup (1 stick) unsalted butter, softened
1/3 cup cherry pie filling
1/2 teaspoon almond extract
1/2 teaspoon vanilla extract
4 cups powdered sugar
2–3 tablespoons milk, if needed

In a medium-sized mixing bowl, beat cream cheese and butter on high speed, until light and fluffy. Mix in cherry pie filling and the almond and vanilla extracts. Add in powdered sugar, mixing until it reaches desired consistency. Add in milk, if necessary. Spread or pipe on cooled cupcakes. Garnish with a maraschino cherry, if desired.

BANANAS FOSTER CUPCAKES
A banana rum cake with banana buttercream frosting and a rum caramel drizzle.

1 1/2 cups flour
1/2 teaspoon baking soda
1/2 teaspoon baking powder
1/4 teaspoon salt
1/2 cup (1 stick) unsalted butter, softened
3/4 cup sugar
1 1/2 teaspoons rum extract
2 beaten eggs
1/2 cup milk
2 medium bananas (1 cup), peeled and mashed

Preheat the oven to 350 degrees. Sift the dry ingredients together in a medium bowl. In a large bowl, mix the butter, sugar, rum extract, eggs, and milk. Add the dry ingredients, then mix in the bananas until batter is smooth. Bake for 15 to 18 minutes or until golden brown. Makes 12.

Banana Buttercream
1/2 cup (1 stick) salted butter, softened
1/2 cup mashed banana
1/2 teaspoon lemon juice
4 cups powdered sugar

In a medium-sized mixing bowl, beat butter on high speed, until light and fluffy. Mix in bananas and lemon juice. Add in powdered sugar, mixing until it reaches desired consistency. Spread or pipe on cooled cupcakes. Garnish with rum caramel drizzle, if desired.

Rum caramel drizzle: Melt one cup of caramels in a double boiler, adding one teaspoon of rum extract. Allow to cool and thicken, using a fork to drizzle over the cupcakes.

ABOUT THE AUTHOR

Jenn McKinlay is the *New York Times* bestselling author of the Cupcake Bakery Mysteries, the Hat Shop Mysteries, and the Library Lover's Mysteries. As Josie Belle, she writes the Good Buy Girls Mysteries, and as Lucy Lawrence, she wrote the Decoupage Mysteries. She lives in Scottsdale, Arizona, with her family.

The employees of Thorndike Press hope you have enjoyed this Large Print book. All our Thorndike, Wheeler, and Kennebec Large Print titles are designed for easy reading, and all our books are made to last. Other Thorndike Press Large Print books are available at your library, through selected bookstores, or directly from us.

For information about titles, please call:
    (800) 223-1244

or visit our website at:
    gale.com/thorndike

To share your comments, please write:
    Publisher
    Thorndike Press
    10 Water St., Suite 310
    Waterville, ME 04901